A TIME OF DARKNESS

BOOK ONE: SCATTERING THE ASHES

ROBERT BARTLETT

authorHOUSE®

AuthorHouse™
1663 Liberty Drive
Bloomington, IN 47403
www.authorhouse.com
Phone: 1 (800) 839-8640

Published by AuthorHouse 03/09/2018

ISBN: 978-1-5462-3262-9 (sc)
ISBN: 978-1-5462-3261-2 (e)

CONTENTS

PRELUDE

DAY ONE, GROUND ZERO

His breath is strained and short, consisting of small quick gulps of air as he struggles in the chill of a pre-dawn, rocky mountain morning to restart the fire that the two young lovers (in their attention to each other) had let die during the night. Watching him from a distance, she admires his tenacity at not wanting to give up on restarting the flames. Smiling to herself as she recalls the way he had lectured her the night before saying repeatedly as he struggled to light the fire the first time; "This is the way it's supposed to be done". She had been a little surprised when he succeeded in getting the fire to start by hand last night using the primitive bow drill method he had stumbled across while watching survival videos on You Tube – and by the look on his face, so had he. His persistent nature never ceased to amaze or impress her. He approached everything with passion, doing the best he was capable of in all that he did. Be it digging a hole in the backyard to bury their cat LuLu or building a primitive fire out in the middle of nowhere Wyoming. To her, it was one of his most attractive traits.

"Damn it!" She hears him shout at the little pile of kindling he was bent over working feverishly trying to re-ignite the flames. Discouraged and annoyed the outburst is followed by the unmistakable sound of sticks shuffling across the ground as he throws them in his moment of irritated frustration.

"The damn sticks must've gotten wet in the night dew or something and to make matters worse, I broke the damn bow string. I'll have to try to think of something else." Sitting back on his haunches, out of breath and panting he lets out a heavy, frustrated sigh through his nose, his aura thick with disappointment.

"Ok baby that's fine. Let me know if there's anything I can do to help. It's freezing out here this morning."

She wonders if this is the right time to tell him about the cigarette lighter she has secretly stowed away in her backpack. Smiling, she decides against it as she turns to see him walking over to retrieve the sticks he threw, then grumpily he restarts his efforts on bringing the dead campfire back to life.

"Yeah, a little chill really settled into the valley last night," he offers as he sits heavily back down on the ground Indian style next to the small pile of tinder. Blowing into his hands too warm them up, he begins trying to fix the bow string that had broken on the fire starter. Wearing a nonchalant, mischievous grin he quietly adds, "I guess that's what we get for coming to Yellowstone at the end of September instead of in the middle of July." His voice thick with more than a hint of sarcasm.

"True… but the way I see it, is that this is your punishment for not finding me and marrying me sooner," she shoots back, wearing a wry grin of her own. Then, with a cute shrug of her shoulders, she adds matter-of-factly, "So…. ultimately it's still your fault that we're out here freezing our asses off in early fall instead of running around half naked through the mountain pastures of summertime wildflowers in mid-July." His short but honest laugh fills the campsite as he laughs at himself and his wife's own quick wit. She loves his laugh, and of course they would have come in July, but they weren't married in July. They had gotten married in September, which was the same month they had met in six years ago, on a blind date of all things! Her best friend Kelsey had been the one to set the meeting up for her. He cheeks flush with color as she thinks back about how she had bitched and moaned for the entire ride over to the little cantina in Huntington Beach just south of Los Angeles where they were going to meet Kelsey's boyfriend Matt, and his cousin John. Whining about how pathetic she thought she must look for not being able to find a date on her own and had essentially needed her best friend to set her up with one. She smiles warmly at the memories of the humble beginnings that would become the relationship between Carly Smith and John Foster. The relationship that had quickly transformed into the wild, romantic whirlwind affair that had ultimately led to them being married only one year later. She had insisted that they wait at least a year before they were wed, making him jump through all the hoops of courtship in the process; even though she had known from the very first time she had heard his laugh that she had fallen completely and madly in love with him. The same laugh that had just echoed through the campsite. Honest and genuine it was nothing short of contagious to anyone that was close enough to hear it.

"It could be wishful thinking, but I think I just saw a thin line of smoke," John calls over to her breathing heavily, leaning over the pile of tinder he had placed strategically in the center of the makeshift fire pit hard at work with the newly fixed bow drill.

"Good job baby. Breakfast will taste much better cooked. I'm not much into raw eggs and bacon," Carly calls back sarcastically before she settles comfortably back into her thoughts, content to stay there for the time being. No campfire was currently keeping her warm, but her thoughts certainly were. She looks affectionately over at John still hard at work hunched over the fire pit, sawing feverishly trying to create the ember that will bring warmth and comfort to their chilly little mountain campsite. John had always dreamt of coming to Yellowstone, so how could she say no to him after he had surprised her by planning this whole trip for their fifth wedding anniversary? He had been so excited! Like a child whose parents had just told him that were taking a family trip to Disney World or something. Carly sighed at the sweetness of the memory. She wasn't exactly the outdoorsy type, but aside from the cold front that had decided to wrap them in its arms last night, she had to admit it was beautiful out here in the middle of nowhere. It had a peacefulness to it that she hadn't expected. It was serine in the way that something is serine when it was pure; untainted by civilization or by any form of technology. She had been amazed by the vastness of the night sky as they had laid underneath the stars the night before. It was an awe-inspiring sight to a city girl, who had lived her entire life within the comforting glow of Edison's greatest invention (or Tesla's, depending on your own point of view).

"Any more smoke yet Davy Crockett? I hear spring is right around the corner," Carly good heartedly calls over to the slumped over form of her husband, still trying desperately to get the bow and sticks to form an ember.

"Yeah, yeah. Go ahead, make fun of the guy trying to get us warm. Not to mention the fact that I just *love* anniversary jokes at my expense," John cheerily calls back, smiling despite the cramps currently plaguing his forearms. Laughing out loud as he thinks to himself; "At least something over here is burning", although he would prefer it to be the kindling and not his muscles.

"I actually do think I'm making some progress smart ass. You just get ready with that breakfast you were threatening me with." John continues, still smiling as he once again begins the back and forth sawing motion of the primitive fire starter.

"Oh ok. I'll get right on that Paw, since I am doing such an *amazing* job at embracing this frontiersman's wife persona for you," she calls back over her shoulder, smiling affectionately as she makes her way back towards their tent.

Her smile still melts his heart even after five years of marriage. He can't believe he got her to agree to come out here camping with him in the middle of nowhere for an entire week. Carly hates the outdoors. At least she hasn't had any lizards run up her leg while they were sitting around the camp fire sipping wine this time. Well, at least not yet anyways. You could place bets safely against the odds in Vegas that if something were going to happen between nature and humans while they were doing anything outside, it would most assuredly happen to Carly. Lizards, snakes, spiders, she is the pied piper of nature's mishaps. It is a testimony to how much she truly loves him that she agreed to come out here at all to celebrate their fifth wedding anniversary, especially in the middle of September. He hoped the new diamond ring he planned to surprise her with on their hike later would make up for any creepy crawly disaster that was inevitably going to happen. He already knew it would fail at expressing the depth of his passion and love for her; but in the diamonds defense, no material object could. His love for her was spiritual on a cosmic level, she truly stirred his soul.

"Here stud, why don't you give this a try," she says as she walks over, gently placing her hand on his shoulder as she dangles the stowed away lighter in front of him tauntingly. Then wearing the sly smile that she knows always makes his heart flutter she adds,

"My appetites getting bigger, that fire isn't." Kissing him quickly on the top of his head, she bounces away giggling at herself as John's laughter booms out full and throaty once more. They both magically fill the countryside with an innocent incantation born of true love and happiness.

"Ok, ok…." He says, throwing his hands up in mock surrender. "But let the records show that I still hold to my belief that this is cheating. However, in the interest of my city princess needing a hot meal, I suppose that just this one time I can make an exception." He is still smiling as he admiringly watches her walk over to the pile of fallen branches and old logs they had collected the day before. Gathering up some of the wood she carries it back over to him and drops it next to the circle of rocks that make up the perimeter of their little campsite fire pit. Fuel for the fire that was now only a thumb flick of the lighter away. John kneels and strikes the lighter at the base of the little pile of kindling he had prepared. Smiling broadly, he knows that he is now and has always been, completely in love with his wife. He knows that the "today, tomorrow, and forever" anniversary band he has picked out for her as an anniversary gift is exactly the truth; he will love her from the deepest recesses of his soul for all of his life. Even if he is blissfully unaware, that at that very moment the flame that is his life, is approximately only an hour away from being extinguished.

The trail is clear and easy to follow as the couple makes their way toward the Octopus and Mushroom Hot Springs located in Yellowstone's lower geyser basin. Both sides of the trail are littered with beautifully colored local wild flowers and birds. John pauses at an opening in the trail for a moment taking some time to admire his surroundings. Smiling to himself at how lucky he is to have stumbled upon such a beautiful setting to present his anniversary gift of the ring to Carly.

"Come on slow poke!" Carly teases as they approach the clearing that signals that they have almost reached their first destination. Laughing John checks his pocket one more time to insure himself that he hasn't forgotten or lost the ring. The exertion of the hike, coupled with the heat that was rising from the mud pots and hot springs, has quickly burned off last night's chill. Stripped out of the jacket she had put on that morning to fight back the cold, Carly walks in front of John a little further up the trail. Dressed now in only a pair of khaki cargo shorts, an army green tank top, and a comfortable pair of hiking boots with warm cotton socks (which were now making her feet sweat) pulled up to her knees. With her jacket tied about her at the waist Carly absently fingers the gift that she has secretly hidden away for John inside the left pocket of her shorts. She was trying to figure out exactly how she was going to be able to sneak it out without him noticing when she hears him stop on the trail behind her and call out,

"Damn, it got hot quick. I'm burning up now." John laughs trying his hardest not to sound too obvious as he tries to set up his own excuse to pull out the ring and present it to his wife. "I don't remember it getting so hot this fast yesterday. I've got a couple bottles of water in the back-pack, would you like one?" He calls up to her.

"I would love one actually," Carly responds, thinking that this just might be when John plays right into her hands and allows her the opportunity to sneak out her surprise for him undetected.

"Ok, why don't you go on up ahead and see if there's a bench or something where we can rest our feet and take a break for a minute while I pull 'em out of the pack. I'll be right behind you, then we can enjoy one of nature's many wonders together." He knows that she'll think he means the hot springs, but diamonds are truly one of the wonders of nature as well. He is smiling to himself at his cleaver play on words as he squats down to open the pack. Carly stands at a bend in the trail marveling at the beauty of their surroundings. She calmly bends down pretending to tie her shoe as she slips her hand slyly into the left pocket of her shorts.

John stands up from his backpack stretching his tired back, the two bottles of water in one hand and the diamond ring secretly hidden in the other. He could see Carly bent over tying her shoe just up the trail a little way up ahead of him. She stands up placing her hands on her hips catching her breath as she glances back over her shoulder calling back to him.

"Hurry up Johnny, this place is absolutely INCREDIBLE!" She runs on up ahead as smiles spring onto both of their faces. Her shouts filter back down the trail to reach him as Carly makes her way up around the next bend, jogging the final leg of the trail that led out to the hot springs. John, seeing no real reason to run after her just yet, stops to pick a bundle of the colorful wildflowers that decorate the landscape along both sides of the trail. Smiling in anticipation of giving the ring to Carly he hopes the beauty of the flowers would add to his presentation. John is still bent over picking flowers lost in a debate with himself over whether he should get down on one knee or not in a re-enactment of his proposal to her when he feels the earth tremble for the first time. Moving back from the flowers John stands in the center of the trail wearing the stern mask of concentration mixed with confusion. He furrows his brow as he looks down at the trail paying close attention to the ground beneath his feet. As the seconds' tick away turning trepidation into uncertainty, he starts to second guess himself on whether he had felt a tremor at all. Standing there wondering if his imagination had gotten the better of him, his doubt is quickly extinguished as the earth begins to move for the second time. Longer and more violent than the first. The bouquet of Rocky Mountain wildflowers that he had just picked of Wyoming and Sulfur paintbrush, Monkey flowers, and Sand Verbena's hits the ground as Carly's screams begin to filter back down to him along the trail. Breaking him out of his dazed and confused state, her screams propel him up the trail towards his wife at a full sprint. He rounds the bend just as the ground begins to move and shake for a third time, bucking and vibrating in a long, continuous undulation of earth and rock causing him to lose his balance and fall. He catches sight of her as he stumbles, losing his balance he falls skinning both of his knees in the process. Confused he's not exactly sure of what it is he is seeing at first. Carly looks as if she has been blanketed in a hissing cloud of steam as it explodes from beneath the ground behind her, shrouding her in a hazy, ghostly nightmare. Her screams begin turning into harsh whispers as her throat and lungs became seared from the heat of the steam. The tremors were now continuous as the magma continued to roll and shift deep beneath the Wyoming Mountains. The turbulence causes the earth to split, opening a fumarole only yards behind his wife in a section of the trail that had recently been cleared away to make it easier for more inexperienced hikers to traverse. Carly was been facing away from the steam vent as it opens at her back, thankfully she had been facing back down the trail leading to the first hot spring watching for John after she had felt the first tremor. Scared and confused, unsure of what exactly was happening, a full third of her body is flash cooked in an instant as the steam hits her exposed backside with all its devilish force. The earth continues to shake and buckle growing more violent as John finally reaches her; both the flowers and the ring lay in the dirt long forgotten as Carly collapses into him. Her partially cooked body no longer able to support her weight during the next powerful series of earthquakes. It is all John can do to hold it together as he tries desperately to comfort and cradle his lovely, dying wife. Her eyes begin to glaze over as she stares blankly up into the sky. Her hands and arms convulse involuntarily as she slips deeper and deeper into shock. Trying to stop Carly's convulsions John looks around frantically, calling out in vain hoping beyond reason that someone would hear his desperate cries for help. Finding no reply, John tries not to panic in the knowing that they are helplessly alone out here in the middle of nowhere. Slowly, what is exactly happening around them begins to dawn on him as he struggles to keep his emotions together as the knowing of their inevitable death is waking up and bubbling to the surface all around them. The ticking time bomb that is the Yellowstone super volcano was no longer ticking. It was now what Mother Nature had always intended her to be; she was now just a bomb. A bomb like no other on the face of all the earth. In the calamity and violence that begins to surround them John bows his head and for the first time in his life he begins to pray to a God he could only hope was listening. He opens his eyes to look down apologetically at his dying wife as he notices something clenched tightly within her left fist which she had pressed tightly to her chest, over her heart. Prying it gently from her hand, he sits there staring at the item for what seemed like an eternity before he bends over and kisses her on her exposed stomach. The tears that had been welling up in his eyes and threatening to fall suddenly burst forth to stream down his face. He is no longer able or willing to hold the tears back as he looks up lovingly into Carly's face allowing the tears to flow freely down his cheeks as he kisses the positive pregnancy test that his wife had been holding within her dying fist to surprise him with.

-And the sun turned black as if covered in shadow, the moon turned red as if covered in blood.

~Revelations 6:12

SCATTERING THE ASHES

CHAPTER ONE

YEAR ONE, DAY ONE

Jeff Stevens sits casually behind his computer terminal at the NASA volcanic research facility located within the mono-basin region of the southeastern California and the western Nevada border. Bored, he pays far more attention to the I-pad he has resting on his lap and the game of angry birds he is currently playing than on the beeps and flashes of the computer screen that he is stationed at. Stevens is an unassuming man straight out of Cal-Tech. Standing just under six feet he is around the average height for a man these days, with a head topped with curly, greasy dark brown hair. He is thinly built, but non-athletic, with a little pot belly beginning to form from his marathons of sitting behind a computer monitor. His light brown eyes sit behind thick lensed glasses that do little to cover up the intelligence that lives behind them. His constant unhealthy diet of potato chips, mountain dew, and candy bars from the breakrooms' vending machines gives him far more acne than a man in his middle twenties should ever have. But, with that being said, Stevens had been a great addition to the research facility. Genuinely liked by both his supervisors and his peers alike; despite his addiction to pointless smart tech video games.

"Still trying to rid the virtual world of little green pigs Stevens?"

"Hey what's up Watts! I didn't hear you come in," Jeff says, responding cheerily to the facilities day floor manager Kelli Watson as she brushes past him on her way to check the monitoring instruments at the end of the aisle. Technically this was Jeff's job, but around here everyone gave a hand in completing the daily mundane "chores". Not much excitement typically happened around the observatory aside from the occasional middle school field trip. And even on the rare occasion that something did show up that was unusual all it typically meant was that someone had to make a phone call to the main office of NASA's science division located in Washington D.C. No one was sent running to the bat cave for the deployment of top secret equipment to save Gotham city or anything. But still, what they did here *was* important. The research done at the facility served as an early warning system for all the volcanic activity in an area nicknamed the "Ring of Fire" that encompassed the entirety of the Pacific Ocean. Monitoring earthquakes and analyzing the percentages for the possibilities of potential devastating tsunamis had also fallen to them after the tragedy of the Indian Ocean megathrust in 2004. That one disaster alone had taken the lives of approximately 250,000 people and had held the world in shocked horror at the destructive power hidden within the mega wave. The planet had learned the hard way that an early warning system was desperately needed for such potentially large and devastating natural disasters. As early as possible that is, no one could perfectly predict or do anything to sway the actions of an angry Mother Nature. Kelli's sigh of indifference is audible as she reaches the end of the aisle and begins to examine the latest readings that were systematically being printed out by the facilities monitoring equipment.

Stevens watches after Kelli longingly as she strides down the aisle away from him. By all accounts Kelli is still a very attractive woman, even in her middle forties. Although the infidelity and subsequent divorce from her husband of over twenty years coupled with the worry of her own now uncertain future had done its best to leave its mark on her. But her resolve had seen her through and had made her even more of an inspiration to everyone at the observatory. Blonde with big brown eyes the divorced mother of two was by every definition the cog in the wheel that made this clock tick so efficiently with such little effort. Kelli is humming as she bends over to read the latest TOPSAR (topographic synthetic aperture radar) readouts. This is the equipment that gives the facility the latest analysis of volcanic deformations and hazard warnings from the volcanoes that litter the Pacific coast lines and islands. The Pacific Ring of Fire is what is where the world's most active and dangerous volcanoes still lived and breathed. Kelli stops humming as her eyes narrow. She furrows her brow as she begins to read the information that is on the latest printouts. At that same moment, almost as if on cue, Stevens' computer begins to beep and flash a warning alarm. The alarm startles Jeff awake from his game and his thoughts of the lovely Miss Watson causing him to jump and drop his I-pad on the floor.

"Shit!" Jeff exclaims.

"What's the screen flashing Stevens?" Kelli calls from the TOPSAR.

"Um...well...I'm not exactly sure Watts. I've never seen readings like this before," Stevens answers shakily from where he was sitting at the other end of the aisle.

"Well then get sure damn it! Because I've got some really strange readings down here that we all need to start praying *AREN'T* what I think they are." Kelli's hands are shaking as she continues trying to decipher the printouts she is holding. She tells herself to calm down, that she can't be reading them right. That the calibrations are off or that it's just an unusually large blast from the rock quarry in the next county over. She holds them up into the light foolishly hoping that will change what she is reading on the printouts.

"Um…. Watts, I think you need to come down here and take a look at this." The shock and disbelief both evident in Stevens' voice even from where Kelli was standing in front of the TOPSAR equipment. She drops the printouts letting them fall to the floor as she hurriedly makes her way down the aisle to where Jeff is sitting, examining his computer monitor. Her eyes widen subconsciously as she the reads the monitor over Jeff's left shoulder. Mumbling under her breath as the screen confirms her worse fears.

"Kelli… is… is that *Yellowstone*?" Jeff stammers as Kelli studies the screen.

"Print this out then copy it in an e-mail and send it to me, Washington, and Florida. Please do it as fast as you can Jeff, this is big." She quickly turns away from Jeff's computer monitor as she finishes giving him her instructions walking with purpose as she heads out of the monitoring room in the direction of her office.

"Hey! Where are you going Watts? You didn't answer my question!" Stevens calls out after her nervously when he notices she has walked away from his work station.

"I'll be in my office. I've got a lot of phone calls to make," Kelli answers. She hoped her voice didn't give away the truth of the despair she was truly feeling inside or the fear that was quickly gathering there.

"Who are you going to make those calls to?" Stevens asks, stopping her in midstride. Kelli stands there blinking in disbelief as she answers without turning around to face him, her voice barely above a whisper.

"To anyone, and everyone, that I can get to listen."

"In a few hours' no one in the western part of the U.S. will need to listen. All they'll have to do is look out of their windows." Kelli hears Jeff say, almost apologetically, as she continues down the hall and steps into her office closing the door behind her. Bowing her head and covering her face with her hands, she tries to calm herself, steeling her nerves against what she knows is coming. Taking in a deep breath through her nose she covers the short distance from her door to her desk quickly as she begins looking for the number to her supervisor's office in Washington D.C. Finding it in the back of the rolodex that she keeps on her desk for nostalgic reasons she reaches down to pick up the phone from its cradle sitting on her desk. As she holds her hand out just above the receiver, she can't help but to notice, that it was still shaking.

CHAPTER TWO

Kelli sits down heavily at her desk as she hangs up the phone, staring blankly out of the windows that line the west side of her office facing the Sierra Nevada Mountains. She sits in stunned disbelief as a storm moves in from the west, lightning playing and dancing across the mountain tops. She jumps involuntarily, startled as the sound of thunder rolls across the observatory. She closes her eyes, shocked in the fact that she is about to witness what could arguably be the most destructive force ever given to mother nature and what it will do to change the surface of our planet. The Yellowstone super volcano will be the largest natural disaster ever to befall mankind in its recorded history. Not since the Lake Toba super eruption in Indonesia 74,000 years ago has man, or the planet, faced such a threat of utter annihilation. And while she sits there in her office looking out at the mountains, she knows that right now, at that very moment, in OUR country, it was happening. The caldera that lies beneath the Yellowstone National Forest has awakened. After 640,000 years of relatively peaceful slumber with her true power buried and hidden deep below her pristine exterior. A power that was only hinted at by the mud pots, hot springs, and geysers like Old Faithful that littered her landscape accompanied by the occasional small earthquake. The volcano now sets out upon the task of reminding mankind of how fragile and small it truly is. Only a few truly knew what Yellowstone was truly hiding deep beneath her primeval outer coverings; an unimaginable force like no other on all of the earth. Even among her peers she is a giant. This will be the very definition of what the Volcanic Explosivity Index classifies as a level 8 super eruption; an eruption that will spew the equivalent of 1500 to 1800-cubit miles of debris up into the atmosphere.

"What's going on Kelli?" Jeff asks from her door.

Sullen, lost within the despair of her own thoughts she hadn't even heard Jeff open the door. Jeff's question draws her grudgingly back to reality as Kelli slowly turns away from where she has been sitting and staring out of the window to face him. In the calmest voice that she can manage she quietly asks him,

"Gather everyone together in the break room please Jeff. I'll explain everything then." Then dismissively and without another word of explanation she turns her back to him to stare out of her office windows once more.

"OK. Are you alright Kelli?" Jeff asks her the concern evident in his voice. She starts to speak but is forced to stop to clear her throat, so that her voice will actually work.

"Yes, Jeff I'm fine. Thank you." She inhales and exhales sharply trying to give him a reassuring smile that is faltering at best.

"I just need to run to the ladies' room to get myself together before I address everyone, then I'll be right in." Kelli stands up from her chair and using the window glass as a sort of mirror begins smoothing the front of her skirt and blouse with her hands, trying to wipe away the wrinkles that had set in the fabric as she sat staring out at the countryside. Walking with awkward strides she tries her best to hide the nervousness that had settled within her shaky knees. She brushes by Jeff, who was now standing just inside the door, and touches his arm re-assuredly as she exits the room. Moving quickly down the hall, she can feel Jeff's eyes stay on her until the door to the women's restroom swings shut. She barely makes it to the toilet before the nausea overtakes her. Sitting there afraid and alone on the tiled bathroom floor, vomiting up bile and coffee, Kelli begins to cry. She covers her ears and shuts her eyes as thunder once again reverberates through the building.

The muttering of the curious and the confused alike ceases as soon as Kelli breaches the entryway into the small and brightly lit breakroom. So bright in fact, that it took Kelli's eyes a moment to adjust as the storm outside continued to roll in under quickly darkening skies. This was the only time in the history of the Solid Earth Science Working Group (or SESWG for short) that anyone could recall that the entire on duty staff had been called together for a meeting creating an overlying atmosphere that was both anxious and inquisitive. All eyes were watching her. All ears were listening to her. Everyone is waiting for what it was that was so important that would cause Kelli to call them all here together like this as she walked to the front of the room and turned to address them. With the tension thick about her Kelli clears her throat and begins to speak in a controlled, measurable tone.

"Today approximately 30 to 45 minutes ago, the super volcano that makes up the Yellowstone caldera awoke and began to erupt." She pauses for only a moment to take in a deep breath before she pushes on through all of the audible sighs and gasps, "The eruption appears to be a total and complete inclusion of the entire caldera basin. It is by every definition what Volcanologist classify as a VEI-8 super eruption. This eruption will spew 1500 to 1800-cubit miles of ash and debris into the air reaching up into the upper levels of the atmosphere possibly breaking through the Stratosphere into the Mesosphere. It will release so much ash that it will cover approximately half of the connected United States and Canada. It will also simultaneously kill 1.5 to 3 million people in an instant; literally blowing some to pieces while flash incinerating others. Everyone within a 75-mile radius of ground zero is already dead. Anyone unlucky enough to have been caught inside the 75-100-mile range of the epicenter is now dying from the largest and most devastating pyroclastic flow ever to be witnessed in recorded history." Her voice trails off as the gravity of her words begin to weigh on the people gathered together here in the facilities small cafeteria. Kelli's' speech waivers just long enough to allow a tearful, college aged woman named Mary to stand up and ask a question.

"Mrs. Watson? I'm sorry but I don't understand any of this. What does all this mean? Why are so many people dying?" Mary Jensen was the young, part time receptionist that answered the phone and greeted people at the front desk as they entered the building. She had taken this job to supplement her income as she worked her way through college; partly because the pay was decent and partly because it was easy to study at a front desk that rarely received even the occasional visitor or phone call.

"I…. I'm sorry Mary," Kelli's stumbles. Her offered smile to the group is somber but genuine as she begins to explain in more detail exactly what it is she's been trying to describe.

"For those of you here who may not know, a pyroclastic density current or what is more commonly referred to as a pyroclastic flow, is a fast-moving cloud of hot gases, ash, and debris that races out from the volcano's center as it erupts at speeds of up to 450 mph. With recorded temperatures that can reach up to 1800 degrees Fahrenheit, pyroclastic flows consist primarily of two parts. The basal flow, which makes up the base of the cloud as it hugs the ground and moves outward, and an ash plume that lay's just above the basal flow due to the turbulence between the basal flow and the overlying air." Kelli stops to catch her breath, fighting back the visions that continue to invade her mind of the unfortunate helpless millions of people that she knows have already been caught in its path.

"Nothing stops it. Not even water. It will destroy almost everything that lies in its path. The flow will knock down, shatter, bury, incinerate, or carry away nearly everything that it encounters. Any living creature unlucky enough to find itself in its path will be flash incinerated at temperatures that can literally cause the body to spontaneously combust. Studies done on the skulls found on the island of Pompeii from the Mount Vesuvius eruption have shown scorch marks on the inside of the victim's skulls, literally caused by the brain itself catching on fire." Kelli's voice is barely above a whisper as she finishes speaking but it still booms in the silence that has settled about the room. As the grim reality of the situation takes its hold, the uncomfortable silence slowly begins to be broken by the soft whispers and quiet disbelief of many of its occupants.

"Ok, so now what Mrs. Watson? What the hell are we supposed to do now?" Breathing heavily, Fred Carter the overweight security guard stands up to ask. Not much more than a glorified mall cop, he breaks the tension that had settled throughout the room, voicing out loud what most of the them were already thinking. His gruff voice cutting through the thick atmosphere of uncertainty that has settled about the room like a dense fog as all eyes turn to first land on Fred, then turn to land on Kelli, anxiously waiting for her answer with nervous apprehension.

"That's a good question Fred. What I think all of you should do now is this; I think you should all go home to be with your families and friends if you can. Everyone should leave here to go be with the people you love and with those that love you. Go do whatever it is that you love to do. But fill these moments with all the love and happiness that you can. Sadly, we don't know how many of these moments we have left anymore." Kelli's voice is flat as she finishes, driving home her point. She looks sympathetically into each of their faces as they begin to filter out of the room going to wherever it is that they have chosen to go in this unprecedented moment in time.

The guilt of having to share such devastating news eats at her as each of her co-workers and friends file out wearing looks of disbelief and confusion. Kelli finds herself wondering morbidly if they truly understood that they were leaving the observatory to go and live out what was most assuredly their last days on earth. Kelli knows that their last days will most likely be filled with darkness and violence as society crumbles and its infrastructures begin to falter and fail. She understands that these coming days will be filled with the pangs of hunger and thirst that accompany dehydration and starvation as first the food stores ran out, followed by the water supply. She sighs heavily in the inauspicious recognition of the knowledge of how many days that would be however, no one truly knew.

The room finally clears as Kelli reaches down and places her hands shakily on a nearby table to steady herself. She takes a moment to catch her breath and is about to leave when she notices Stevens sitting alone in the back of the room by the vending machines absently sipping a mountain dew.

"Hey Stevens, I almost didn't see you sitting back there. Why haven't you left yet?" She asks him, trying to keep her voice steady and reassuring.

"Because I don't have anywhere to go," Jeff answers sadly, never picking his head up to look at her. "What do you mean? I thought you were from the San Fernando Valley area?" Kelli asks quizzically.

"I am. La Crescenta to be exact. Just outside of the Angeles National Forest, "The Balcony of Southern California," Jeff says mockingly in a poor Mexican accent. Then taking in a deep breath through his nose and blowing it out through his mouth he unsuccessfully attempts to get his emotions in check before continuing. Leaning his head back to stare up at the ceiling he closes his eyes for a moment before he can begin.

"My parents died in a car crash coming back from a weekend trip to Lake Tahoe when I was a sophomore at Cal-Tech. I was never very close with any of my other relatives, my family is originally from Virginia and I'm an only child, so I don't have any brothers or sisters. Kelli I'm going to die alone!" Jeff sobs, barely getting out the last word before he breaks down uncontrollably slumping from the chair to land heavily on the floor, knocking the chair over in the process. He places his head against his knees as he breaks down, hugging his legs close to his body in an upright fetal position like a scared child. Kelli rushes over, and squats done to sit next to him, wrapping her arms around him as best she can in an awkward attempt to comfort someone that already knows what fate has in store for them. They sit together on the floor surrounded by the air of distress and dread that is brought on by the knowing of what the future has in store for them when between his own muttering sobs Jeff manages to choke out a concerned question of his own.

"Besides, why aren't you on your way home to go be with Beth and Ethan?" The tears that had been threatening to escape from her eyes for the last 20 minutes' spring forth like a geyser to flow down her cheeks as Kelli softly whispers her answer.

"Because they're spending the week with their father and his new twenty something year old girlfriend."

"Well can't you just go be with them anyway? Given the situation I'm sure they would understand Kelli." His own sorrows momentarily forgotten as he tries to understand what Kelli is trying to tell him. He has to strain his ears and lean towards her just to hear her answer as she breathes it to him more than speaks it.

"I wish I could, but I can't. They were spending the week together camping and rafting just outside of Jackson Hole, Wyoming." Now it is Jeff's turn to wrap his arms around his friend as he desperately tries to find any words of comfort to offer her but they all escape him. They sit together on the floor in silence that is broken only by their shared weeping, holding each other alone in the observatory in mutual understanding. Jeff weeps in his disbelief, Kelli weeps in her despair as they lean on one another sharing their dismay both empathetic to each other's feelings of being abandoned and left behind by everyone in this world that they had ever truly loved.

Somewhere in rural western Montana, a father fills his truck up with gas. Smiling at the memory of how excited his two young sons had been that morning when he told them about the weekend long fishing trip he was going to take them on as a treat for school starting back up. In eastern Idaho, a young mother sings Disney carols with her daughter as they make their daily morning commute to her pre-school; practicing for the fall concert that the school put on every year with the three and four-year-old classes celebrating the Eastern Idaho State Fair in Blackfoot.

In western Wyoming, a farmhand works on repairing a section of fence that has been damaged by a herd of pronghorns migrating through the valley the previous evening as he enjoys the quiet serenity of a cool rocky mountain morning. And in the suburbs of northern Utah a young woman is beaming with an excitement that can't be altered even by the thick, morning rush hour traffic as she drives to the first day of her new job, her new career, since graduating from college that summer. All over the tristate area of Montana, Wyoming, and Idaho that are connected to Yellowstone; into northern Utah and the southern Canadian provinces of Alberta, British Columbia, and Saskatchewan, life on this fateful morning begins as normal. Businesses open, and morning shifts begin as night shifts end. Young teenage girls on their way to school whisper to their girlfriends about their first kiss at last Friday night's football game while young teenage boys brag to their friends about theirs. All of this is extinguished when the volcano erupts. Instantly killing millions in a flash of earth, lava, and violence. Some die while changing the radio. Others die while standing in line waiting for their morning coffee. Most die having no idea of what has even happened, mercifully dying with very little pain or fear. But they all die just the same. Death is swift and efficient as it carries them on its wings into the afterlife and begins to single handedly write the next chapter of human existence in its own blackened vision. Death spews ash all the way into the stratosphere where the jet stream, caused by the rotation of the earth, plays its role by carrying the ash all over the globe swiftly laying an ash cover too thick for the sun to penetrate even at its zenith. In just a matter of days' death wraps its arms around mother earth in an embrace of malicious intent blanketing her in complete and utter darkness.......

"I take mine into contemplation and so secure myself,
by making my recourse to my God, who is our security."

–John Donne

"Ask not for whom the bell tolls, for it tolls for thee."

CHAPTER THREE

Year One, Day Thirty-Eight

Kelli's eyes flutter and close as the energy of her life continues to ebb away. She is too weak and dehydrated to truly be able to tell if she is awake or asleep, the lines that separated the two worlds of consciousness and unconsciousness having blurred together into one existence a long time ago. She and Jeff had scavenged through the observatory as best as they could after the eruption collecting and storing away everything edible and drinkable that they could find. Looking mostly for the things people had stowed away at their work stations or in their breakroom lockers. Sadly, a box of saltine crackers, a few multi-grain bars, some bottles of water, and a medium sized tin of mixed nuts (which had already been opened) were the only booty to be found in their treasure hunt for survival. Couple all of that together with what they had broken out of the vending machines (which had thankfully been recently stocked) and one could easily, but foolishly think that they had found enough to sustain them for several weeks, possibly months. Months unfortunately, had ended up being just a handful of weeks even with careful rationing. Kelli's eyes flutter back open, even the small act of blinking only taking place now with tremendous effort. The horizon still has an orange glow from the fires set by the rioters and lynch mobs that had formed in the initial panic after the eruption. The glow stands out in stark contrast against the backdrop of darkness against the small city outline. The government had quickly declared Marshall Law of course but it had done little if anything to contain the panic and violence of the ravenous hordes of maniacs. The overwhelming lawlessness that had all too quickly begun to define the city was one of the main reasons she and Stevens had initially decided to try to make their last stand here at the observatory. A noble attempt to hold out up here on their little hilltop hidden in relative safety until things either calmed down or as mobs like this often do, people just lost interest. The cities police department and the National Guard sent to keep order in the city had lost control in just a matter of days, over run by the sheer number of people out of their minds with fear and panic. The sounds of sirens used by the fire department and paramedics trying to put out the fires and stop the bleeding also no longer wailed. Only occasionally did they even hear gunfire now. The city, once a haven in these mountainous foothills, was now broken and destroyed. Leaving what pieces of the city that were left to be run by the rapists, murderers, and thieves that had inherited it from the government once they had pulled out, leaving the city to suffer alone in the hands of its own fate. Staring out at the glow of the city her eyes flutter closed again;

"Hello Mom." An angel beams down at Kelli, surrounded by a brilliant and beautiful, comforting light.

"Beth? Is that you? I thought you were with your father for the week, rafting in Wyoming?"

"I was, but I'm home now Mom. We all are. We have been here waiting for you."

"Oh Beth, I'm so happy to see you! I thought that I had lost you forever!"

Kelli's eyes flutter open again. She is not greeted by the angelic image of her daughter as she hoped but instead they open to land on Stevens who was sitting directly across from her propped up against the opposite wall. A rat that had been eating what was left of Stevens nose now perched itself up on his half-eaten face by using his gnawed and widened bloody nostrils as foot holds, its head buried up to its shoulders in Jeff's right eye socket. His breathing comes in slow ragged gasps as his left pointer finger twitches spastically in what was surely a subliminal registry of pain. She had hoped he had already slipped away when she noticed the first rat appear early this morning. Or was it late yesterday evening? Time ceased to have any true meaning in the ever-pressing darkness and hunger that now enveloped everything. A movement caught within the gloom of the red exit sign that still shown bright draws her attention back to the moment. She shudders at the thought of the vermin eating Stevens while he was still alive. The wet sounds of his gargled breathing sicken her but just like Stevens, she is far too weak and close to death herself to do anything about it. So, she sits there. Lacking the ability to help herself or Stevens she drops her head, feeling sorry for them both. Watching the rats devour her dying friend causes what acids that had managed to form in her belly to roll and turn threatening to come up. She would cry if she could, but her body hadn't the energy or the fluids to spare to offer her such a luxury of release. What fools she and Jeff had been. The food they had found in the offices ran out first. Then the food and sodas from the vending machines had run out. Then when the water had stopped running from the faucets, they had run through what water bottles they had managed to set aside in just days. Both naively thinking that the water would eventually get turned back on, neither of them realizing just how bad things had in fact truly gotten in the city. In an act of desperation, they had foolishly used the water to try and ward off the hunger pains that threatened to eat them away from the inside. Thankfully, almost mercifully Kelli's eyes flutter closed again.

"You didn't lose us Mom. We were just separated from each other for a little while."

"Where is Ethan? Is he here with you?" Kelli gasps as she frantically looks around for her son.

"Yes, Ethan is here with me. See? Look over there. Can you see him standing there on that hill top waiting for us?" The angelic figure of Kelli's beautiful daughter steps back to reveal a lovely sunny spring day shining down over a brilliantly green grassy knoll that stood behind her in the distance covered in dazzling wildflowers. She sees a group of people gathered there and standing in the middle was Ethan, smiling and waving his arm in his mother's direction.

"Can you see him Mom? He's right there in the middle waving to you."

"Oh yes, I can see him! Ethan!"

Kelli's eyes flutter back open with her son's name still on her lips as she tries to call out to him. The dry crackle that manages to escape her throat in life however momentarily makes the rats that were still steady at work on Stevens pause for just an instant. The fiend that had been buried in Jeff's right eye socket now peered out at her from his left eye socket, its nose twitching in her direction sniffing the air. The tail that wiggles joyfully against Stevens cheek reminds Kelli of a worm trapped on a section of sidewalk after a hard rain, as it hangs out of the eye socket it had used to enter the soft, gray matter of his skull. Thankfully his finger had stopped twitching, and his chest no longer expanded, his lungs finally stopping their efforts at trying to force air into an already dead body. Kelli's eyes fall closed, just as she feels Beth reach down and grab her by the hand.

"Come now Mom, we've kept them waiting for us for too long. You've fought hard enough. It's time for you to come with me now." Beth helps her to her feet and embraces her, then turning towards the knoll they begin to walk towards the others. Hand in hand, mother and daughter, they both wear broad smiles upon their faces. Cruelly, her eyes flutter open once more as her body selfishly clings to a life that the soul had given up on long ago. With a ragged exhale (which was a pitiful attempt at her daughter's name) she looks down at the hand that she would have sworn had been in Beth's grasp just moments before and looks directly into the red rimmed, doll black eyes of the rat that was now perched in her palm. Blood is evident around its nostrils from breathing in the ashes that still fell like snow flurries outside, the microscopic shards of glass reaping their havoc on even nature's most perfect opportunist. At first, she thinks it is the same harbinger that had aided Stevens on his journey into the afterlife but a painful glance over at her pitiful friend reveals otherwise. The tail of the tiny blood-soaked monster still hung from Stevens's right eye socket waving in the air like the side walked trapped worm, the weight of the rat causing his head to lean to one side sickly causing his jaw to drop open revealing his black and swollen tongue. Kelli feels the weight in her own hand shift, bringing her attention back to her side of the room. Mercifully the movement causes her eyes to flutter back shut for the last time, she has become far too weak now to hold them open any longer.

"We're almost there, Mom. Don't stop now, you're doing great."

"OH Beth!" Kelli exclaims, clutching at her daughter. "I thought you had gone away! Please don't make me go back there again. I want to stay here with you and your brother!" She is almost shouting in her desperation. Her sobbing pleas to her daughter almost incoherent as she cries for her to never let her go again.

"SHHHHH its ok, you never have to go back there again. You're home now. Here with us, forever."

15

Kelli Watson; the blonde, green eyed, divorced mother of two walks slowly over the grassy knoll and slips out of sight. Holding her sons hand in her left hand, her daughters hand in her right, the trio follows behind the rest of their beloved family members that had come to welcome Kelli home. At the observatory, the resourceful rat begins to gnaw its way into the thoughts and dreams of a still, blonde haired, emaciated form precariously leaning against a vending machine that had long ago gone empty.

"People are like stained glass windows. They sparkle and shine when the sun is out, but when the darkness sets in; their true beauty is only revealed if there is light from within."

~Elizabeth Kubler-Ross

CHAPTER FOUR

YEAR ONE, DAY THREE HUNDRED AND TWENTY-TWO

The road is dark and narrow as the group makes their way through the lightly falling rain and ash mix that falls out here in the Ashland. The streaks left on the windshield by the wipers back dropped with the perpetual darkness of a sunless sky makes it hard to truly define anything as they travel along making their speed slow and methodical. Disaster had already taught them the harsh lesson that caution was more important than speed when they were away from the safe confines of the compound. You could be driving down what you thought was a road one minute, only to discover that it had once been a boat ramp in the world before and find yourself dangerously standing waist deep in an ash mud lake with the same properties and voracious appetite as quicksand the next minute. The volcano had effectively turned what was once some ones Saturday morning little piece of Heaven into a death trapped cesspool. Where fathers had once sat with a pole in the water and their young son fidgeting next to them dreaming of monster catfish and bass delighted in the fact that his father had included him in something that he instinctively knew was special. A lake that had once created precious memories and fed guilty pleasures now sits dead and silent. The color of life having been drained away only to leave behind the shadowed black and grey memories of days gone past. The lakes and waterways had died quickly. Almost overnight they had become unable to sustain life any longer due to the oxygen choking ash and the acid rain that had continuously fell from the skies initially after the eruption to run down their banks and flood their depths with death.

Without prejudice between animal or plant life the rain and ash had fallen from a blackened and sunless sky, slowly but efficiently poisoning and killing almost everything. Three members of their party had been horribly lost to this lake the first time they had all agreed to venture out into the Ashland to scavenge for supplies. Clay had tried to warn Roger to take it slow and easy while they felt their way around, but some people even in this version of our world still had to learn things the hard way. Except that now learning the hard way could mean ending up dead. They had been driving along the road that led around the lake to a small fishing camp on the far side when Roger unexpectedly made a right-hand turn onto what appeared to be a winding back road, foolishly believing that he had discovered a shortcut. Unfortunately for them the shortcut ended up not being a road at all but ended up being an overly wide path that led down to a large public fishing dock that was once used to rent canoes to weekend warrior's that liked to get their weekly exercise rowing their kids across the lake pointing out the wildlife and shrubbery that decorated the banks like some sort of cheap public access nature show. Now however, in the aftermath of the volcano's destruction it was just a dilapidated, old broken down wooden reminder of what life had been like before the apocalypse. Partially collapsed and falling apart what was left of the dock stuck out of the muddy and ashy slurry water like the half submerged pre-historic skeleton of someone's broken dreams and forgotten pleasures. In the extreme dark with flurrying ashes mixing with the lightly falling rain Roger had literally driven the car right over the edge of the derelict dock causing the car they were traveling in to do a slow-motion flip in the air, landing on its roof. There it began to sink torturously slow into the gruel colored muck that now defined the lakes contents. The consistency of the liquid that now made up the lakes "water" making the car sink far more gradually than it normally would have, slowly dragging its occupants down into the depths in a cruel and tormenting death. The rest of the group were greeted by the screams of the dying and the frightened alike when they arrived at the accident far too late to be of any help. Blinded from the dark and to cold and wet from the icy rain that had now begun to fall heavily pelting them with big, fat rain drops. The heavy rain clears away some of the falling ashes caused by the volcanic winter that now cloaks the planet as they stand together mortified in their helplessness. The car was already half way swallowed up by the muddy water when they had arrived at the scene and hating to admit it they were sinfully thankful when the liquid death finally filled enough of the car to muffle the agony it contained inside of it. It was a gruesome reminder to all that witnessed the lake drag the car down to its depth of the constant dangers that threatened to greet them around every corner out here in the Ashland. *The Ashland.* The name the group had playfully adopted calling the area that began in the foothills of the Ozark mountain range in western Arkansas to where they assumed the initial blast of the volcano had destroyed and incinerated almost everything and everyone. An area they had heard reported before the power went out that encircled an approximate radius of one hundred and fifty miles around what was left of the Yellowstone National Forest in western Wyoming.

"Hey Dad, if I'm reading the map right we should be getting close to where we lost Roger's group the last time out." Clay's oldest son Levi updates him from the passenger seat momentarily pulling him out of his reflections. He doesn't think he'll ever get used to how his sons voice sounds through the mask they all are forced to wear when they are out here around fallen or falling ashes. To Clay it makes everyone sound detached and distant.

"Thanks. I was afraid that was about where we were. That's a day I wish we all could forget," Clay responds.

"Yeah, well Uncle Roger should've known better than to drive like a maniac out here. Especially in an area we hadn't been able scout out yet," Levi says trying to ease the guilt he knows his father still feels from the death of his mother's little brother.

"I know but try telling that to your mother. It was my responsibility to look out for him, remember?" Clay says with a heavy sigh. Levi lets it drop with a casual shrug of his shoulder as he says,

"I know, but she'll get over it eventually. It'll just take her some time. Besides, Uncle Roger was always kind of an asshole anyways." Clay laughs, lightly hitting his son on his shoulder. Under their masks, they were both smiling as they continued down the ash covered road. The head lights from the vehicles cut a shallow path through the darkness as they make their way past an ominous right turn that didn't lead to anywhere but memories of death and gloom.

CHAPTER FIVE

Two days had passed since the group had left the safety of the compound. No longer able to spare the gas to run the generators that would supply the power for the UV lamps that lined the ceiling of the makeshift greenhouses they had initially constructed they hadn't been able to grow any food on their own for quite some time now. With supplies running dangerously short they had been forced to start going out on supply excursions to rebuild their stock of food rations, bottled water, and medical supplies. At first, they had been able to find most of what they needed in the local areas surrounding the compound. But after their early success in the surrounding countryside their explorations into the smaller cities within short driving distance started coming up empty. Finding anything of use had become increasingly more and more difficult to the point that they were finally forced into having to make their way to, and then down, highway 270 towards Malvern and Interstate 30. The utter destruction of the larger cities they passed was a shock to everyone at first. The simple, but real fact of what pampered and spoiled suburbanites would do to their own neighbors when faced with the uncertain reality of not knowing where their next meal or their next drink was coming from or when they would receive it was quite disturbing, even to the most hardened pessimistic. The looters had destroyed more than they had taken in their initial wave of panic. Deranged hoards made up of the overweight and over medicated population of privileged suburbia fighting over their diet coke and anti-depressants. They rolled over and destroyed virtually everything like a terror stricken obese tsunami. And what they didn't manage to destroy, they unknowingly made whatever little was left behind unusable. Between the panic of the suburbanites and the fires set by the rioting governmental dependents pissed off about their useless EBT cards and the handouts that were no longer coming there was very little left behind in these over populated areas that was of any real use. Not to mention the fact that what people were left behind in the cities more closely resembled small roaming groups of opportunistic rapists and lunatics that needed to be avoided than they did real people anymore. But for those few left behind and savvy enough to escape the cities to less populated areas or for those lucky enough to have family or friends already set up in remote areas of the country, survival was a daily responsibility taken on by the strong willed, strong minded, and strong backed. Clay Stratford and his wife Veronica along with their two sons Levi and Cain were one of the savvy ones lucky enough to escape out of the city to the higher ground of the Ozark mountain range where they were also lucky enough to have Veronica's doomsday prepping younger brother Roger. Always preaching about governmental conspiracies and the New World Order, Roger had also thankfully practiced what he preached and had been prepping for years on land he had somehow acquired just outside of the Ouachita National Forest. The volcanic eruption hadn't been the event he was preparing for but "Crazy" Roger's compound had saved all their asses just the same. In the beginning, right after Yellowstone had spewed its hate out onto the world, Clay had no idea of how he was going to care for his family and get them through all of this. It had been Roger that had come through for them. He had supplied them with a place to stay, a place to try to hold up in the aftermath. But most important of all, he had given them *a place to survive*. Sadly, in what had to be the most classic example of irony, it had been the moonshine making, marijuana growing black sheep of the Owens household, drunk on his own brew, that had driven himself, his like-minded best friend Lee, and Kim (the only woman that Clay had ever known that could put up with all of Roger's bullshit) right off of a broken-down dock to die in an ash mud lake. Roger had been too stubborn to listen to the ex-military, city boy that came from "cushy city living and a gym membership" when it came to mountain survival. So, in the end the unlikely savior of Clay's family, the only one of them that had possessed the fore sight to set aside a place of hiding and preparation, was indeed just an asshole.

"Ok dad, it looks like we're past the part of Ouachita lake where the accident happened and should be coming out of Hurricane Grove. Joplin is just up the road a little way past that." Levi calls out pulling Clay back to the present once again.

"Alright, sounds good. We'll pull over here to set up camp and work our way towards Joplin. Don't forget to circle Hurricane Grove so that we know we've already searched there. Levi, can you make out what the sign for this place says it is? It kind of looks like a doctor's office.

Maybe we can find something in there that we can use if it is," Clay says to his son as he slowly pulls the jeep into what they hoped was an abandoned parking lot.

"Um… let me see. I mean it's kind of unfair to ask the guy with poor vision and dyslexia to read what a sign says in the dark just because he's in the passenger seat, but hey what do I know," Levi says jokingly to his father. "I guess that's what I get for calling shotgun. Oooo, wait a minute… maybe we can get some use out of this place after all!" Levi exclaims excitedly. Turning towards his father for effect, he adds sarcastically, "It's a chiropractic office. Do you think they're open? I could definitely use an adjustment." Everyone in the car laughs this time, a choir of Darth Vader's thankfully still able to find some humor in an otherwise humorless world.

Clay slowly maneuvers the lead vehicle around to the back of the building for better concealment from the road, also he makes sure that the Jeep is carefully positioned pointing back out the way they had come into the parking lot, just in case a speedy get away became necessary. Everyone is scanning the area for anything that could be of any harm or use as they make their way through the parking lot. All the laughing came to an end as the time to get to back work and be alert, began. Clay brings the four door Jeep Wrangler they had found the first time they had left the compound for supplies to a stop turning off the engine as he sets the parking brake. They had been lucky enough to find the Jeep sitting in front of a local drug store with the keys still in the ignition. Parked just outside of the drugstores front door, the back loaded down with beer, wine, and energy drinks. A materialized vision of a high school boy's wet dream it was a forest green 4x4 with a small lift kit and big off-road tires. They had found the driver of the Jeep dead in front of the pharmacy. Apparently shot trying to steal what was left of the OxyContin and Xanax. Evidently, the would-be thief hadn't been completely satisfied with only the alcohol and energy drinks that he had already taken. The jeep seated four comfortably and had unquestionably become an essential tool in excursions for the survival of the compound. On this trip out the four chosen to ride in the Jeep were; Clay and Levi, who were seated in the front, with Paige Harris and Jim O'Conner seated in the back. Jim wasn't one of the regulars that normally went out on these trips, Jackson was. But, with his wife Gracie being pregnant and so close to giving birth, it was decided that he should stay behind to be with her in the event that she happened to go into labor while they were out. Needless to say, Jim wasn't exactly thrilled at being the unasked volunteer to fill the vacant fourth spot on the team. They always went out on these excursions in two teams of four, both for safety and practicality. Two of the four were equipped with compound bows and side arms. They ran point on the explorations for supplies while the two that guarded the rear were equipped with shotguns or carbines along with their side arms. The use of bows by the first two was done to keep things as silent and as covert as possible, while the heavy firepower of the rear guard was to raise all hell if silent and covert was no longer an option. To ensure that they could in fact get away in the face of the horrors of the Ashland or when the shit had just completely hit the fan. It was simple and effective. Everyone on both teams had their own job to do. Four would scout around the predetermined area for anything that could be of use, while the other four stayed behind siphoning gas from the abandoned cars in the parking lots. These four would also protect whatever they were using as a base camp as well as protecting the ever increasingly important vehicles they had become so dependent on for these supply runs.

Clay and his group were just beginning to climb out of the Jeep Wrangler as Ray idles the black Toyota Tacoma crew cab 4x4 that made up the second vehicle of this miniature convoy directly behind them. Already in an unspoken understanding behind the strategic positioning of the vehicles Clay raises a hand to his friend as he closes the driver side door and stretches for the first time in what seems like days. Ray returns the gesture as he puts the truck in park and kills the engine. The occupants of the truck that make up the second group, the ones responsible for the vehicles and for scouting the parking lot are Ray Jones, his son Grant, his oldest daughter Laura, and Colt Kingston. Ray, along with his wife Sophia and their other two children twelve-year-old twin girls Lily and Rose had become fast and close friends to Clay and his family over the calamity of the last several months. Along with Paige, whom Ray, and Sophia had taken in after the loss of her family, and with Clay and Veronica taking in their youngest son Cain's best friend Dylan Glosser, they were as close as two-family units could be during such an unprecedented time of uncertainty. Not to mention that it had been Ray's experience as a car mechanic that had directly led to them being able to equip and maintain the vehicles on these long trips away from the protection of the compound. He was the one that had known that the cars would continue to work just fine as long as they kept the air and gas filters clean from the engine choking ashes. Ray had his group clean out the air filters every time they stopped for the night. Plus, by making sure everyone kept ashes from falling into the gas tanks as they filled them up each morning, keeping the gas filters wasn't that hard. Keeping in mind that evening and morning were relative terms in the world they now lived in of course. It would've been more accurate to describe it as dark and darker as the dull globe that now defined the sun rose and fell across a world that was blanketed in a perpetual gloom.

"Slow going coming around that shit hole of a lake," Ray says to his friend as he approaches him from the side, extending out his hand. Clay grasps the man's hand fondly.

"You can say that again. Those maps we found at the burned-up Quickie Mart are the only things that even made this trip possible at all. After the last time, I'm not sure I would've been brave enough to try it without them," he answers, dropping his gaze to look down at the ground when his statement is finished.

"Well I think you and your young navigator there did one hell of a job getting us all the way through Hurricane Grove with no mishaps. And stop doing that, there isn't anything to drop your head about Clay. Despite how Ronnie feels about things right now, Roger wasn't your fault. One day she'll be able to let it go, you need to do the same." Finishing, Ray puts a hand on his friend's shoulder giving it a light squeeze before he turns to walk back to the truck. Everyone begins unloading supplies as Clay looks after his friend smiling, appreciative of the gesture of good will.

"Hey dad, Paige and I are going to scout the front of the building see if there's anything to see," Levi says from behind Clay startling him.

"Ok son, that sounds good. Keep it quick. Keep it silent. I'll have Jim briefed on the way things work on these house sweeps by the time you two get back. If it's too much for him, we'll have to take Colt instead. I figure we can enter the office through that door over here," Clay says as he gestures towards a back door set off to the far side of the building that led out to the dumpster paddock. "We do a quick sweep and clear to make sure there's no one home then we do a more thorough search to see if we can find anything that's of any use to us or the group."

Clay and Levi both nod in understanding and agreement as they part. Clay watches Levi as he walks away to go find Paige and inform her of their agenda. Left standing in the parking lot alone Clay is encircled by the utter and complete silence that was left after Levi's departure. You didn't realize how noisy the world was until everything was shut off. The electricity had stopped working not long after anything requiring a satellite link had stopped working. Since the satellite signals were unable to penetrate the ash cover to reach the towers they were the first piece of modern technology to stop working. So, the world that was once blossoming in technological wonders was put into a perpetual darkness and silence. Not only was the sky blackened by Mother Nature herself, but humanity had also been removed from under the false security blanket of electricity. Nothing to chase away yours fears at the flick of a switch. No cell phones, no GPS, no XM radio, no internet, with no electricity to power the pumps there wasn't even running water. Literally ***everything*** that a so called civilized society had come to depend on every day -and consequently took for granted – was gone; effectively setting the worlds civilizations back at least two hundred years. Nevertheless, it really wasn't the lack of all the pleasantries that affected you. It was the absolute silence. The world had gone quiet and that was the un-nerving persistent reminder to Clay that their lives, that the ***world***, has been forever changed, and that their previous way of life was in fact like the silence that surrounded him -**dead**. Standing in the midst of the dark and quiet that now defined their existence Clay reflects on how proud he is of his sons and how much they have grown during the last year. He can't help but smile as he reflects on the obvious infatuation that was growing between his son Levi and the lovely Miss Paige Harris.

The budding romance between the two youths left him hanging on to hope for the world's future. That something beautiful could still find root in the dead, grey ground despite the hardships that they all now faced on a daily basis for survival. Levi and Paige slip off around the corner of the chiropractor's office sticking close to the building trying to stay concealed within the dead bushes that had once decorated it as he turns around, holding onto his smile, he begins walking to where the others were waiting at the back of the Tacoma to begin laying out the plans for the rest of the group.

The couple returns just as Clay is finishing up his part of the pep talk to the group and Ray takes over continuing to drive home how important their diligence was to the details and for everyone's safety.

"OK, just so everyone understands, we actually make a small puncture in the left rear corner of the gas tank to filter the gas out. That way we're certain to get all that we can get out of it, always making sure to run it through the cheese cloth. That will filter out any debris that's settled at the bottom of the tank over time," Ray is saying to everyone as Clay jumps in,

"Look, we know most of you have heard all of this already, but this is Jim and Grant's first time out. Plus, it's also an excellent way to tell if we've already visited an area. We have the map gridded out to hopefully prevent that from happening again, but a little insurance policy never hurt anyone. It's cold and dark out here so mistakes are inevitably going to happen. Not to mention that I think all of our map reading skills got a little rusty with the invention of map-quest." The group laughs at Clay's last comment as Ray brings the lecture home.

"So, if you go to siphon a car and it's got a hole in the bottom left rear corner of the gas tank, we've accidentally revisited an area that we've already been to. If, or should I say when, that happens find myself or Clay and we'll all get together and try to figure out where we made a wrong turn and move on to an un-scouted spot."

"Ok let's wrap this up, does everyone understand what they're supposed to do and what their responsibilities are? Two of you work together on siphoning the cars while the second two stand guard keeping a watch over them and the area for anything threatening. As well as keeping an eye on the trucks. With the exception of Jim and Grant we've all been out here before. Let's collect what we can and get back home quick and safe. Everybody got it?" Clay finishes as the group answers with a mask muffled chorus of "Got it." Now that the assignments had been given out Jim quietly pulls Clay off to the side.

"What's up Jim?" Clay asks as the others disembark.

"Hey Clay, I don't think I'll be of much use in there with you guys. I've never handled a bow before and I'm not much better with a gun," Jim says as he and Clay continue to walk away from the others who were all now in the midst of getting ready for their assignments.

"All I'm saying too ya is, that I'm a hell of a lot better at being a mechanic than I would ever be at being a soldier."

"I respect your honesty Jim. The last thing anyone wants is for you to do anything you're not comfortable with. Knowing how much you help out Willy back home at the compound I was kind of already expecting this conversation." Gripping Jim's shoulder reassuringly he adds,

"I've already asked Colt if he wouldn't mind switching with you in case you weren't good with going inside."

"What did he say?" Jim asks hesitantly.

"He said that it wouldn't be a problem at all," Clay answers, giving his friends shoulder a happy pat.

"Well alright then. You have no idea how relieved that makes me Clay. Thank you… and thank Colt for me too if you wouldn't mind. I just figured I'd be a hell of a lot more useful outside helping Ray instead of being a liability inside searching with you guys. You know what I mean?" Jim says, his mood visibly improving.

"I understand completely my friend, no thanks are necessary," Clay says, slapping Jim good heartedly on the back as they turn to make their way back to the rest of the group and inform every one of the changes. Clay, Levi, Paige, and Colt will enter the Dr.'s office to gather anything of use from inside and to clear the building of any possible dangers so that they could set up base camp. Meanwhile the rest of the scouting party; Ray, Jim, Laura, and Grant will start going through the parking lot refilling the gas cans and rummaging through the abandoned cars that were abandoned there for anything useful. The party splits into their collective groups all with the understanding of how important what they are doing out here truly is.

The back door is locked tight as they had expected it would be after Levi and Paige's scouting trip to the front of the building had found the front door and windows to all be the same way. The fact that the windows and doors were still secure made this an even more attractive selection for base camp as Clay eases the crowbar between the door and the door frame as far in and as silently as possible. Then slowly, Clay begins to apply pressure, leaning on the crowbar. At the same time, Levi puts steady, controlled pressure on the door trying to get it to "pop" as quietly as possible. Clay is beginning to add more pressure onto the crowbar just as the door swings in with a jolt, not as silently as they were hoping for, but the goal was accomplished all the same. They split into two smaller versions of the main group to enter the building two by two. Clay leads the group into the building with an arrow notched ready to be released if necessary. Levi follows closely behind him armed with a Mossberg 500 12-gauge pump shotgun held at the ready to aid his father if the need arose. Colt follows them in with his bow held at the ready and an arrow notched as well with Paige positioned as his rear guard armed with an HK GSG-5 .22 caliber semi-automatic carbine. All of them together are collectively tense, filled with nervous anxiety at the possibility of any unknown dangers that could be waiting for them inside the building as they enter it. The door opened into what was once a break room slash storeroom. Inside the room there was a small round table with two chairs slid in underneath it, a microwave and toaster oven, a small refrigerator (like the ones you would see in a college dorm room designated for beer), a single row of cabinets, and a handful of chairs all taking up one side of the room. A tower of boxes stacked on top of one another, assorted cleaning and disinfecting supplies along with some filing cabinets and empty shelving took up the other side. They hold steady in focused concentration with the main body of the building still needing to be swept and cleared even when faced with the hopeful possibilities that there could be food, or first aid found within the cabinets. There would be plenty of time to investigate what was in this room later. After a quick, glancing inspection of the room Clay spots a door standing slightly ajar at the far end of the room. Figuring that this was the door that will lead them out into the main hallway of the building they stay in formation and begin to approach the door with determined purpose. Colt and Levi switch positions as the group forms back into one unit. Clay reaches the door in only seven careful strides and slowly begins to push the door the rest of the way open. He tries without succeeding to keep the creeks and moans of the unused door to a minimum as he does. The hallway that greets them just beyond the now fully open door was thankfully empty and showed no evidence of being used in quite some time. They check and clear each room in turn as they make their way down the hallway towards the office's main waiting room and the door that lead to the doctor's personal office. Finishing their initial sweep and clear of the rooms lining the hallway they are all able to breath sighs of relief as thankfully each room was yielding the same results as the break room they had used to enter the building. They were all relatively empty and unused.

Approaching the end of the hallway it is the smell that first tips them off to what awaited them just behind the closed office door of Dr. Tyler Blackburn. The unmistakable smell of death accosts their senses even through the dust masks they still wore filling this area of the hallway with the thickly sweet and sickening smell of decay. The door to the office swings open slowly as Clay and Colt take up the doorway (one kneeling, one standing) and are the first to be confronted by the half-decomposed body of the late Dr. Blackburn. The .357 magnum that was lying on the floor at his feet and the hole clearly visible in his skull, left little doubt as to what had been the culprit of his demise. Clay, afraid of how the shock of finding such a gruesome scene like this will affect the young members of his scouting party, does his best to hide his own emotions as he calmly walks over and bends down to pick up the handgun. Never acknowledging the gore that covers everything behind him, Clay speaks with simple indifference as he comes around to the front of the desk, using himself as a barrier between the rest of the group and the body, testing the weight of the revolver as he bounces it in his hand.

"This could come in very handy. The best thing about this being a magnum instead of just a .38 is that it will shoot both .357 and .38 special cartridges out of it. So, we basically just lucked into two guns instead of one. I'll start checking around in here for anything of use, like a box of bullets for this much-needed newest member of our arsenal here for example." Clay holds up the Ruger LCR .357 magnum they had just discovered for everyone to see as he finishes the statement.

"You three go and start collecting anything we can use out of the examining rooms working your way back to the break room we entered through. I'll give the waiting room a once over just to make sure we don't leave any stone unturned and meet you all there. We can update Ray and the others then. Be especially on the lookout for any antibiotic salves, bandages, and disinfectants like peroxide while you're searching." Clay gives these orders quickly, doing his best to get the group out of the room and their minds onto something, ***anything*** else other than the brains and bits of bone that were splattered all over the library of medical books that sat on the bookshelves directly behind the desk of the late chiropractor. As the group turns around in unison thankful to get away from the scene they now stood in front of, Clay stoops down to get a closer look at something that had caught his eye when he had picked up the magnum. The thighs and calves of the dead doctor appeared to him as if they had been gnawed upon. But gnawed upon by what, or the more disturbing possibility, by ***whom*** was the question.

CHAPTER SIX

Lost in his own contemplations of the possibly partially eaten right leg of the dead doctor, Clay walks right past the door that leads to the unexplored waiting room as he is leaving the office. An opened box of .357 caliber bullets for the Ruger his only bounty from his search of the room. Colt, picking up on the fact that something clearly has Clay rattled, reaches out and gently grabs Clay by the upper arm as he walks past without ever seeing him.

"Hey Boss. You still with us?" He asks Clay as he walks by the waiting room door, his head down in obvious deep thought.

"Huh? What? Oh…uh…yeah Colt. I'm sorry. Yes, I'm still with you. Just got a little lost in mapping out the rest of the search," Clay stammers in response.

"You sure about that chief? You're walking through here like you're on the surface of Mars" Colt says as he and Clay share a halfhearted laugh.

"Yeah…. I'm fine. Sorry about that. Thanks Colt," Clay says as he looks Colt in the eye and gives him a short appreciative nod.

"No worries. Come on I'll check the waiting room out with you. Levi and Paige have the examining rooms covered," Colt offers as he returns Clays nod.

"Are they finding anything useful?" Clay asks with cautious optimism.

"Oh Yeah!" Colt exclaims, "A few ace bandages, some gauzes, latex gloves, some cotton balls, a couple bottles of disinfectant, mostly stuff like that so far; but definitely all stuff we are in desperate need of." Before the event, these things weren't exactly what some one would think of as important in everyday life but when everyday life becomes the survival of the fittest (or as in the case of the compound, the survival of the best prepared) little things like cotton balls and ace bandages could be the difference between being able to live or not.

"Sounds great. This place is quickly turning out to be a pretty-good score. Oh! Has anyone spotted a restroom yet? How great would it be to find a dozen rolls of toilet paper," Clay sighs longingly as they start to turn into the waiting room. The wishful desire for a commodity that was so often taken for granted evident in his voice even through the muffling filter he wore.

"Well it is the little things in life that you miss the most when they're gone," Colt replies jokingly. They both share another short laugh as they slowly open the door and step inside the offices quaint waiting room.

The room is bigger than they had expected it to be as they shine their red lensed lights around inside trying to get a feel for the layout of the room. The laugh they shared which was already awkwardly uncomfortable in the gloomy overcast of the world's current situation is ominously cut short as they both sense the uneasy feeling the room ebbs outward towards them like a thick haze. It slams into them as soon as they cross through the doorway into the room almost as if they have just entered a thick invisible fog. Clay motions for Colt to go to the right as he takes a step in the direction of the receptionist's desk which sat off to their left. Following this pattern, they should come back together at the front door which would give them the opportunity to check the strength and security of the locks. They were hoping to be able to use the office as their base camp of operations while they were exploring this section of the town. Clay, along with Ray and Colt, had gridded out the map yesterday when they had stopped to rest, placing this small core of office buildings grouped in the grids center. Hopefully optimistic that at least one of them would be secure enough to afford them safe shelter as they scavenged the local area. Clay, who had just reached the front of the reception counter and can't help but to notice the receptionist's name plate standing in the center next to the sign in sheet, stretches to look over the counter top to peer into the area behind it. The blood is instantly recognizable in the red glow of his light from where it has turned black over time. He can see how it coats the chair and had even pooled on the floor beneath it. The blood also seems to be splattered all over the computer monitor and desk top that the chair sits behind. The fact that the .357 he had found was short two rounds left little doubt to Clay as to what exactly had caused the blood splatters. Whatever had happened to the unfortunate soul that had once occupied the receptionists chair, Clay still has his suspicions. It appeared the gunshot hadn't killed her right away, evidenced by the drag marks Clay can make out on the carpet where she had apparently drug herself out from behind the greeting counter and into the main area of the waiting room. "Or something else drug her out from behind the desk" his inner voice offers warningly, causing him to shudder as the thought creeps into his mind, doing his best as he tries to push it away. He is walking over to investigate the drag marks, attempting to determine the destination of the now deceased Mrs. Deloris Scott, when he hears the muffled scream come from behind him, followed by the unmistakable sound of shattering glass.

Levi and Paige are filling and re-filling their packs as quick as they can get to the support vehicles and unload them. It had been a preverbal odd and end goldmine in the examining rooms. The rooms had been full of survival essentials like bandages, disinfectants, latex gloves, paper towels, bedding, tissues, etc. The tissues and hydrogen peroxide had drawn the biggest whoops of excitement from Laura and Grant when they were announced to the group outside as they were helping them unload their bounty. They were already finished draining the gas from the vehicles in the parking lot, which had filled up two of the six, five-gallon gas cans they carried with them and part of a third. Not too bad when you considered that there were only four cars in the parking lot, but it only provided a portion of the fuel they had hoped to find before their return trip home. Laura and Grant now stand guard over the fuel they had been able to collect as well as the vehicles and the fresh supplies being collected by the group inside. They also would lend a hand unloading the packs whenever Levi and Paige brought out a fresh load of the welcomed and much needed supplies. Ray and Jim were busy taking advantage of an unexpected opportunity by pulling the battery and other parts they could salvage from off of another Toyota Tacoma that happened to be parked in the same lot. Levi raises a hand to Jim who glances over at them for a brief second. He hastily raises his own in response, then just as quickly lowers it as Ray seems to ask him for assistance at the same moment. Levi smiles understandingly beneath his mask; he had also found himself on the other end of Ray's strong work ethic and sharp tongue. Ray's desire to get a job done quickly and efficiently often outweighed his willingness to use manners and other pleasantries. But say what you want, Ray always seemed to accomplish both so very little was ever said when the orders he gave came out with a curt, no nonsense directness. He was both blunt and demanding, but he was also knowledgeable and fair, which is pointed out by the fact that no one ever worked with him that didn't come away with more awareness and understanding about whatever it was they were doing than they had when they started fixing whatever it was that was broken. Levi turns away from the two men working in the parking lot and walks back into the office building, following Paige as she re-enters the hallway on her way to the next examining room designated for exploration. There is a lighthearted feeling in the air due to the quality and quantity of supplies they were finding when the unmistakable sound of breaking glass fills the hallway, stopping them both in their tracks. The sound is almost deafening in the otherwise dead, silent world instantly putting them both on high alert.

It takes them mere seconds to figure out that the sound that had just filled the corridor had come from the direction of the waiting room where Clay and Colt were still checking for supplies. Knowing that were also testing the security of the doors and windows to see if they could set up here as a make shift base for the duration of the sortie makes the tension and worry rise to even higher levels. Levi passes Paige in the hallway to reach the room first in his desperate attempt to make sure that nothing horrible has happened to his father. Shock and concern cause Levi to stop so suddenly just inside the room that Paige crashes into him from behind causing them both to stumble farther into the room. Levi is trying to figure out exactly what is going on and who was lying on the floor in an ever-widening pool of their own blood as Paige, regaining her balance, takes in the gruesome scene that is unfolding in front of her, blurting out, "Oh my god Clay! What happened to Colt?" And just like that, she sets all of Levi's worries to rest with that one simple question.

CHAPTER SEVEN

Colt slowly creeps around the perimeter of the waiting room staying close to the wall. Clay is off to his left, he can see the red beam of his flashlight scanning the area directly in front of him, as they explore. They used red lenses while they were searching un-scouted areas because the red doesn't interfere with their night vision, allowing their eyes to stay as adjusted as possible to the dark. Their eyes that were already evolving to the constant dark, worked hard enough as it was as they constantly tried to adjust to the almost pitch black that consisted of their days to the absolute pitch black that now made up their nights. With no sun, no electricity, no moon, or stars to shine down on them their days and nights were almost utterly and completely dark. Talking with his wife Holly about it one night as they lay in bed straining to see their hands that they knew were right in front of their faces, their young daughter Belle fast asleep in the bed next to them, Holly had likened it to what she thought it would be like to be blind. As he had lain there listening to the slow, soft, and rhythmic breathing of his little girl he conceded that he had to agree with her. This indeed must be what it was like to be blind. He shivers at the memory and is thankful, not for the first time, for the light the red capped flashlight offered him against the black backdrop of their existence. His thoughts shift to his lovely, young wife and his longing to be back at the compound with his family when something catches his eye just at the edge of the red glow that leads him around the room. It's hard to make out any real detail in the dim ambience of the red light as he struggles to figure out exactly what it is he sees taking shape in front of him. Taking a cautious step forward he begins to make out what he thinks are, shoes? Another cautious step forward shows him that yes, they are indeed someone's shoes! Colt instinctively crouches lower in surprise as he draws back his bow causing the mounted light to shake for a brief, tense moment. His finger rests just above the quick release trigger ready to release an arrow at the first sign of anything threatening. He has no qualms about instituting the "shoot first, ask questions later" motto he had read on bumper stickers plastered to the backs of a thousand pick-up trucks growing up in the wild and wonderful state of west Texas. As he edges ever closer to whomever it is he has stumbled across sitting on the floor he allows himself a quick glance over in Clay's direction to check his position in the room (information that he may need in the event that back up became necessary) and sees him coming out of a crouch to peer over the top of the receptionist's counter and inspect into the area behind it. With Clay's position noted Colt again puts his attention to the task that literally sits on the floor in front of him. Cautiously thinking out each step before he takes it he begins to inch his way forward towards whomever, or whatever it is that is waiting far to patiently for him to arrive.

"Hello?" Colt whispers to the form as he gets close enough to see their calves and shins now, not truly knowing if he wants a return answer or not.

"Hello?" Colt whispers once more, again to no reply. He inches closer.

"Hello? Is someone there?" he says it a little louder this time as his courage begins to rise slightly, due mostly to the fact that he hasn't been able to make out any signs of movement as he's inched steadily closer. He takes one final step as the mutilated form of the rotting, dead receptionist Deloris Scott enters fully into the beam of his flashlight, repulsive in all its vile and putrid glory. Her entrails are strung out and laying about her like the tentacles of some horrible nightmarish, Lovecraftian beast from where she had been eviscerated. The upper portions of her thighs had been gnawed down to the bone. What is left of her breasts are exposed, her left one having been completely eaten to the point that her ribs showed signs of scoring from the teeth that had worked away all the flesh that had once clung to it. The open mouthed and sunken eyed mask of death stares back at him grotesquely as his light scans the rest of the way up the corpse to land on her face. The vileness and horror of the mangled and partially eaten form continues to manifest in front of him as he is overtaken by the shock of it all, like the wave of a mile-high tsunami. He stumbles backwards, a muffled scream escaping his throat as he struggles to gain control of himself. The glass topped coffee table that sat in between the two lines of chairs catches him just below the knees unexpectedly causing him to sit down violently. Instinctively, he throws his arms back to break his fall, releasing the arrow he had pulled back to impale the mutilated would be attacker as he inadvertently thrusts both arms through the plate glass that makes up the top of the coffee table. An action that successfully slices through the artery in his right wrist while severing all the tendons and ligaments in his left arm with a gash that runs the length of his forearm, the glass makes surgeon like incisions. Colt lies on the floor in a fast forming, shallow pool of his own blood; the smashed remains of the coffee table lay beneath him, as the mutilated corpse of Deloris Scott still sits indiscriminately in front of him. Laying there, staring wildly at the ceiling and in obvious shock, he begins to yell for his wife Holly in the shrill voice that so often accompanies panicked screams. Confused he wonders why she isn't responding to his pleading cries for help while his arteries rhythmically pump out his life. No longer merely lying in the ever widening and quickly deepening pool of his own blood, now he was bathing in it.

"We have to stop the bleeding!" Clay exclaims to Paige as she reaches the center of the room to squat next to them. The blood that is still pumping in steady spurts from Colts severely severed limbs covers everything in a gruesome crimson sheet that appears black in the darkness.

"What should I do Mr. Stratford?" Paige asks Clay, trying to be heard over the screaming Colt.

"Talk to him. Try to keep him awake, he's in shock. I've got to find something we can use as a tourniquet. His artery has been cut in his right arm at least. I can't tell about the left one." Clay gives the orders to Paige as he stands up searching desperately for anything that could be used as a makeshift tourniquet.

"HOLLY! DON'T LEAVE ME!" Colt screams as Clay stands up. In his shock and panic he has begun to hallucinate.

"SHHHHH Colt its ok, everything is going to be ok. It's me Paige. Colt, I need you to listen to me ok, I need you to try and stay awake for me. Ok? Do you think you can do that for me? Clay is going to find something that we can use to help us stop the bleeding, but I need you to try and stay calm so that we can help you. Do you think you can do that for me Colt?" Paige talks to Colt in the most soothing voice that she can muster in the chaos that now makes up the waiting room. At the same time, Clay is frantically searching for anything that they can use to make a tourniquet to try and stop the bleeding. Clay utters a thankful gasp as he spots a lamp sitting on a table in the far corner of the room. Crossing the space to the lamp in four swift strides, he draws out his knife as he walks. Grapping the lamp, he hastily cuts the cord that sticks out of the back and jerks the plug out of the wall then turns and hurriedly makes his way back to where Paige has been doing her best to keep Colt as calm as possible.

"Ok Paige, lift his right arm up as high as you can. I have to tie this above his elbow" Clay explains. Paige does her best to help but Colt is lost in his shock and delirium, unable to understand what is happening to him, he begins to struggle violently against her.

"I can't hold him Mr. Stratford!" Paige shouts out to Clay in frustration, trying to be heard over Colt's new round of screaming.

"HHHOOOLLLYYY!" He shrieks over and over, "HHHOOOLLLYYY!"

Levi stands frozen in place dumbly staring at the scene playing out before him in childlike disbelief unable to move. Until finally, hearing Colts' screams, watching his frantic father, and the struggling Paige it begins to draw him out of his trance. As his feet finally begin to obey him again Ray and Jim burst into the room with Grant and Laura just down the hall still keeping an eye on the vehicles, but close enough to be there in an instant if their help was needed. Ray rushes past the stone footed Levi seeing instantly the trouble Colt was in as he laid there with Clay and Paige both trying, all be it unsuccessfully, to tie the tourniquet around the right arm of the violently struggling man who was quickly bleeding to death.

"Watch out Paige, let me get to him," Ray exclaims as he reaches them, shouting to be heard over the still screaming Colt. Paige falls to land on her butt then pushes with her feet to scoot back giving Ray access to help Clay, her shoes and hands slipping annoyingly in the blood-stained carpet. Ray's hands quickly get smeared with blood, making getting a firm grip on anything next to impossible. The next few minutes' pass as if they were hours as the two men do everything within their power to help the young man that they have come to feel responsible for. Ever since they had found Colt and his young family living out of an abandoned school bus and had brought them back to live with them and their families already living in the compound. All of this is flashing through Clay's mind as thankfully Colt's energy finally begins to wane, the heavy loss of blood rapidly beginning to take his life as he begins to slip mercifully into a state of semi-consciousness. Pale and cold, Colt's ragged breathing becoming more labored thankfully dropping his struggling in both strength and frequency. Clay looks down at his dying friend, thankful that he was finally able to get the tourniquet tied around his arm. All he can do now, is pray that it wasn't too late. Colts eyes flutter open as he tries to speak. He licks his lips slowly, the motion seeming to take great effort as he tries to speak in a hushed whisper.

"I'm sorry Clay. I'm so sorry. Tell Veronica I'm so very sorry." Slowly and mercifully, Colt slips fully into unconsciousness as he finishes his apology to Clay. Curious faces turn to look at Clay as they all try to catch their breath in the now eerily still room. Colt has ceased his screaming and the silence that follows is broken only by the raspy, labored breathing of their mortally injured friend.

CHAPTER EIGHT

The arrow slams into Clay's right side like a hammer, momentarily stealing the breath away from him. The blow to his ribs is instantly followed by the panicked screams of Colt and the violent sound of shattering glass. Clay falls forward to lean against the counter struggling to catch his breath before wearily easing himself down onto one knee. He is wearing one of the Kevlar vest they had found inside the trunk of a wrecked police car left sideways in a ditch about 5 miles outside of the compound as he gingerly feels for the arrow that he knows has pierced his right side through the protection. The vests were one of the first significant finds they had stumbled upon once they started venturing further away from the compound for supplies. They had since found a few more that they all took turns wearing, depending on their responsibilities. Clay thankfully had been assigned one for this search. He finds the arrow that has pierced his side and carefully begins trying to pull it out, praying to any God that will listen that Colt hadn't placed one of the razor hunting tips that Roger had hoarded on the end of his arrows. The breath he is finally able to find hisses through his tightly clenched together teeth as he tries to bite back the pain. The arrow begins to slowly slide out of his body, using his blood as lubrication. Kevlar was great for stopping bullets, but all it did for piercing weapons, such as knives and razor tipped arrows for instance, was to slow them down just enough to hopefully keep you alive. Clay could feel the arrow exiting his body as he gradually works it out from between his ribs. Ribs that were now bruised and painful, but hopefully not broken. He quietly whispers a thank you to whatever God had listened to his prayer as he realizes the arrow was tipped with the smooth sided heads used for target practice and not the hunting arrow tips he was afraid of. The arrow finally works free of his body as Colt's siren like screams continue to fill the waiting room, growing in volume and intensity. Through his pain and the screams, he can also make out the sounds of Levi and Paige barreling up the hallway in the direction of the waiting room. Undoubtedly Colts screaming, and the sound of the shattering glass alerted them to some sort of danger. Clay drops the arrow on the floor to land at his feet as he stands up to run to Colts aid. Not yet knowing or understanding what exactly it was that has happened, he runs only in the understanding that his young friend was in dire need of whatever kind of help that he was capable of giving him.

"While I thought that I was learning how to live, I have in reality been learning how to die."

~ **Leonardo Da Vinci**

CHAPTER NINE

YEAR ONE, DAY THREE HUNDRED AND TWENTY- THREE

The sun. Once the center of the universe for the tiny blue planet that had miraculously been hung inside what was known as "The Goldilocks Zone" by the supreme powers of the cosmos that we called home. Worshiped by our ancestors, the bearer of light and warmth, the sun had provided the energy that allowed plant and animal life to cover our lands and to fill the wonder that was the oceans for over four billion years. It was the rising symbol that signaled the farmer that it was time to work the fields or to milk the cows. It was the hero that rose to chase away the nightmares that haunted little children in the dark. Veronica looks at the dull globe that hangs precariously in the sky just above the horizon. The ash clouds that stream across its surface stand as a visible reminder of the villain that has, at least for the moment, triumphed over the hero that once hung in the heavens. What was once the brightness of midday, now is about as bright as midnight with a half moon. You could see enough to maneuver and function in open spaces but the dark corners that surrounded you always gave rise to the primal fears that still reside in all of us. Those of us fortunate enough to have been spoiled by the constant ambient light of civilization and technology, anyway. The adult inside you keeps telling you not to be afraid, that there isn't anything in the shadows at night that isn't there during the day. Only now, there isn't a day. There is only a constant and perpetual night. Expectedly the child that lives in you re-appears to overpower the ability of reason, telling you that it's never daytime anymore, that it is only darkness that lives in this world. And in the black that is the darkness, no one ever truly knows what lies waiting for you just beyond your distance of sight, waiting for you in the black cover of watching shadows.

Veronica pulls her coat up tighter trying to keep out the cold and fear that creeps up the back of her neck. Another day in the life of this current evolutionary stage of the world. She absently pokes at the fire beneath the pot she has hanging from a tri-pod over the flames. The rest of the compound remains asleep with the slumber that accompanies an endless night and an ever increasing cold. The longer the ash cover kept the sun blocked out the colder it got, slowly spiraling the planet into the mini ice age of a volcanic winter. She pokes at the fire again, keeping the flames just high enough to lick the bottom of the pot that holds the coffee she is brewing as the aroma of the morning necessity slowly starts to matriculate through the camp. It's been three days since Clay and the others had gone out on another trip searching for supplies. She hated it when they were gone, outside of the relative safety and security offered by the compound. They were fortunate to have the ability to have all they needed to be comfortable within the confines of the shipping containers that strategically outlined their perimeter and served as storage. Thankfully, Roger had been more than diligent in his preparation of the compound. Roger. The memory of his death causes her to take in a long, deep sigh as she looks around, taking in what she could see of the compound in the dark and the misting morning rain. Despite his countless quirks, she had loved her little brother. Sometimes loving him because of his quirks. Like when he had saved them all with this compound they had ridiculed him for building over the past ten years for example. She had been so upset with Clay when he told her the news of his demise. Hell, who was she kidding... she had been downright cold and cruel to Clay lately; a crude, flesh and blood incarnation of the world they all fought so hard to survive in now. She hadn't even been there to see them off when they pulled out of camp three days ago. An action she now deeply regretted, for the sake of her husband as well as her oldest son. She knew Roger's death hadn't been Clay's fault, but the news had caught her so completely off guard when he had told her, that she didn't know how else to react. I mean, Clay hadn't said that Roger was hurt or lost. That he was off on some wild excuse for a party that only he and his little band of friends would have defined as entertainment. No, Clay had told her that her quirky little brother was in fact dead. Drowned in a lake of mud of all things. She absently wipes a tear away as she sits wallowing in her own personnel pool of regret; both for her actions to her loving husband and the absence of her dead brother. In her selfishness and self-pity for losing some one that almost everyone else in the world that had known him would most assuredly think of as an asshole, she had treated the one man left in this world that would lay down his own life for her and their children like a royal bitch. Worse yet, she had done it over something she knew he had no real power to prevent. But in her grief for the loss of her brother, she had to blame somebody, and unfortunately, that somebody had been Clay. All despite knowing in her heart that no one except her arrogant, half-baked baby brother was to blame.

"Well you're sitting out here by the fire like you're awake, but that faraway look in your eyes tells a completely different story."

"Oh, hey. Good morning Willy," Veronica says warmly chuckling softly, greeting the camp handy-man as he enters the little circle of firelight.

"I think I'm about fifty-fifty right now. I'll be able to give you a more honest answer after I get this first cup of coffee in me," she finishes as they share the cheery laugh that only close friends can share as she pours them both a steaming cup of the coffee she had been brewing. William Hocker was a 62-year-old, grey haired, and balding man with a shaggy, untamed beard. Small in stature only, Willy was the camps adopted Mister fix-er-upper and father figure. Between William (or Ol' Willy as the guys around the camp liked to call him) and Jim, there was little around the camp that stayed broken for very long. Veronica thought she had heard him say once in passing that he had been a farmer in the world before the darkness and had made his living knowing how to fix, repair, or grow almost anything. She found herself wondering now and then if that had been his connection to Roger before everything in the world went to shit. Willy had never exactly said what it was he had *"grown"* on his little farm. Only Willy had known about this little fortress tucked away in the Ozark Mountain Range outside of Kim, Lee, and Roger's immediate family. Willy coughed and spat as he continued to sip his coffee trying to wake himself up.

"I hope to hell someone runs across some sugar this trip out. It would go a long way to weaken this up a little Ronnie, your brew's so strong it would curl the toes of Hercules." Veronica chuckles dreamily as she agrees with him.

"Mmm hmm and some non-dairy creamer. It'd be nice to drink a cup of coffee that wasn't as dark as this damn sky the swirls over our heads every day," she adds, closing her eyes and hugging the warm cup of coffee to her chest.

"That it would my dear. Hey at least it's not raining.... Much," Willy says this last part looking up as if the skies would open up on them at any minute just by him mentioning the damned acid rain. They both subconsciously pull their coats up a little closer around their necks and close their hands a little tighter around the cups of coffee they were holding trying to fight back the cold they could both feel closing in around them.

Veronica had never seen such violence in a storm like the storms that now raged across the mountains they called home. She had experienced tornados as a child growing up in Oklahoma, so she knew first hand that nature could be violent, and the volcano had done its part to hammer home the power of nature's unpredictability. However, the thunderstorms they dealt with now were something different entirely. They were in a category all to their very own. Violent and long lasting, they carried with them strong gusts of wind, almost hurricane like in their intensity. Thick bolts of lightning reached across the heavens like the fiery fingers of God, or the pitchforks of the devil depending on your own personnel point of view. The rain was far too acidic to be suitable as drinking water but the men of the camp, led by Willy, had engineered a filtration system that sat at the base of a runoff channel on the far side of the mountain about two hundred yards away from the main entrance to the compound. The system itself was simple enough; it started with a fifty-gallon water barrel that Clay said was used by people who wanted to collect rain water so that they could use it to water their plants and yards with. Inside the barrel, they lined the bottom with as much cotton as they could afford to spare, that was preceded by a heavy layer of sand, then a wide layer of charcoal taken from the fires after that. Small rocks filled the barrel to the top and represented the beginning of the filtration process. Finally, the water was strained through another stack of cotton t-shirts finishing the process. This filtered the water enough to allow it to be used for cleaning and laundry, but it stilled needed to be boiled to make it safe enough to drink. Willy and Jim had been busy working on a way to distill all the water that was collected, but that had been put on hold while Jim was out on the supply run covering for Jackson. Right on cue, almost seeming to read her thoughts Willy asks,

"How is Gracie feeling Ronnie? Is she doing any better?" She looks up at her friend and sees the honest concern flickering within his eyes alongside the firelight as she replies,

"Holly stayed with her last night so that I could try to get some rest. Belle stayed with me and the boys." The whole camp had been doing everything they could for Gracie and Jackson over the last few weeks. Anyone could look at Gracie and tell that she was going to pop at any second and she was naturally struggling to keep up with her daily responsibilities at the compound. Everyone was pitching in where they could to give her and Jackson a hand with whatever was needed, for the compound, and for their soon to be new arrival.

"She's still pretty uncomfortable then?" Willy says, his voice tinged with the worry of an experienced father and with the uncertainty that a man has about being pregnant.

"Yes, unfortunately she is. I feel bad for her, but we can only do so much to cut the pain. As far as we can tell, she can go at any minute," Veronica answers.

"Well isn't there like a test we can perform on her or something? Wave a branch over her or tie a ring onto a string and hold it above her belly or some crazy shit like that?" Willy asks, scowling with worry. Veronica's hearty laughter echoes through the camp causing her to have to gain control of herself before she is able to respond.

"There are, but I don't know exactly what to do and I don't think we have any witch doctors wandering about to perform any of your suggestions." She bursts into laughter again enjoying her own joke at Willy's expense. Willy joins in, throwing his own head back and slapping his knee.

"Well my young Mrs. Stratford, in my day men stayed the hell out of the way and paced around the waiting room where they belonged," Willy says as his laughter subsides, jabbing his finger in her direction for emphasis.

"We could tell how far along she was if someone knew how to check to see if her cervix was dilated," Veronica offers with a slight shrug.

"Check her what? To see if it's what?" Willy asks more confused than ever, a tinge of disgust apparent in his voice. Veronica's laughter flies through the camp this time like a mini sonic boom. Willy looks at her sideways with pursed lips, muttering, "Cows and horses are a lot less complicated than what ever the hell you just said."

"I hope that coffee has the same effect on us," Holly jokes groggily as she and Jackson stroll into the glow of the firelight, red eyed and weary from spending the night doing all they could to help keep Gracie comfortable.

"I seriously doubt it," proclaims Willy with a sideways look at the now hysterical Veronica. The rest of the camp begins to filter in from out of the dark and congregate beneath the pavilion they had erected to act as a central gathering point in the center of the compound. It wasn't much protection from most of the elements but at least it kept the rain off of you. Not that there had been much rain lately, aside from the sprinkles and light mist that fell this morning. Lately to the dismay of everyone, the rain had begun to mix with snow as winter started setting in far too early this year. Not the pure beautiful white snow we all know and love, not the snow that little children all over America used to dream about on Christmas morning. This snow was grey and dirty as it fell slowly from the skies to cover up the dead grey ground. Acting as nature's little maids it gently scrubs the air, slowly filtering out all of the poison and ashes the volcano had seemed fit to cover the world in. Cain and his best friend Dylan were next to enter the pavilion followed closely by Belle; Colt and Holly's five-year-old daughter who had stayed with them the night before while Holly filled in for Veronica with Gracie.

"Well don't you two look nice and chipper this morning," Willy says with a sly smile directing his sarcasm at the two young men who were obviously disappointed to be awake when they both clearly thought that they should still be fast asleep.

"Belle said she had to go to the bathroom," Cain and Dylan both say in groggy unison.

"Mommy!" Belle gleefully shouts from behind them as she spots Holly at the edge of the fire pit.

"Good morning baby doll! How did you sleep? Were you good for Mrs. Ronnie and the boys?" Holly asks her daughter as she scoops her up for a good morning bear hug.

"Yes ma'am." Belle answers in the sweet voice of innocence. Innocence that both Colt and Holly hoped wouldn't be tainted by the harsh, cruel world that they knew their lovely young daughter would most likely spend her entire life struggling to survive in. As if Veronica could read her thoughts she whispers into Holly's ear, just loud enough that only she could hear.

"The sun won't hide forever. One day the world will correct itself, the sun will shine again on the lands and waters and life will begin again as new." Holly smiles warmly at Ronnie, mouthing the words "thank you" to her for the words of encouragement as Belle nestles herself deeper into Holly's neck.

"Has anyone seen Sophia and the twins yet this morning?" Willy asks no one in particular.

"Not yet, they may have gone to the wash house before coming over to the pavilion," Veronica says.

"I have to take Belle over to the washroom anyway so she can use the potty and brush her teeth. I'll check to see if they're in there," Holly offers.

"Thank you, Holly. I'd appreciate that," Veronica says as she hands her a fresh, hot cup of coffee.

"Thank you for the coffee Ronnie, I'm gonna head on back and sit with Gracie," Jackson says as he stands up, holding a cup of the brew in each hand. "I'll see if Gracie wants a cup, maybe the warmth of the coffee will help her fell a little better." Jackson states as he holds the cup of coffee up in a mock salute to the group, "And if she doesn't... I know I sure as hell can use an extra cup this morning." The group laughs together in sympathetic agreement as Jackson turns away and strolls towards the bunker (or "Hobbit hole" as Jim had fittingly nicknamed them) that he, his wife, and their soon to be born child all call home.

"Above all else guard your heart, for everything you do flows from it."

Proverbs 4:23

CHAPTER TEN

Jackson sits in the chair across the room from his wife watching her sleep and feeling increasingly guilty that he can do nothing to help her with her discomfort. The battery powered lantern that they used when they were inside their bunkers radiated just enough light to make out her anguished face as it twisted and contorted in obvious agony as his poor, beautiful wife tried to rest. They had been married for seven years now, wait, or was it eight? Hell, he couldn't tell what time of day it was much less what the date was in this damned eternal darkness. And now as the brightest light in his life lay in front of him squirming in pain and discomfort he sat there helpless, unable to do a damned thing about it. Jackson wrings his hands in nervous anxiety as he quickly stands up with hasty disgust and walks over to his pitiful wife, dabbing her forehead with a cool wet cloth. He bends and pulls the blanket back down to cover her feet; which had become exposed as she writhes around in the bed, unable to find any position that would even temporarily ease her suffering. Jackson thinks back to when he and Gracie had met. It was at his Cousin Pat's wedding; who lucky for him, had been marrying Gracie's stepsister Julia. Neither one of them wanting to be there but both felt bound by moral family obligation to be there, they ended up being each other's company at the reception by keeping the bartender at the open bar constantly in work the whole night. Instant friends as they entertained themselves by picking apart all the other attendees clothes and hair, intoxicated and laughing at themselves as the drinks continued to go down far too easy. They exchanged numbers and were calling and texting each other by the next day, dating by the next weekend, and engaged by the next spring. She was and is all he has ever truly wanted. He loved her not only for who she was, but also for who he was when he was with her. They had everything a young couple could have wanted or asked for. A lovely little house filled with love, with the white picket fence that lined a plush, well-groomed lawn, and a two-car garage. Both had blossoming careers (hers in real estate, his in teaching), financial stability, and were living both happy and healthy lives. All they seemed to need to complete their little puzzle of the American dream was a family of their own. That last piece of the puzzle though, had unfortunately ended up being a lot harder to obtain than either one of them had anticipated. After the first miscarriage, they were both still optimistic that everything was fine. That it had just been one of those unfortunate things that happened to fortunate people. By the end of their fifth one however, they had both grown frustrated and confused as the pessimism began to set in, making them both come to the morose realization that completing their puzzle may not be a possibility for them. Regrettably, it had also strained their relationship to a point that neither of them would have ever thought possible. At first, she had blamed him. Then he had blamed her. Then they had blamed God, the doctors, and anyone else that they could think of to project their pain and frustrations onto. But in the end, it hadn't been anyone's fault. The doctors said that they couldn't figure out why Gracie's body kept rejecting the fetuses. They told them that both of them were perfectly healthy, and that medically, Gracie should have been able to bear children. Then with their next breath the doctors had gently informed them that it was also dangerous for them to keep putting Gracie's body through the physical and mental strain of the miscarriages. Thus, in the end and under the constant strain of disappointment and depression *and* now the added risk to Gracie's health, they had simply just given up. Then the volcano had erupted, turning the world upside down and dropping it on its head. It was here, amid all of the chaos and death of this living hell, caught in the struggle of starvation and destruction that the entire planet had transformed itself into, that they had been delivered a miracle. After all they had gone through trying to have a family, it was here, in this imperfect dystopian version of the world, that they had finally been given their chance to complete their puzzle. To start a family of their own. Jackson smiles to himself at the irony of it all. Standing up from his chair he walks across the room to stand at his wife's bedside, dabbing her forehead once again with a cool cloth.

Jackson looks down at Gracie as she moans and whimpers pitifully, then bends and lightly kisses her tenderly. Softly whispering words of encouragement to his suffering wife.

"It's ok baby, I'm right here if you need me. Just imagine Gracie that any time now, in spite of all that we've been through together, you and I are going to be parents! We're going to have our own little beautiful baby to love and cherish. We'll finally have the last piece of our puzzle, a miraculous symbol of light and hope in this otherwise dark and hopeless world." Gracie opens her eyes wearily, looking up at Jackson, she manages a weak smile.

"I know lover." Her voice is barely loud enough for him to hear it as her throat crackles from sleep and lack of moisture.

"Hey, you," Jackson breathes excitedly as he wipes her brow and face with a damp cool cloth.

"I thought you were asleep."

"I was," Gracie whispers. "I was dreaming."

"You were? What were you dreaming about doll face?"

"I was dreaming that we had a beautiful, healthy baby girl, and that we named her Marie." She raises her husband's hand to her lips softly kissing the back of it.

"What a wonderful dream," Jackson says leaning over and kissing her on her cheek.

"Marie huh?" Jackson chuckles as he pulls back from the kiss, "I thought we weren't going to consider names until we meet him or her in person?"

"I can't control my dreams Jaxy," she says, smiling up at him sweetly meeting his gaze as he gazes down on her affectionately. Returning her smile, he laughs lightly saying,

"Well at least we have a girl's name picked out now. Can I get you anything? Are you thirsty?"

"Yes, can you get me a glass of water please?" Gracie asks weakly.

"Of course you can beautiful, coming right up. Would you like that room temperature or room temperature? We offer only the best of mountain luxuries here in Hobbit Hole Hotels," Jackson says playfully winking at his lovely wife.

"Don't make me laugh butthead," Gracie chuckles dryly.

"Sorry baby doll. Would you like me to get you some more aspirin?" Jackson asks before standing up to go pour her a glass of water. As Jackson reaches the water basin, Gracie cries out, her voice still hoarse and raspy from sleep.

"Oh my God Jackson! I think my water just broke!"

Jackson drops the cup he was holding as he fully absorbs the weight of her exclamation.

"What? Really? Are you sure?" He clamors, stumbling over his words as he turns around to stare nervously at his wife. Gracie is sitting up in bed with her legs spread wide underneath the covers Jackson had laid over her to fight back the chill; between them is a widening pool of amniotic fluid and blood.

"Gracie is that normal?" Jackson shakily asks his wife who has gone pale in the light of the lantern, his voice thick with worry. She looks up at him teary eyed and confused as she clamors,

"I don't think so…maybe…I'm not sure…maybe a little but not this much… shit I don't know Jackson!" She screams, growing hysterical in her pain and panic.

"Gracie! Oh my god baby, what do I do? Please tell me how to help you!" Jackson says as he begins to slip into his own hysteria. Seeing the stress flooding onto Jackson's face Gracie slowly begins to calm herself down letting herself lie back down on the bed taking in several slow, deep controlled breaths. "It's going to be ok Jaxy, but I need you to go get Veronica and Sophia."

"When you are in the midst of chaos, it is then that you need to find the stillness that lives within you."

~Unknown

CHAPTER ELEVEN

Holly runs into Sophia and her twelve-year-old twin girls, Lily and Rose, washing up and brushing their teeth in the designated area of the wash room for women. She uses the opportunity to catch Sophia up on the status of Gracie before they fall into discussions about the plans for the days' list of chores. A list which mostly stays unchanged from day to day and consists of collecting firewood, cleaning, cooking and rationing out provisions, making the daily morning and evening runs to the water filtration station, and doing laundry. Using the terms day and night still seemed funny to them but Clay had insisted that everyone still used the accepted names for the designated times of the day. He hoped it would provide an air of normalcy to their existence in the dark. Even though in truth you could no longer tell the difference between dawn and dusk, morning from evening. There was only dark and darker that now separated day from night. The only way anyone was truly able to keep track of the passing days and differentiate morning from evening was by monitoring the time on your watch or by the time on the wind-up clocks they all kept in their hobbit holes. Clocks that they had all become quite fond of if they were being honest and most would now find it very difficult to sleep now without the monotonous tick tock sound the clocks made as they ticked away the days and nights of their lives.

When everyone's daily responsibilities came to an end, everyone met under the pavilion to have supper together as a family and as a group. The group at the compound was small and tight knit as the tragedy of their current circumstances had brought them together out of necessity. They carried out the ritual of gathering under the pavilion every day to remind themselves of what family should have meant before the event; not to mention that for most of them, as far as anyone knew anyway, each other was the only family they had left in this sinister world. Plus, it helped to build and keep the comradery between them, adding the sense of belonging that a truly successful community needed. It aided in creating an old-fashioned sense of caring and responsibility for one another. According to Jim and Willy that sense of togetherness was the only good thing to come out of the calamity the volcanic eruption had created. It had recreated a true sense of fellowship. A sense of belonging to something greater than just one's self as they all fought to survive together in the aftermath. Veronica hated to admit it, but she had to agree with them. Meeting together under the pavilion every "morning" and every "evening" also was a great time to share the details about your day with one another and it offered a time to bring up any issues that needed attention within the camp or its inhabitants. A forum of sorts for making suggestions on how to make things better or to mention if something needed fixed. Not to mention that it was just a good time for everyone to check on the wellbeing of everyone else they had all come to care so much about. Those whose lives depended on each other's abilities to take on and complete the daily chores that was life in the community. A throwback to the way the whole country had been a couple hundred years ago. A time when your family, your neighbor, and being a part of *your community* had truly meant something.

Aside from the missing group out scavenging, that night's supper and subsequent round table discussions had been business as usual. Nothing out of the ordinary happened regarding the itinerary and agenda that they all normally followed on a day to day basis. They were all dragging a little more than usual from picking up the vacancies in the chores left by the inability for Gracie or Jackson to participate and the other missing compound members, but outside of that it was a normal evening. Small talk was made but there was a glaring hole left in the story telling without Ray, Clay, and especially Jim there to put their entertaining spin on something as mundane as collecting firewood, making it sound grandiose like they had just single handedly logged half of the Ouachita National Forest. Needless to say, without their stories and tall tales, the topic of conversation quickly turned to the exhausted Jackson and the deteriorating condition of Gracie. Veronica updated everyone that they both had seemed fine and in good spirits earlier when she last had taken a late lunch in to them so that they could eat together in their bunker. Regrettably she admits that she hadn't been able to get back and check in on them since but stated that to her Gracie seemed too tired and uncomfortable to try to make it out to the pavilion to eat with everyone else at supper time and Jackson of course wouldn't want Gracie to eat alone. As supper concluded everyone exchanged their nightly pleasantries and retired for the evening. Making her way back to her own bunker Veronica stopped to check on the condition of Gracie one more time, out of habit or motherly impatience she couldn't really be sure. Gracie and Jackson kept insisting that they were fine and that everyone should go sleep in their own bunkers that night so that they all could get some much-deserved rest. Jackson and Gracie kept re-assuring her and Sophia (whose own motherly instinct had prodded her to drop in to check on the expecting parents) repeatedly that they would be just fine until the morning. Veronica was too tired to argue anymore so she finally submits to the couples wishes and bids them both a good night. She tiredly exits the bunker dragging the still protesting Sophia in tow behind her.

Later, while lying in her bed, Veronica lays alone missing her husband and the warmth of his body lying next to her as the night slowly drags along. Listening to the rhythmic breathing of Cain and Dylan in the other rooms she marvels at how only teenagers could drift off to sleep in just a matter of minutes regardless of the day's events. Going over the rations for tomorrow and the events of her own day, she slowly tries to will herself to drift off to sleep. Finally beginning to relax, her thoughts start drifting dreamily towards something Willy had been talking about that night sitting around the fire as they all shared a nightcap of cheap bourbon before she and Sophia left to check on Gracie. He was talking about how he felt that the world had needed to be "reset". That social decency and morality had become as black before the eruption as the darkness that swirls around them now. He spoke about how families used to gather together seated around the breakfast and supper tables engaging in each other's lives. He sighed sadly as he described how that turned into sitting around a television set or with their faces stuck in their phones, if they sat together at all. He mentioned that he felt that kids had lost their positive role models and that without the structure and stability in their lives that all young minds crave, they had fallen into listening to what did give them attention: Facebook, MTV, and other social media outlets. Parents weren't exempt from Willy's reflections tonight either as he pointed out how they too often detached themselves from their children's lives to spend it brainwashed by Dr. Phil and ridiculously pointless reality TV shows. There they could watch strangers throw their personal lives into the faces of everyone else while saying to themselves, "Oh I'm glad that's not us, that would never happen here." All the while, little Janie is sneaking out of the upstairs window to drop ecstasy and get knocked up by Bobby down the street. Nothing was private anymore as hedonism and pornography ran rampant, made easy by the internet, all while marital dedication and monogamy drowned in a whirlpool of immorality. Veronica and the others had hung onto every word as Willy spoke that night, seamlessly moving onto what would have been the inevitable collapse of the American petrol dollar as well as the complete and utter disregard the current government had been showing for the Constitution and the Bill of Rights…. Veronica sighs, wiping away the tears that had formed in the corner of her eyes. She pinches the bridge of her nose to stop a fresh flow of them from falling. The guilt she was carrying for her mistreatment of Clay rises up in her now like flood waters threatening to burst through her emotional levy, causing an uneasiness that was making sleep impossible to find tonight. After what seemed like a small eon, with thoughts of the love for her husband coupled with the world being "reset" dominating her thoughts she finally falls into the uneasy, light slumber of the guilty and overly exhausted.

It seemed to Veronica as if she had only been asleep for seconds when she began to hear frantic pounding on their bunker door along with the panicked shouting of her and Sophia's name. In her sleep deprived state, she couldn't quite make out exactly whose voice it was calling out for her. At first, she thought it had been Clay and for a moment her heart skipped excitedly at the thought that the scouting party had gotten back much earlier than expected. But no… she was wrong it wasn't Clay, it was… **Jackson.** Oh my God it was Jackson! It seems Gracie must have finally gone into labor! A new form of excitement fills Veronica as she jumps up to run to Jackson and Gracie's bunker. Smiling happily, she slips on her boots and coat before she steps out into the frosty cold, pulling up her hood to protect her head from the bitter, icy rain that fell from the heavens. She can see Jackson already running towards Sophia and Rays bunker to wake up Sophia. Her warm smile returns brightly as she rejoices in the fact that the community was about to welcome its newest member. The purest symbol of innocence and hope; the birth of a child. Her smile broadens as she nods to herself thinking that yes, the world was in deed being reset. Like a gigantic magic eraser, the volcano was scrubbing the earth clean of all the atrocities that man had done to her during its pathetically short existence.

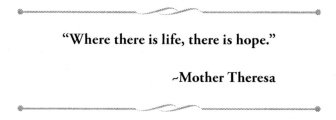

"Where there is life, there is hope."

~Mother Theresa

CHAPTER TWELVE

YEAR ONE, DAY THREE HUNDRED AND TWENTY- FOUR

Gracie's screams filter through the compound as Veronica, Sophia, Holly, and even Willy (who was calling on his experience in helping to deliver calves and colts growing up on his family's farm) all attempt to help deliver the baby that has been trying to come into the world now for almost eleven hours. With nothing but ibuprofen to give her for the pain the quartet does their best to help comfort Gracie, but regrettably, despite all their efforts, nothing they were doing seemed to have much of an effect.

"She's having strong contractions now, about nine seconds apart. I think we're finally getting closer," Holly calls out from Gracie's bedside where she was busy swabbing her forehead with a cool wash cloth and holding her hand. Calling up all she could still remember from the Lamaze classes she and Colt had taken during her pregnancy with Belle, Holly helps Gracie breath and push during her contractions and tries to help her relax in-between them. Willy had finally been able to gently coax Jackson out of the room and wait under the pavilion while they tried to help his struggling wife give birth. The amount of blood Gracie was losing was making Jackson panicked and increasingly more worried about the well-being of his wife and unborn child. Willy rushes back into the room, having just escorted Jackson outside, saying sternly as soon as he enters the room,

"Something's not right. I've never been a part of delivering a child before, but even I know this much blood is NOT normal." Willy stays firm as he gently pushes his way to stand between Sophia and Veronica.

"I know but I can't see what's causing her to bleed so much," Sophia explains shaken and visibly frustrated. "She hasn't torn and if you look, the blood seems to be definitely coming from inside of the womb. With as long as she's been in labor we should be able to see the baby beginning to crown by now and we still can't see anything." Willy's face goes somber as he stoops to get a closer look trying to figure out what the problem could be. The seconds tick by as the room waits, tense and anxious until finally Willy stands up looking only at Gracie's contorted and anguished face, the realization of what he thinks could be happening evident in his eyes. As calmly as he can manage as he struggles with his emotions and with a deliberately monotone voice Willy begins to put his fears into careful words.

"I think the placenta has detached itself from the wall of the uterus and is trapped underneath the baby stopping the baby from being able to fully enter the birth canal. That's what's causing Gracie to bleed so much, because the placenta is being pushed out first. Which also most likely means," Willy pauses uttering an exasperated half sob, half moan, "That the baby is probably breech."

The room goes into slow motion as Willy's words begin to sink in. Seconds tick by followed by minutes, the only sounds in the room coming from Gracie as she lies there in the agonizing throws of a difficult childbirth.

"Are you sure Willy?" Holly is the first to finally break the uncomfortable silence to ask the obvious question that is on all of their minds. "And if you are… can't we like… turn it or something?"

"No, I'm not positive. I've actually only witnessed this type of stuff with animals. Cows, horses, things like that… So, someone will need to feel for the baby's head for us to be absolutely sure," Willy answers. "But I can't in good conscience feel inside the private parts of my friend's wife. I'm too old fashioned for that. I won't do it." Willy looks at them all in turn before continuing.

"One of you will have to do it. If the placenta has detached itself, we won't be able to feel the baby's head and we won't have any way that I know of to try to get it to turn. We can't move the placenta out of the way without hurting Gracie or the baby. Unfortunately, we're not doctors in a hospital Holly, I wish we were."

"I'll do it Willy. I'll feel for the baby," Sophia volunteers. "Or at least I'll try to do it. I took beginners classes in high school to be a CNA when I thought I wanted to go into nursing, so I have a vague understanding of what I'm feeling up there. But I'll still need you to walk me through exactly what it is I am feeling *for*. Ok Willy?" With a heavy exhale, Willy nods slowly at her while Veronica and Holly move to try and comfort Gracie. They both do their best to explain to her what is happening, and that something might be wrong.

"Now don't overlook the fact that it's been a very long time since I was in high school while we're doing this Willy," Sophia warns as they begin the examination.

"Believe me, I won't. It's not like this is gonna be routine for me either. We'll just have to feel our way through it together."

"Pun intended?"

"Actually, no. Ironic coincidence." Willy's demeanor quickly goes serious as he begins to quietly whisper instructions to Sophia as she probes around inside of Gracie. After several fretful minutes, they stand back from the bed, the answer to what they were searching for held in the tears that had begun to stream down Sophia's cheeks. The baby was in deed breech and trapped behind the detached placenta, leaving them with no way to manually turn the baby.

"Ask her not to push anymore until we figure out what the next step is," Willy asks Veronica and Holly sadly.

"I'll go out to the pavilion and get Jackson. I think they need to be together while we attempt to explain what their options are here."

"And what exactly are their options Willy?" Veronica asks viciously, already fearful of the answer.

"We can abort the baby and try to save Gracie, we can do a primitive emergency C-section and try to save the baby, or we can let nature take its course and hope for the best," Willy answers.

"Every single one of those options ends up with us either losing the baby or losing Gracie Willy," Veronica states more than asks.

"I know that Ronnie. We either try to save the baby, or we try to save Gracie. I don't think we can save both, she's too far into labor and we don't have the necessary equipment," Willy says somberly.

"So you're about to bring a man in here and ask him to choose between the love of his life and the life they both prayed for to love." Veronica spits at Willy. Sobbing openly now, sympathetic to the absolute horror of the situation. She is fraught with the emotions over what two of her closest friends were about to go through, and angry that she was completely helpless to prevent any of it from happening.

"Yes," is all Willy says as he turns stiffly and exits the bunker to begin making his way to the pavilion. The fact that they could lose both Gracie and the baby wasn't lost on Willy as he goes to tell his friend the hardest news he had ever had to tell anyone in all of his 62 years.

***

-And then I saw a new heaven and a new earth for the first heaven and the first earth, which had passed away.

-Revelations 21:1

***

CHAPTER THIRTEEN

"But I don't want to go with Lily and Rose to get the dumb water." Belle continues to protest to Cain, even after the fourth time he had turned to scold her for trying to follow him and Dylan out into the woods to gather more firewood for the camp.

"Well you can't come with us out into the forest Belle, you're too little. I can't have you running off and getting lost." Cain tries to explain, "Besides, you're not strong enough to carry any of the wood back anyways."

"Yes-huh I can too! My daddy lets me carry the little pieces back for the fire all the time!" Belle retorts, saying this last part with a little humph and pride in her voice.

"Lily, Rose, will one of you please come get her? You know she can't go with us out into the woods," Cain pleads with the twins. Exasperated, he pinches the bridge of his nose between his thumb and pointer finger. Dylan, who is fifteen, along with the twins, who are twelve, are all laughing at the childhood crush that Belle, who just turned five last month, has for some reason bestowed upon the fourteen-year-old Cain, much to his own frustrations. Belle's had been the first and only birthday that they have celebrated at the compound thus far. No one was exactly sure what the actual date was, but they were doing their best to keep track of these types of things as they moved through the perpetual cold and dark. With a scavenged pack of Twinkies and five small twigs from the kindling pile they had celebrated in the best that they could, given the circumstances they all live in. Finally, it is Lily that comes to Cain's rescue.

"Come on and go with us Belle. You don't want to be around these smelly ol' boys anyways. All they'll do is give you cooties." Lily says this last part while making a silly face at Belle who is still distraught and protesting over Cain not letting her tag along. While in the background Rose echo's

Lily's statement attempting to aid her sister in coaxing Belle to come along with them to collect the morning water rations from the filtration station. Belle finally turns away from Cain, stomping her foot angrily.

"Oh, fine!" She takes Lily's offered hand as she begins to lead her away down the path that takes them to the barrels that they use for collecting water. After they take a few steps away from Cain and Dylan Belle quietly asks, "Lily, what are cooties?" A new round of laughter escapes from the twins, filling the countryside as they try to explain the age-old disease of cooties that all young boys have infected young girls with since the first little cave boy said "Uga" to the first little cave girl many, many millennia ago. Cain shakes his head as he and Dylan, who has also begun to laugh, turn and begin walking up the path to collect the firewood from a patch of woods on the other side of the clearing that rests on the hilltop. The silence and dark set deeper in around them the further they get away from the compound entrance, causing the two little bands of would be helpers to unconsciously fall into an uneasy alertness. Both parties begin to whisper their conversations without even realizing that the octaves of their voices had instinctively dropped.

"I wonder how Gracie is doing," Dylan mentions to Cain. Concern is evident in his voice as they reach the top of the hill and cautiously begin to cross the clearing, keeping their eyes open for anything unusual.

"Yeah me too. My mom seemed pretty nervous about it this morning. I could tell by the way she kept telling me that everything was going to be 'OK' when she woke us up. It was like she was trying to convince herself more than me. You know what I mean?" Cain answers.

"I do, she kept doing the same thing to me when she was asking me if we would organize gathering the firewood and water for today." Dylan agrees, seeming to walk a little slower as an obviously painful memory appears to creep into the forefront of Dylan's thoughts.

"Yeah, it should be a lot quicker though without Ol' Willy constantly trying to describe what every dang tree and blade of grass out here used to look like and what it was called before the volcano erupted," Cain says with a little chuckle, trying to raise the spirits of his friend. Picking up on the sudden drop off in the mood of the normally upbeat and positive Dylan as the memory of something or someone had painfully begun to bother him.

"You make fun of him about it as much as everybody else," Dylan says. A small, quick smile briefly cracks the newly acquired stone-faced expression he was wearing before sadly disappearing just as fast, as the memory takes hold of him again.

"What's up Dylan? You look like your puppy just died or something," Cain asks his friend still trying unsuccessfully to lighten the mood.

"You know how I only had a dad? I mean when we started hanging out, only my dad and stepmom were around, not my real mom?" Dylan asks his friend, so softly that even in the maddening silence Cain can barely hear him.

"Yeah I remember. I always thought your dad was pretty cool," Cain offers. Thinking that it was the loss of his father that had sparked the memory that had gotten Dylan so upset.

"I guess he was alright. He was really kind of a dick most of the time if you ask me. After my mom died anyways. Before that...yeah, I guess he was pretty cool," Dylan says. Finally looking up to meet his friends gaze.

"I'm sorry Dylan. I never knew what happened to your mom. You never really talked about her and I never thought to ask. I didn't know that she had died," Cain says looking down at the ground. He no longer wants to look his friend in the eye from feeling guilty about always having his mom and dad around while Dylan it seems, at the young age of fifteen, had already lost both of his.

"Yeah I know. Dad didn't like to talk about it. He just drank himself into a stupor every night. I never told him but at night after I would go to bed, I could hear him crying and talking to my mom in his sleep." Dylan says this last part with more than a little animosity as he begins to cry. The pain and hurt of the memories that were flooding his thoughts as they continued conjuring up emotions that he had buried down deep inside of himself a long time ago.

"He always cared more about himself and drowning his own pain than he ever did about me or what I was going through," Dylan spits the words out through angry sobs and clenched teeth. "He never bothered to see that I was hurting too!" Cain walks over to sit next to his friend who had stopped to sit on a fallen tree. Cain listens to the pain in Dylan's voice as he recounts one of the worst things that could ever happen to a child.

The premature loss of your mother. Dylan wipes at his cheeks angrily before he continues.

"He just couldn't function without my mom. She was the one that had always taken care of *everything*. Then, just like that," Dylan snaps his fingers in the air for effect, "she was gone. And after she was gone, it wasn't long before he was gone. There wasn't anyone there to take care of *anything* anymore. First dad lost his job. Then he lost his motorcycles, the cars, he lost *everything*. He even lost our house. I can remember coming home from school one day and these guys I had never seen before were carrying out all of our furniture and stuff, I didn't know what was going on so I called the cops. *I thought we were being robbed!* As it turns out, they were just there to repossess all the stuff my dad hadn't been making payments on. Do you have any idea how embarrassing that was for me?" Dylan pauses to swipe at a fresh stream of tears that had started running down his cheeks before continuing.

"My dad lost everything my mom had worked so hard to make sure we had in less than a year. So, there I am this confused and scared kid sitting on the curb in front of what used to be our house by myself, waiting for my dad to show up. I wasn't allowed to go in the house at all, they wouldn't even let me go into the backyard to sit on the damn swing set!" Dylan slams his fist angrily into the open palm out of his pain and frustrations over the experience. After several, very tense minutes Cain finally gathers up the nerve to speak to his hurting best friend.

"Dang. What happened after that?" Cain gently prods. You could hear the animosity in Dylan's voice and the angry scowl he wore on his face was apparent even under the dust mask and the dark as he answers.

"My dad never showed up at all. There I am just sitting there on the curb with my head between my knees watching these ants crawl around and kind of poking at them with this stick I found, wondering what the hell I'm supposed to do now when I feel some one sit down on the curb next to me. I look up and see my Aunt Ivey and my Uncle Don sitting on either side of me. They said that dad had to go away for a while and that I was going to go live with them until he could come back. So… that's what I did."

"Damn dude, I had no idea. I knew your dad wasn't always around but he always seemed pretty cool to me," Cain says softly, almost apologetically.

"By the time you started coming around I guess he was alright again. He had changed a lot by then," Dylan says wiping at his cheeks again sighing heavily, blowing out a cleansing breath through his mouth.

"How long did you stay there?" Cain asks. "I mean, when we started hanging out you lived with your dad and stepmom."

"A little over two years. All of fifth and sixth grades. They lived over on the other side of town where they owned this little convenience store and gas station." Dylan stops talking for a moment to take in a deep breath, exhaling heavily he tries to clear out the fog threatening to settle in his head.

"Then one day, just like that my dad shows up out of the blue married to my stepmom Rebecca and says that everything is cool again and that I'm going to come live with them." Dylan looks up at his friend for the first time since recounting the loss of their house and moving in with his aunt and uncle.

"That's how I ended up moving into your neighborhood. Rebecca already owned a house over there before her and my dad got together. She was actually pretty cool."

Cain nods his head in agreement, then after a brief pause curiosity gets the better of him and he apprehensively asks,

"What happened to your mom? I mean how did she die?"

Dylan looks up in surprise as he realizes that he had totally forgotten to finish the story he had started out to tell in the first place. Before the animosity he had developed for his father had surfaced and taken over, diverting the story in its own brooding direction.

Dylan draws in a deep breath and exhaling it slowly he begins to finish his story;

"My mom died when I was nine. We had just moved into a house on the edge of downtown, out on Cherry Blossom Dr. Things were going really good. My dad's handy man business was booming and my mom was pregnant with my little sister. We knew it was a girl because they had found out the baby's sex with one of those sonogram things at one of mom's doctor's visits. Mom wanted to know ahead of time what they were having so she could have everything ready. They had already picked out her name and everything. Dad had decorated the baby's room exactly the way mom wanted it, with these big purple and pink flowers painted everywhere.

And mom had hung these little bubble fairies all over the place, hanging from the ceiling and around the windows." Dylan pauses and sighs at the pleasant memories of the house and his little sister's room.

"Anyway, one day when I came home from school mom was already home from work, which was really unusual. She said she didn't feel well and that she needed me to be quiet until dad got home while she lied down and tried to rest." Dylan sighs again, taking in a long breath and exhaling it slowly collecting his thoughts. Cain can sense that even though Dylan's voice remained steady, his friend was crying again.

"Dylan, you don't have to tell me about it if you don't want to. It's cool dude, I'd totally understand," Cain says offering his friend a way out of finishing the story. The memories of which were still clearly upsetting and painful to him.

"No… I'm Ok. It actually feels kinda good to talk about it really," Dylan says as he continues.

"By the time my dad gets home moms feeling even worse. He called my Aunt Ivey to come over and stay with me so that he could rush mom to the hospital."

"She was the one you went to live with for a little while? When your dad went AWOL?" Cain interrupts to ask.

"Yeah, she was my mom's older sister. Anyway, evidently the baby had pooped inside my mom's belly and no one knew so it turned into some kind of bad infection, I can't remember what they called it. She died in the hospital three days after she gave birth. I never saw her alive again. They wouldn't let me go to the hospital room so I never even got to say good-bye." Dylan wipes at the fresh round of tears that were now rolling down his cheeks in a steady stream wetting his dust mask and causing his nose to snot.

"I… I am so sorry Dylan. That really, really sucks man," Cain says, no longer attempting to cheer his friend up. Embarrassed now that he knows the extent of Dylan's pain. His previous immature attempts to do so, suddenly making him feel silly and childish.

"Hey! What happened to your little sister? Did she die too?" Cain asks suddenly. Then seeing the anguish lingering within his friend's eyes he chastises himself (again), quickly wishing he could take back the question.

The silence settles in tighter around them. Minutes seem like hours in the melancholy thickness that surrounds them before Dylan finally says,

"No, she didn't die. She was ok. Dad said that he couldn't ever look at her without remembering what she had done to mom. I guess he had to blame somebody for my mom dying, so he blamed the baby. He signed away his parental rights and gave her up for adoption. I never even got to meet her."

"Damn dude, that's cold." Was all Cain could manage to say. They both sat there together in silence, letting the dark that surrounds them mix with the darkness of the story as it fully sank in. Finally, Cain stands up from the fallen tree they had stopped to sit on to start heading back down the path that lead to the woods. Turning around to face Dylan a question springs suddenly into his head.

"Hey Dylan, did they ever tell you what her name was going to be?" Cain was surprised that he hadn't thought to ask Dylan before now, then not wanting a repeat his previous mistake he quickly adds,

"I mean…. what would your sister's name have been if… you know… if your dad hadn't of put her up for adoption?" Dylan stands up so suddenly that it startles Cain making him jump and stumble over backwards, tripping over some unseen obstacle to fall hard onto his butt. Dylan takes off down the trail with long purposeful strides as Cain sits in the ashes and mud collecting himself. From down the trail he hears Dylan call back over his shoulder;

"Marie. Her name was supposed to have been Marie."

Lily does her best to keep Belle focused and moving forward. She is technically too young to be of any real help with any of the chores needed to run the compound on a day to day basis. Consequently, she has never had a reason to venture out to the filter station before today. In the typical model of all young, curious children Belle wants to explore everything. And whatever she doesn't want to explore, frightens her. The battle of keeping Belle on task is as futile as fighting the ebb and flow of the ocean's tide. One minute she's rushing about excited, wanting to touch and see everything. The next minute she's cowering and timid, afraid to take another step forward. So there they were, stuck in the middle of the trail just like the ever-changing tides of the ocean. Continuously at work but never succeeding in actually making it anywhere.

"Oh... my... *GOD*!" Rose exclaims angrily. "What's wrong with her now?" Rose asks Lily visibly frustrated with their little tag along.

"She says she keeps hearing something rustling in the leaves just outside of the lamplight. Like something in the woods is following us." Lily answers looking around nervously, quite a bit more understanding of the situation than her far less patient twin sister.

"That is ridiculous. How many times have we been out here to collect the water? How many times have the others came out here?" Rose snaps the question at her sister more than asks it.

"A lot, but never without an adult with us Rose," Lily snaps back nervously.

"That doesn't matter and you know it. We know this path backwards and forwards. Besides, when was the last time you saw anything, or *anyone*, that wasn't from the compound out here anyway? Weeks? Months? We don't even see squirrels or birds anymore." Rose exclaims, growing more annoyed by the second. Visibly upset at how long it was taking them to reach the water station she sighs out of frustration before stating flatly,

"Now the little weirdo is creeping me out too. I'm not wasting any more of my time out here Lily. I'm going on ahead by myself. I'll just meet the two of you there. I'll start filling up the jugs and you can just help me carry them back. Besides, as long as it's taking little Miss Creepy Mc'Creeperson to get down there I'll probably be done by the time the two of you get there anyways." Rose turns and stomps off down the path without giving Lily time to say anything, frustration clearly clouding her judgment.

"Rose, wait! I don't think we should split up!" Lily shouts at her sisters back as she continues to hustle away from her and Belle, who has fallen silent huddled up at Lily's side tightly clutching the bottom of Lily's raincoat.

"Rose! Come on Belle we shouldn't let her get too far ahead of us." Lily utters, coaxing her young travelling companion to hurry along down the path.

"But Lily, I heard something again." Belle whispers so softly that Lily can barely hear her over her own breathing. Lily didn't get frustrated this time though, or question Belle about what it was she thought she was hearing, because this time… she had heard it too.

Rose stomps off down the path putting distance between herself and her sister. Lost in her own frustrations and lack of patience in the annoying chattering of Belle, who in her mind was only succeeding in slowing them down. She already hated being out here. Something about it always made her feel uneasy, like there was some hidden insidious presence lurking in the dark waiting to steal her soul away in every shadow. All she wanted to do was to get the water and get back inside the compound as fast as possible. If Lily wanted to play baby sitter with the little fraidy-cat that heard noises and saw forms in every shadow and around every corner, then Lily could have it. She wanted nothing to do with it. Completely blinded by of her anger and frustrations, Rose is too lost in her own fears to notice the slender, ravenous forms that have begun to close in around her from the dark.

"Dylan! Hey man wait up!" Cain calls out, hurrying after his friend as he continues to dust himself off from his fall over the dead tree branch." Do you know what happened to your aunt and uncle after you moved back in with your dad?" Cain asks, still looking down as he brushes the last bit of dirt from his pants.

"I saw them every now and then. They would stop by, or we'd go over there for a barbeque or something. The air of sadness and disappointment never cleared up between them and my dad. I think he felt shameful for how things went down with mom, me, and especially my sister, and he should have. But it made their visits kinda uncomfortable really."

"I can see how that would make holidays a bit touchy."

"Yeah, then the volcano erupted and everything went to shit. Everyone was running around panicking, freaking out. Some losers came into their store and tried to rob them. When my Uncle Don fought back and refused to give them anything the robbers shot him in the back. F'ing cowards. They shot my Aunt Ivey too, even though she didn't do anything to stop them. I guess because she was a witness. The crooks were too dumb to know or they simply just didn't care that the security camera had recorded all of it. It ultimately didn't really matter anyway. Things got so messed up in the city with everyone acting crazy the cops never had a chance to do anything about it anyhow." Dylan shakes his head sadly, re-opening the wound of the memory stinging him all over again.

"My step-mom Rebecca was killed in a car crash trying to hurry home after they announced that Marshall Law had been implemented. A delivery van t-boned her car right on the driver's side door. She was dead before she even knew what happened. When my dad got the phone call telling him about what had happened to Rebecca he just stood up and told me to stay at the house, that he'd be back home in a little while. But I knew he was never coming back the minute he closed the door. I had already seen that look in my dad's eyes once before. It was the same look he had after my mom died. That's when I packed what I could and came to your house. Your mom asked me where My dad and Rebecca were when I showed up alone…. I feel bad now for lying when I said I didn't know." Dylan falls uneasily silent as he finishes. Cain abruptly runs head first into his back, never noticing that Dylan had unexpectedly stopped dead in the center of the trail. A loud "Humph!" escapes from Cain as he falls to land in the dirt for the second time that day taking Dylan down with him.

"Dude! Why did you stop in the middle of the trail like that?" Cain calls out from the ground annoyed. They had both fallen from the collision, Cain grunts aggravated at the fresh layer of dirt that now coats his pants taking the place of the last layer of dirt he had just finished brushing off. Dylan ignores Cain's complaints as he jumps up and rushes back to where he had been standing before Cain had slammed into the back of him, driving them both to the ground.

"Damn it Dylan. What the hell are you looking at man?" Cain asks annoyed as he walks over to see for himself whatever it was that had Dylan so distracted. Dylan stands rooted in place. Not turning around to look at Cain, his only answer is to point at the ground that lay directly at his feet. Cain comes to stand next to him and following Dylan's finger he lets out an involuntary gasp at what stands out clearly in the muddy, fallen ash on the ground in front of them. Shocked, they both stand stone still, staring at the ground until finally, unable to hide the quiver in his voice, Cain quietly mutters; *"Holy shit."*

CHAPTER FOURTEEN

"What exactly are we supposed to do with him then Ray?" Jim close to shouts as the group stands huddled around the quiet form of the dying Colt lying on the floor in a shallow pool of his own blood. They had done the best that they could with the lamp cord tourniquet, but Colt was still losing blood at a dangerous rate.

"I don't know what we're going to do with him Jim. But I'll tell you what we're not going to do, we're not going to leave him here on the floor of this god forsaken waiting room to fucking bleed to death!" Ray shoots back angrily.

"Alright, alright…now everyone just needs to calm down," Clay interjects as the tension steadily grows inside the room. "Unfortunately, I think it may be too late for us to stop him from bleeding to death now Ray. Look at all the blood he's already lost and it's not like we can hook him up to an I.V. We don't exactly have a supply of plasma laying around."

"But Clay," Ray pleads, trying to state his case before Clay holds up his hand cutting him off.

"Let me finish please." Everyone falls silent and waits for Clay to continue. "Now with that being said; Colt *is* a part of our community. And being part of said community, he deserves a hell of a lot better than to lie here and die on this damn floor in a pool of his own blood." Clay pauses to drive his point home as he looks from one face to another before continuing. "So now that we *all* understand that; *this* is what we are going to do with him. We are going to pick him up and move him into one of the examining rooms. There we are going to make him as comfortable as humanly possible so that if this is Colt's time to go, his passing will be as easy on him as we can make it." Clay raises his eyebrows as he finishes, "Is that acceptable to everyone? Can we all agree with that? That our friend, *our brother*, deserves at least that much?" No one says anything as Clay slowly turns to look them all in the eye one by one. "Ray? Jim? Anyone? Can you live with that?" The room grows eerie in the silence that follows until finally Clay nods his head adding, "OK then. Let's gently pick him up and get him moved. Levi, you and Paige have been in most of these rooms already. Is there one that the two of you think would be better than another to comfortably lay Colt in?" Clay looks first at his son, mentally willing Levi to get it together and re-focus. Quietly hoping the shock of the day's events won't have any lasting effects on his oldest, but still impressionable, son.

"Huh? What? Uh sorry dad. I don't know, um I'm not sure. They all pretty much look the same..." Levi stammers. Clay closes his eyes and sighs as he hears a female voice interject. He silently hopes that Paige's strength is enough to propel Levi forward in the coming days.

"Examining room three Clay. It's the biggest so that would give us the most room around the bed to work on Colt's wounds. Aside from that all the beds in the rooms are the same," Paige says, jumping in and helping Levi. Picking up on growing anxiety and uncertainty inside of Levi she quickly adds, "Levi and I can go get the room prepped for you guys to bring Colt in. It's the second door on the left as you move down the hallway back towards the break room."

Paige pulls Levi out of the room as Clay turns to the rest of the group, quickly giving everyone instructions on the other items they would need in their continued attempt to help Colt. Blankets, pillows, antiseptic, etc. When they all begin to separate and carry out their own individual missions Clay softly calls out,

"Hey Ray, can you hold back for second and give me a hand? I think we need to dress these wounds up a little better before we try to move him." Ray's response of a small curt nod is all the evidence he gives that he had even heard Clay. An action that showed Clay that his friend was still quite distraught with the rest of their group. Upset about how they were so dismissively able to already come to terms with what the outcome of Colts wounds would most likely be. Clay knew, that in Ray's mind it wasn't so much that Colt would die as much as it was that everyone had seemingly been fine with leaving Colt to his own fate, to leave him in this room to die alone. Content to basically stand back and do nothing as he laid there on the floor with some blankets and pillows. That they were content to leave him here to die and rot on the floor of this waiting room. Clay could see in Ray's posture that it had both disgusted and saddened him to see the lack of compassion displayed within the group when the debate of what they should do with Colt had initially begun after the accident. With drooping shoulders and his head looking down staring at his feet, Ray makes his way back over to where Clay still squats on the floor next to Colt. Clay would have to talk to him about all of this later, try to set his mind at ease about everything. Maybe he would suggest that he and Ray take the first watch tonight so that they could sit and talk over a warm cup of coffee after everyone else had turned in for the night. But first things first, and the first thing that they needed to do was to get Colt moved out of this blood-soaked nightmare of a waiting room where this ménage of horrors had been created. With the already departed Mrs. Deloris Scott painting her blood stains and leaving pieces of her flesh to lie on the carpet, to the now unfortunate Colt who lies dying in his own contributions to the blood stain artwork on the floor. And soon enough, the group would find out that Clay too has been leaving his own contributions to the morbid masterpiece that had become the blood covered chiropractic waiting room that the three of them had all been adding their own personal brush strokes to.

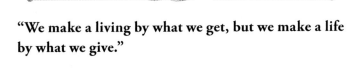

"We make a living by what we get, but we make a life by what we give."

–Winston Churchill

CHAPTER FIFTEEN

"Belle please hurry-up!" Lily pleads as she half carries, half drags Belle down the path in pursuit of her twin sister. "I can't see the glow from Rose's lantern anymore."

"But I don't want to go that way Lily. That's where I hear the noises coming from now! Can't you hear them?" Belle pleads at Lily's back, struggling to free herself from the vise like grip that Lily has on her wrist. Lily too had picked up the fact that the noises had moved off in the direction of Rose as soon as she had stomped impatiently down the path, frustrated and alone. Separating herself from Lily and Belle and the added safety that their numbers seemed to have been offering them against whatever it was that has been trailing them in the dark. Ominous forms that now only seemed to dangerously be trailing the preoccupied, defenseless, and *solitary* Rose who was now so far ahead of them that she was beyond their field of sight walking alone in the dark.

Dylan places his finger over his lips in the universal gesture that symbolizes to be quiet as he and Cain both begin to understand the extreme level of danger that they and the girls are all in. The footprints made by the roaming pack of wild dogs stand out clearly, visible on the ground at their feet in the mixture of mud and dusting of snow. Dylan and Cain silently begin trying to figure out how fresh the tracks are and in what direction they were headed when the first series of howls and yips begin to fill the air. Horrifying in their savagery and desperation, they sing like the personal choir of the devil himself coming straight out of the deepest pits of hell.

"Oh my God Cain...They're trailing the girls! COME ON! WE HAVE TO FIND THEM!" Dylan shouts over his shoulder as he begins to run in the direction of the water station. Cain falls in close behind Dylan, already in a sprint of his own. Feeling more and more guilty for how he had treated Belle that morning with nightmare visions of her being ripped apart by frantic and starving wild dogs haunting his mind with every fleeting step.

Rose hears the attack begin as the dogs come barreling down the hill towards her entirely too late to have any real chance of being able to flee or defend herself. The lead dog hits her behind the knees biting at her calves as a second dog slams into her chest driving her to the ground. All while the third and final member of what was left of the motley pack savagely tears at her throat and face as she lands in the mud, ash, and freshly fallen snow. It all happens so quickly that Rose is only able to release a single gargled scream as her throat is slashed and her life force begins to bubble out in thick crimson spurts. She begins to flail wildly at her attackers in a futile attempt at saving her own life. She slams her fists down over and over again on the bottom dog, the one who had taken her legs out from under her in the initial start of the attack, but it is to no avail. The starving dog had already begun to open up her midsection to get at the nutrient rich entrails that it instinctively knew lay hidden inside of its fallen prey. The third and lead dog of the pack begins to lap at the blood spurting out from her neck like a thirsty jogger at a community park water fountain while the second dog returns to its target after recovering from slamming into her chest and begins to grab at the flesh of her upper right thigh ripping off mouthfuls of flesh. Like a zebra on the plains of Africa being taken down by hungry lions, Rose slips into the dying stillness of shock that nature mercifully created for all prey animals. Lying there in a pool of her own blood and gore, Rose Jones, the twelve-year-old less patient and ill-tempered twin sister of Lily Jones, dies listening to her own flesh being devoured. Her own blood being lapped up greedily. Her own bones being snapped and broken in the very jaws of the nightmares that had always haunted her in her fears. The fear of what could be waiting for her just beyond the light of the lantern. Waiting for her crouched hidden within the shadows. Waiting behind closed closet doors or from underneath her bed. Insidious and opportunistic the patient horrors of the dark that had always been waiting to devour her life and soul.

Be alert and of sober mind; for your enemy, the devil prowls around like a roaring lion looking for someone to devour.

–1 Peter 5:8

CHAPTER SIXTEEN

Jackson stumbles clumsily into the room, weak kneed and red eyed, his face swollen from the tears that still stream steadily down his flushed cheeks. Willy's eyes are also red, as he shares in his friend's pain and grief. The eyes of Veronica, Holly, and Sophia, who all have come to love Jackson and Gracie over the course of the past year, also show the tell-tale signs of grief and sorrow for their friends.

"Jackson, we are so sorry. We've done everything that we know how to do for her," Veronica says to her devastated friend. Just the sight of him causes her tears to start anew as she goes over to help Willy hold him up. Sophia and Holly stand silent and morose as they watch the love and disbelief flood Jackson's eyes as he looks at Gracie lying on the bed in her anguish and suffering.

"I…. I…. know." Jackson barely manages to say through his choking, heartbreaking sobs. When he is finally able to pull his eyes away from his wife he turns to them and says in the awkward voice of the unknowing and the unsure,

"Thank you all very much for all that you've done and for trying your best. We both thank you. And if the baby could I'm sure it would thank you too." Jackson breaks down once again, collapsing to one knee. Willy and Veronica rush to help ease him into the chair that they had set next to Gracie's bed so that Jackson could sit as close to her as possible as they tried to make the difficult decision that laid before them. Softly, barely above a whisper, Jackson murmurs between sobs,

"Is…. is Gracie awake? Is she aware of what's going on?"

"Yes Jackson, she knows. We were able to briefly explain it to her between contractions when we were trying to get her to understand why she needed to stop pushing," Sophia answers, wiping her own tears away as she speaks.

"We've given her a small shot of morphine to help ease her pain. But we explained things to her first to make sure she was fully aware of what we were trying to tell her. We couldn't give her the shot before because we needed her to stay awake and help with the delivery," Holly adds, rubbing Sophia's back as she weeps.

"What did she say when you told her?" Jackson asks, looking up at Holly with hopeless despair.

"She asked about the health of the baby…."

"And, I asked for you," Gracie says softly from the bed interrupting Holly.

"Can everyone please leave? I need to be alone with my husband for a moment," Gracie asks through clenched teeth, still struggling with the amount of pain she was fighting against. Everyone nods in unison like a grief-stricken line of bobble head dolls, fresh tears stream down their faces as they turn to exit the bunker leaving the two heartbroken lovers alone to share in their grief together.

Dylan and Cain break over the top of the hill in a full sprint, stumbling and falling over the dead limbs and fallen trees that lay hidden under the ash and light snow fall as they attempt to get to the girls as quickly as they can. Running through the woods with reckless abandon they fear the worst, but hope for the best as the horrific sounds of killing propel them ever faster towards the trails end near the water station. Everything had gone eerily silent as they break into the expanse that had been cleared away to allow for the filtration barrels, figuring that was the most likely place the dogs could have cornered the girls. Finding the clearing empty, they hastily begin working their way back up the trail towards the entrance to the compound systematically searching the trees that line both sides as they go. Both Dylan and Cain pick up sticks they hoped were big enough to use as weapons in the fight they knew was coming against the dogs as they run along the trail. In their panicked flight, with their eyes straining against the dark a fresh chorus of screams and howls filters down the trail towards them, floating in the darkness. Adding energy to their strides they move ever faster along the trail as the girls' desperate cries guide them on their frantic quest to find Rose, Lily, and Belle.

"Gracie! I'm so glad that you're awake baby, I wanted to be able to tell you that I love you so very much!" Jackson confesses to the love of his life as he buries his head into her neck breaking down into sobs once more. His words are muffled and barely decipherable as Jackson moans into Gracie's neck. "Please tell me what to do Gracie! I don't know what to do! I can't lose you…. either of you!" Jackson heartbreakingly pleads into her neck and pillow.

"Shhhh honey it's going to be ok. It's all going to be ok," Gracie says trying to comfort her grieving husband as she too begins to cry. Resting her cheek against the Jackson's head she rubs his arm affectionately.

"This is what's best Jaxy. This is what I want. My last wish is for you and the baby to have the possibility to live long, wonderful lives together."

"But I can't do it without you Gracie, I just ***can't***. I don't ***want*** to do it without you Gracie!" Jackson cries, his heart begging his wife to try to hang on. To change her mind. That there had to be another option. "I can't live without you! We don't know what will happen, we could do this and I could lose you and the baby."

"Yes you can Jackson…. you can. I know you can, because I ***believe*** in you. You'll have to. We must take this chance Jackson. And if something unfortunate happens then you'll just have to love the baby enough for the both of us," Gracie tells him, softly kissing his forehead as she strokes the back of his head. "I love you so very much Jackson. I will always be with you. In your thoughts, in your heart, and in the eyes of our baby." She pulls him back so that she can gaze into his eyes, "I will never leave you. In this world and the next our souls will always be intertwined." She kisses him on his cheek and then his lips as she places her forehead against his and whispers to her heartbroken husband,

"Now…. please go get Ronnie and the others Jaxy." Jackson pulls back to return her gaze as he runs his left hand down the right side of Gracie's face before he kisses her desperately on the lips. Long and passionate, the kiss holds all the years of his love and the love for all the years he now knows he may never get to show her, within it. He stands up and kisses her hand as he lays it against her chest. Bending over he quietly whispers into her ear,

"I love you Gracie. I will always love you. Everyday." Then pulling away from her he quickly turns and walks away from the only woman he had ever truly wanted and exits the bunker.

Their flashlights slowly reveal the scene like a strobe light horror show as Cain and Dylan come upon the dogs and their victim. The small bend in the trail is covered with blood and little scraps of flesh and bits of bone mixed in. The two dogs that were still working on the corpse, thin almost to the point of starvation and dehydrated, they cough around bites of flesh as they tear at the body greedily. Their lungs were already partially full of ash cement that forms from breathing the ashes out of the air on a daily basis. Their fur, which was falling out in clumps, showed red splotchy patches of skin underneath as if they were suffering from a severe type of mange. Neither one of the dogs are able to stop their frenzied feeding to notice the two newcomers. Cain skids to a dead stop, slipping in the mud and the blood, the distress and revulsion of the scene that was still being played out before them causing him to become sick. As Cain vomits Dylan stops to stand next to him. Uttering an unearthly scream Dylan suddenly lunges at the dogs with his stick held high above his head ready to crash it down on the first unlucky victim that he was able to release his anger and fury upon. The dogs finally realizing that someone else was there, view the newcomers as competition and think that they are there to steal the first meal that they had been able to find in over a week. In instinctual response and desperation, they start tearing off and dragging away whatever bits of Rose's flesh and bone that they can manage to grab, pulling her apart in the process. In their panic to get away from the tornado of vengeance that was now raining blows down on them from above repeatedly, they spread what is left of Rose's body all over the clearing in small bloody clumps of flesh wrapped in fabric. Only her head remains untouched as it lays on the ground staring up unblinking at the swirling, black sky and the falling acid rain now mixed in with the snow. Dylan, and now Cain, were putting all of their strength into every blow that they rain down onto the monstrosities. Powered by pain, fear, and anger mixed with the guilt of not being able to get there in time, their stamina never fades while in the midst of their merciless fury. Their revenge fueled overkill of the dogs that they found over the dead body of one of the girls is only interrupted by a fresh round of screams filtering back to them from further up the trail drawing their attention. They stand in wide eyed ferocity as they hear the blood curdling, terror filled screams of a five-year-old little girl that was currently facing the flesh and blood incarnation of her nightmares come to life.

Willy steps sadly out of the bunker that Jackson and Gracie had called home for the better part of the last year. Blood covers his hands and forearms as well as the front of his shirt and pants. Seeing Jackson sitting alone beneath the pavilion he immediately turns and walks briskly towards the community washroom. Unwilling to chance having to meet Jacksons gaze Willy keeps his head down and his pace fast as he rushes to wash off the blood of his now dead friend as fast as he possibly can. Jackson never picks his head up as he continues to stare at his feet, his tears fall steadily to form a small pool between them. He is thinking about the first time he had ever kissed his lovely Gracie as he waits for someone to come tell him the outcome of the emergency amateur caesarean section that Sophia and Willy were presently performing on his wife and unborn child.

The day was bright and sunny, like most spring days were in the foothills of the Ozarks during late April. It had been warm, but not too warm since a thunder storm had just passed through the night before. The flowers were just coming into full bloom filling the fields with color as the song birds sang giving melody to the wind as it grazed over the countryside. Gracie always loved the rain. They would sit outside in their sunroom, open up all of the windows, and listen to the rain for hours; which almost always ended in them making passionate love as the rain drummed out its beat on the rooftops. This day had been just like that. They had planned an outing to have a picnic and at first he thought the rain was going to wash out their plans for a lazy, romantic afternoon before the clouds parted giving them a break in the storm. The clouds pull back revealing a day that could have been taken straight off of a country mountain post card. They hiked to a spot by the river they had found on one of their first dates, the spot where Gracie liked to feed the ducks as she dangled her feet in the water, and laid out their blanket and basket. Jackson had stopped and picked Gracie a flower on the hike and sitting there on the blanket with Gracie lying next to him watching the clouds and listening to the river, Jackson looked over at her and softly brushed his hand down the side of her face clumsily placing the flower and her hair together behind her ear while he stared longingly into her eyes.

"Well?" Gracie said. The sound of her voice mixing with the sounds of the rushing river. Somewhat startled by the suddenness of the question, Jackson leans back, his brow furrowed with worry and asks,

"Well what Gracie?"

"Well… are you going to finally kiss me or not Jackson? You can't make a pretty girl like me wait forever you know."

Gracie's voice is quiet and sultry surprising Jackson as she rubs her thumb seductively across his lips. A sly, sweet smile spreading across her face as she softly bites her lower lip enticingly.

"Do you want me to?" Jackson shyly asks, both fearing and begging for her answer simultaneously.

"Everyday." She softly whispers as she tugs on his shirt, pulling him closer to her. He submits willingly to her as he slowly bends down and kisses her tenderly on her lips. It had been everything a first kiss should have been; two parts sweet and passionate, two parts awkward and clumsy. Outlining the basis for all of the first kisses they had shared every day since. Their first meeting of the day when they were still just dating and on every morning since their wedding Jackson had brushed his left hand softly down the right side of his wife's face, awkwardly place her hair behind her ear, and sweetly kiss her on the lips. It didn't matter whether she was awake or asleep, he kissed her. And as he pulled away from the kiss he always whispered quietly; "Everyday".

Veronica, Sophia, and Holly emerge from the bunker in unison, all of them wear the mask of empathetic sorrow over their faces. Sophia slowly turns away from where Jackson sat under the pavilion, hesitating for only a moment before she hastily makes her way to the washroom that Willy occupies a part of already to also get herself cleaned up. She keeps her head down in an attempt to hide the tears that continue to stain her cheeks and wet her coat as she walks. Veronica and Holly slowly approach Jackson together, side by side. Leaning on one another for both strength and courage as they approach Jackson to share with him the devastating results of their attempts to save Gracie and the baby. They sit next to Jackson, Holly on his left – Veronica on his right, as Jacksons' tears continue to splash around his feet steadily filling his small broken-hearted pool of lost dreams.

"Was…. was she in a lot of pain?" Jackson asks softly.

"We did everything we could to keep her as comfortable as possible," Holly whispers as her own tears slide down her cheeks to salt her lips. Standing up to squat in front of Jackson, Veronica lays the blood-stained bundle of receiving blankets she had been holding in her arms onto Jackson's lap. Jackson immediately sits up like he has just been struck, looking back and forth between Veronica and the bundle.

"Open the blanket Jackson," Veronica whispers. Slowly he begins to peel back the soft cloth of the bundle to gradually reveal what was laying inside. The baby's eyes are open as he exposes first its head and then its shoulders. As he slowly continues to unwrap and examine the bundle he exposes the baby's arms and hands where he sadly caresses the inside of the baby's palm with his finger. Jackson gasps in surprise as the baby unexpectedly wraps its tiny hand around his finger.

"It's alive! You saved the baby?! You were able to save our baby?!" Jackson sobs, a fresh bout of tears jumping forth to stream down his cheeks.

"She… Jackson. It's a she. She's a beautiful, healthy baby girl," Veronica says, still squatting in front of him as she places her hands over her mouth in an attempt to cover up that she too has once again lost control of her emotions. Regaining her composure, she adds,

"She's your and Gracie's baby girl."

Jackson's sobs begin again in force as he brings the baby up to his chest in a loving fatherly embrace. His sobs are a mixture of the pain he feels for the loss of Gracie and the happiness he feels for the gain of the baby. As he looks down into the eyes of his beautiful new daughter he sees all of the love that he and Gracie had shared contained within them.

"My and Gracie's baby girl," Jackson whispers, looking up at Veronica. "Gracie always wanted a little girl."

"What are you going to name her?" Holly asks placing an arm around him in a comforting embrace. Jackson sits staring into the eyes of his baby girl for what seemed to Veronica and Holly like an eternity. Then suddenly without warning or without uttering a word Jackson stands up, cradling the baby protectively in his arms and begins to walk purposefully towards the bunker where his wife laid. He pauses just as he is about to enter the room mournfully. He knows the body of the recently departed love of his life lies inside, silent and alone. Collecting himself as best as he can, he takes in a big sigh and crosses cautiously into the room, strolling to stand at the side of Gracie's bed. Bending down he presents the baby to too his wife's lifeless body, speaking to her as if he were speaking on a direct line to her soul in heaven.

"Look Gracie, you did it honey. She's perfect, just like you always said she would be." He lays the baby on her chest like he had seen in so many movies as he slowly brushes his hand down the side of Gracie's face. Gently placing her hair behind her ear as he bends down to softly kiss Gracie's still, warm lips. Fighting back the tears that fall once again as he whispers sweetly into her ear,

"Everyday."

Pulling back, he picks up his daughter to once again cradle her in his arms lovingly, never taking his eyes off of his wife as he says,

"Thank you, Gracie, for being you and for making me a better me…. everyday." Jackson turns to face Veronica and Holly who had followed him into the bunker, tears are streaming down all of their faces as he tells them,

"Her name is Marie. Just like Gracie dreamt it would be."

"The most precious possession that ever comes to a man in this world is the love of a woman's heart."

~Josiah G. Holland

CHAPTER SEVENTEEN

Volcanic ash. Fine particles of microscopic glass with the consistency of talc, covers virtually everything like a deathly fine dust in this new version of the world. Water is more valuable than all the gold, silver, or jewels left on the planet *combined.* Life giving and almost impossible to obtain in its preciousness. Cleanliness was a disregarded non-necessity away from the compound. Hand washing and tooth brushing were the only exceptions. Bathing was completely out of the question. They simply just could not afford to spare the amount of water necessary for taking a bath. They are all covered in the dirt, ash, and grime of traveling for three days as they entered the chiropractor's office and began roaming around its parking lot. Unsanitary and unclean bodies wearing unwashed clothes, all of their possessions were crawling with the thriving bacteria that always seems to accompany the filth and the dark. The wayward opportunistic hitch hikers that had found an unexpected easy ride as they hopped onto an errant arrow straight into the flesh and bone of Clay Stratford.

Clay's side throbbed and ached in a constant state of flux as his body goes back and forth in its efforts to fight back the fever and the nausea that now continuously accompany the pain. He breaks out into a cold sweat as he carries the tarp that they kept in the jeep inside. The unfortunate designated funeral shroud for their recently departed dear friend. Colt had passed away in the middle of Laura and Paige's watch last night. Painfully, but mercifully, Colt had passed away while lying in the dark without ever regaining consciousness. His body was just too weak to recover from the massive amount of blood loss and the severe gashes he had suffered in his fall. Short ragged breaths and the soft, barely coherent occasional whisper of Holly's name had been the last verbal contributions Colt had been able to offer to the world around him as he slipped away. Clay had finally gotten through to Ray last night as they had sat and talked over steaming cups of hot coffee. Thankfully able to appeal to his sense of compassion from a different direction; he got him to understand that the pain and loss that they all faced every day coupled with the extreme hardships they had all faced already just to survive to this point, affected different people in different ways. And that they just needed to always do the best that they could to repeatedly remind everyone of the one thing that was the easiest to lose in this desolate dead, grey world. A world where their only goal from one day to the next was to survive. But even in this world gone mad, above all else, they needed to keep their humanity. Lost in the reflections of last night's conversation Clay turns too sharply, foolishly forgetting about his inflamed wound that angrily reminds him of its presence by sending a shockwave of pain rippling up his right side in an excruciating wave of agony. Momentarily blinding him and stealing his breath away as he drops to one knee barely able to stop himself from fully falling over. He catches himself with his left hand as his right hand gingerly clutches at his side. Like a stone thrown into the face of a smooth mountain lake the pain ripples outward from the arrow wound in tormenting shockwaves. Gradually his senses come back into focus from the pain that now undulates through his body. Clay can just make out a fresh round of heated debate beginning inside the office over whether or not they were wasting precious time and valuable cargo space for some one that was unfortunately already dead. The words come in and out as the fever plays evil tricks with Clay's vertigo. The first real sign of what he had feared would happen most from the wound; an extremely high fever caused by the now raging infection that was swiftly spreading throughout Clay's body, traveling through his blood.

CHAPTER EIGHTEEN

Siren like screams rip through the countryside guiding Cain and Dylan on their blind rush through the labyrinth that was once just a path to the water station as they desperately try to find the source of the shrieking. Cain's left hand and forearm burn from the bites he had sustained during the fight to drive the dogs away from what they now knew was all that was left of their poor friend, Rose Jones. Dylan's right leg had also been badly bitten, caught in the jaws of one of the fiends as he threw a kick at it. The bite hobbled him, but only slightly, as his fear and rage propelled him through the dark. Cain was too afraid to imagine what new massacre might await them as they run frantically down the muddy, unlit path.

Cain is the first to arrive. Coming around the corner only a few steps ahead of Dylan, who was also running hard in spite of the throbbing pain that reverberates upward in agonizing stabs with each new step he takes from his torn and damaged calf. The lights from their flashlights fall on a wide bend in the path illuminating the area in a pale, feeble light that does little to fight back the wall of darkness. The lights find Belle and Lily caught in a violent tug of war struggle with a third and much larger wild dog. Lily is straining to hold onto Belle with all of her young strength. Digging her heels into the ground as best as she can in the slippery, unforgiving mud. Her arms are wrapped tightly around Belle's upper torso underneath her armpits in a bear hug of desperation while a third and yet unknown person was attempting to knock the dog off of Belle. Time and time again the newcomer hurls large stones and sticks at the dog's head and its exposed ribs that stand out like protruding shards of bone along the dogs' sides. On the verge of starvation, the dog is in its own personal battle for survival. It had grabbed Belle just above the left ankle and was putting every last ounce of hope and energy that it possessed into the attempt to drag Belle off down the side of the hill and away from the throng of missiles being hurled at it as fast as its attacker could find and throw them.

Lily and Belle can hear the mayhem of the dog attack on Rose well before they can see it. A short solitary scream is cut off suddenly mid-way through only to be followed by the softer, whispering garbles of spouting blood through torn vocal chords. Finally, to be followed by an ungodly, eerie silence broken only by the pitiful whines and desperate cries of the starving dogs. Occasionally they can make out the sound of tearing clothes and the sickening sound of ripping flesh followed by the furious lapping of blood. Lily stops abruptly, gasping loudly as the horror scene surrounding Rose plays out to its climax. Instantly she does her best to block the sight from Belle. The ghastly, grim view that it was; only being spotlighted now by Rose's own flashlight that had fallen to the ground during the initial part of the attack. Lily's flashlight having been dropped and forgotten in her own initial panicked flight towards the haunting sounds of chaos. She grabs and points Belle's flashlight directly into the ground hoping to avoid drawing unwanted attention to Belle and herself. Despite the horror happening in front of them she was still too afraid to turn the light off completely, terrified of losing her solitary beacon of hope. Rose's fallen light however doesn't fail to spotlight the horror show as it continues to stay trained directly onto the feeding frenzy, illuminating the grotesque and ghastly horrors that are currently being performed on Lily's twin sister. Regrettably, Lily is unsuccessful at preventing the scene from burning into the nightmares of her five-year-old companion. Belle's eyes grow wide with fright as her fresh round of screams echo down the path alerting the dogs to their prescience, which was exactly what Lily was hoping to avoid. All three of the dogs stop in the middle of the chaos that defines their meal to look up at them; with blood covered muzzles and desperation in their eyes they drool over the body of Rose as they study the newcomers. Recognizing the lack of any type of threat that the two girls presented to their meal the pack hungrily goes back to their Rose Jones buffet of raw flesh, fresh blood, and bones. All…. except one. The leader, whose posture never altered from its aggressive stance, hadn't taken its eyes off of the girls since their frantic arrival to the kill sight. Lily continues to try to shield Belle from the grisly scene as she begins to slowly back out of the small clearing and start working their way back up the trail bit by frightening bit. This dog alone, who is noticeably much larger than the other two dogs left in the pack, slowly and methodically begins to walk towards them matching their slow retreat step for step. Holding its head down low with its muzzle wrinkled and lips pulled back baring its teeth, a low rumbling growl emanating from deep within its chest. Three feet at the shoulder, the dog was still every bit of eighty pounds and muscular even in this starved state and would have been quite the specimen in the world of plenty before the eruption. Some fur still clung to it stubbornly in small clumps around its shoulders, tail, and down the center of its head giving it a sickly, almost comical Mohawk. A collar was still loosely attached around its neck showing that it had once been part of a family. But in the end, instinct and survival had taken over. Deeply burying all of the memories it may have once had of being the loving pet of some little girl or boy.

Aubrey hears the rustle of the leaves booming out in the silence over the light rain and snow mix that falls from the skies when the attack begins. She holds her breath against the certain death she believes is hurtling through the dark towards her, gasping happily as she realizes that the pack was in fact running in another direction and no longer seemed to be trailing after her. Her relief is short lived however as she hears the chorus of piercing screams filter back to her through the woods. Aubrey recognizes the scream for what it is having already heard it to many times since the world went dark. The scream that can only be made when the realization of your certain and imminent death sweeps over someone's consciousness, knowing that all hope is lost. The initial scream is followed by the frightened screams of what sounded to her like a little girl a few tense seconds later. Aubrey takes off running as gracefully as she can manage in the dark and cold down the trail she had stumbled on accidentally the day before. She stumbles clumsily in her panicked flight toward the new round of screaming, fueled by the unmistakable youth that lives behind the voice. Her hopes that the trail, which showed signs of frequent use, would lead her to an encampment of other survivors that could aid her in her flight from the starving dogs seemed to be accurate. But at what cost she thinks remorsefully. As the sickening, wet sounds of a successful hunt echo through the hills Aubrey realizes morbidly that this new trail seems to be like all the other trails she has taken in her frantic quest for survival. And now, this trail as well appears to be leading her once again to peer into the face of nothing but more death and despair.

The mammoth sized dog continues to shadow Lily and Belle as they slowly back up the trail towards the entrance and safety of the compound. Every step the beast takes is hypnotic almost to the point of seduction, methodical and deliberate as it mirrors the girls every step away from the melee' of Rose. Lily's mouth goes dry as her terror rises higher, the booming sound of her heartbeat drums in her ears drowning out all other sound and dulling her senses. The light in the dog's eyes shines with a demonic illumination, foretelling its evil intentions. Apparently not all of the dog's hunger pangs had been sated with the untimely demise and consummation of her poor sister. She notices with despairing realization that the dog trailing them is beginning to step with its head lower and lower. She sees the muscles in its rear legs twitch spasmodically in anticipation as it begins to crouch ever so slightly, preparing for the spring that would fill its jaws simultaneously with both death and life. All of its strength moving to its haunches for the spring that would end the tormenting pain in its belly and stop the drool that ran out from between its bared teeth and jowls in thick, hungry rivulets. Lily's stomach begins to twist itself into the knots of fear and her eyes uncontrollably begin to fill with the tears of knowledge as she accepts that an attack on her or Belle had become an absolute conclusion and is likely only mere seconds away from happening. Lily drops her gaze to peer down at Belle who hadn't muttered a sound since her initial screaming brought on by the shock and horror of the bloody scene that had greeted them when they came upon Rose being devoured by living, breathing nightmares. She strokes Belle on the top of her head and pulls her closer, whispering to her as assuredly as she can.

"Everything's going to be ok Belle, but I want you to cover your eyes, ok? Can you do that for me?"

The tears of knowing the inevitable begin to slide down her cheeks and fall onto her arms. Belle never takes her eyes off of the dog as she answers Lily softly, her voice barely above a whisper, tinged with fear and disbelief.

"OK. But I don't think so Lily, that everything will be ok I mean. I don't think that everything is going to be ok."

Lily catches subtle movement from out of the corner of her eye. Drearily she brings her head back around just in time to see the monster rock back onto its haunches in final preparation for its assault. Snarling viciously and uttering a dreadful, barking roar it springs into action lunging at the girls in hopes of bringing down its next meal. With the glow from the lantern reflecting out of eyes rimmed in blood from the unrelenting abuse of the ashes the dog is the living image of the monster with the glowing red eyes that haunts you from underneath your bed. The beast that patiently watches, waiting for you to fall asleep from inside the slightly ajar door of your closet. The creature that haunted you from the dark corners of the unknown shadows where childhood horrors lived. But here – in the middle of the dark, blood covered trail – there isn't anyone coming to turn on your bedroom light to chase the dark away. No covers to pull up over your head so that you can hide your face. No one to tell you that everything's going to be ok as the monsters of your nightmares make you begin to cry and scream. When what haunts your dreams as you close your eyes to sleep is alive and leaping at you open mouthed, its teeth bared, and hunger in its eyes. Here on this trail, trapped and held frozen into place as everything around you begins to turn black, there are no mommies or daddies to run to as your nightmares are coming to eat you.

Aubrey strikes the dog in the middle of its leap with the first stick she could find that was big enough to use against the monstrosity leaping to tear at the girls huddled together in the center of the trail. Catching it across the center of its back, breaking the stick from the force of the blow. Unfortunately, the strike isn't strong enough to stop the attack completely but merely throws off the aim of the predator so that it misses the neck and clamps down on the lower leg of its intended prey instead as the dogs leap to falls short of its intended victim; the little blonde haired girl that Aubrey believed to be the owner of the voice behind the screams. The siren like alarm that had thankfully alerted her to the girl's distress at the onset of the attack. Fortunately for the younger girl the blow from Aubrey causes the beast to stumble as it comes down closing its mouth around her left leg just above the ankle. Its vice like hold is strong and set as the bigger of the two girls and the dog begin their life or death game of tug-o-war. Both the life of the dog and the life of the little girl hang in the balance as the game commences, death dances just out of sight patiently playing the waltz while anxiously awaiting to receive its newest soul.

Cain and Dylan finally break themselves out of the hypnotizing trance they had fallen under after taking in the chaos of the scene being played out before their eyes. Shock in the disbelief that the stage for this horror show was a small clearing along a path that they both had taken at least once a day themselves for the past year helping to fill the water jugs.

"LILY, RUUNNNN!" Cain is finally able to shout, his voice cracking from the strain of the yell as he approaches the girls still in the midst of the desperate attack from the dog.

"HEEEYYY! Over Here!" Dylan yells as he waves his arms in the air trying to break the dogs' fixation on Belle, Lily, and the new comer. Dylan takes a giant step forward and strikes the dog in its left hind quarter with the tree branch he was still wielding, putting all the strength he has left within himself into the swing. The blow is placed well enough, and delivered hard enough, to cause the dog enough pain that it releases its grip on the struggling Belle. Yelping and snarling it twists around re-focusing its aggression on its assailant, simultaneously leaping at its new aggressor and snapping at the stick at the same time. Its jaws make an audible "Snap" as they close on nothing but air.

"RUN LILY! RUN NOW! GET BELLE BACK TO THE COMPOUND!" Cain yells trying to get the girls to move now that they are, at least for the moment, free from the grip of the monster they have been fighting against. The dog's attention is purely on Dylan now as it faces him snarling and snapping at the stick in his hands. Guttural growls mixed with the excitement and exertion from the attack causes the dog to start hacking up blood lowering its growl to an even deeper, more menacing octave. In the melee' Cain can see that the dog is wearing a studded black leather collar with a short piece of blue rope still hanging off of it in tattered strings. It is a sight that stops Cain suddenly, rooting him into place. Unable to believe his eyes he sees something printed across the back of the dog's collar. A single word that is barely legible in its worn and tattered state. There, stamped in the leather is the word – **BUDDY**.

"Buddy?" Cain says aloud more as a question than a statement, calling out to the dog. The dog stops snarling and fighting for the briefest of seconds, visibly confused at the sound of its name being said aloud for the first time in possibly a year, allowing Dylan to get a good crack on top of the dog's head in the pause. The force of the blow breaks the stick causing the dog to yelp and momentarily fall to the ground submissively lying on its belly.

"BUDDY!" Cain cries out again to the dog with more urgency. The dog briefly turns its attention to Cain, before turning its attention back to its attacker. Snarling and growling at Dylan one last time for good measure it turns swiftly away to bound off into the woods. Confused, he darts away from the clearing with hunger still rumbling in his belly. Throwing nervous, cautious glances over his shoulder he lopes away from the clearing heading south back towards town and the comfort of the packs lair.

"The saddest thing about betrayal is that it never comes from your enemies.... It comes from your friends and loved ones."

–Ash Sweeney

CHAPTER NINETEEN

YEAR ONE, DAY THREE HUNDRED AND TWENTY-FIVE

Levi and Paige cautiously guide the small group into the second of the three houses surrounding the chiropractor's office that they had mapped out to search for supplies that day. Paige looks sympathetically at Levi as they prepare to enter the living room of the house, thinking to herself about how glad she was to finally see him beginning to act to like his old self again. The group needed him to be on his "A" game out here on the edge of the Ashland as they did their best to find and bring back the badly needed supplies to the compound. The search party that consisted of Levi, Paige, Laura, and Grant continue their exploration of the house being as careful and quiet as possible. None of them say a word as they go from room to room searching first for any threats, second for any survivors, and third for anything they could use for their own survival. Only then, would they go through the house more thoroughly. Taking any and everything they could find that would be of any use to them or the group; either out here on their search or to their family and friends depending on them back home. It felt odd being out here without any of the more experienced adults with them. With the unfortunate – but expected – death of Colt, the age of Jim, and with Clay not seeming like himself, the leadership on this sortie had fallen heavily upon the shoulders of Levi and Paige. With the absence of Clay and Colt they were the only other members of the group that had been on any of the house to house searches that had been organized since scavenging for supplies had become a necessity for the survival of their community of both family and friends back at the compound. Laura and Grant were a little more out of their element away from base camp. Their primary assignments on all of the previous sorties had been to aid Ray with syphoning gas and guarding the supply vehicles. But they were both performing their duties admirably on the sweep and clears of the houses thus far.

"OK guys, everything seems to be ok. Let's start collecting any supplies that we can find," Levi says turning to address the group after the last room had been cleared. His voice sounding muffled through the mask he and all the others still wore every day away from the relative cleanliness of base camp.

"What area of the house should we search first Levi?" Laura asks. "Should we just do it the same as last time?"

"Yeah that's what I was thinking," Levi shrugs. "I thought everything went really smooth in the last house. And we ended up with a lot more stuff than I hoped we would."

"I thought so too. Ok, Laura and I will search the kitchen and bathrooms while Levi, you and Grant search the bedrooms and the garage. We'll meet back here and search any other rooms together. Maybe we'll get lucky and find another full gas can," Paige offers optimistically.

"Sounds good to me," Grant says slapping Levi playfully on the back. "Dude if we find another ATV in the garage like in last one…. maybe we can talk my dad into letting us take 'em."

"Man, I hope so. That would be sweet," Levi agrees with a short laugh. Their youth shining through the darkness in their boyish joy of discussing barreling through the countryside surrounding the compound on four wheelers. They separate into their groups of two falling into quiet, lighthearted conversation about the things they hoped to find as they begin their systematic search of the house.

"Awe man. Dang." Levi hears Grant exclaim.

"What is it?" Levi asks tensely from by the doorway that leads into the garage.

"No ATV," Grant pouts, the disappointment evident in his voice.

"That sucks. Maybe there'll be one in the next garage," Levi says. "On a positive note, check out this awesome hatchet I just found." Levi holds up his prize in the light of the flashlight for Grants approving inspection.

"Heck yeah! That's awesome! Did you see anything else over there that we can use?" Grant asks excitedly.

"Um…. nah, not really. There's a gas can over in the corner by the lawn mower. But that seems to be about it. We should check it to see if there's any gas left in it," Levi says before adding with a sigh,

"I think we already have all the hammers and screwdrivers we need at the compound. Keep your eyes open for anything else that could be used as a weapon though."

"Not a problem," Grant says as he begins to make his way over to the front corner of the garage where the lawn equipment was stored. Scanning quickly around the area as he goes.

"Hey Levi, it looks like there's a doggy door over here in the bottom…" Grant stops in mid-sentence as he spots what looks like a pile of blankets and a sleeping bag arranged on the floor just inside the garage.

"What'd you say Grant?" Levi calls out from the front of the garage, turning to look in Grant's direction. Grant turns quickly towards Levi shining his flashlight on himself signaling for Levi to be quiet. As he does he starts pointing to the floor where he had found the blankets arranged in what appeared to be a make shift bed. Levi crouches instinctively and begins to quickly make his way to where Grant is already standing as quietly as possible.

"Oh, thank you Jesus!" Laura exclaims from where she was bent over rummaging for supplies underneath the bathroom sink.

"What'd you find Laura?" Paige asks curiously from the medicine cabinet she was busy digging through. Laura stands and turns around showing her bounty to her friend like a trophy. They both begin laughing and celebrating at the almost full box of tampons Laura had found underneath the sink. The second such box they had found since they began searching the houses one by one that surrounded the chiropractor's office. A dire need in a world where there isn't a corner pharmacy or supermarket to run to during that "special" time of the month. When general hygiene is hard to come by it made them a terrible necessity – all be it a luxurious one – if you were going to try and avoid illnesses and infections; which was the number one priority after water and food when you lived in a world where getting salmonella, the flu, or even the common cold could be fatal. An unforgiving world where getting dysentery, dying of dehydration or starvation was an actual possibility. Their momentary victory fully celebrated, the two young women get back to work resuming their search for both essential and non-essential supplies; always trying to be aware that all luxuries, great and small, were hard to come by in the current state of things and should never be taken for granted.

Levi probes the poorly thrown together bedding with the new hatchet he has just found trying to see if it was empty or occupied. His sigh of relief comes out heavily as he peels back the last layer of blankets revealing that the bedding is indeed empty. Grant's own heavy sigh echoes Levi's from his position standing beside him as he kneels down watching him investigate the pile. Sub-consciously holding his breath without even realizing it.

"It's empty now, but how long it has been empty is the real question, because it definitely looks like it's been used and used recently," Levi stresses to Grant, a look of concern crossing his brow.

"Agreed. But used by whom?" Grant asks, raising the other obvious question.

"I have no idea. But this is way too close to the dr.'s office for comfort if you ask me," Levi says standing up and scanning his light around trying to see if they had over looked any clues as to who or what had been using this garage to sleep in. Concentration strains his features as Levi tries to figure out their next step. Not for the first time that day he quietly wishes to himself that his father was out here with them as they combed through the houses. Huffing out a heavy breath through his nose he turns to Grant and says,

"Let's go meet up with the girls and get a move on. We still have another house to search today after we finish with this one."

"Yeah... Ok." Grant nods his head dreamily as he turns and leads the way out of the garage and back into the main part of the house, thankful to be leaving the mystery behind them.

"Are you guys sure it was a bed?" Laura asks both Levi and her brother simultaneously.

"You're positive it couldn't have just been an old pile of blankets or something that the past owners of the house threw down and forgot to pick up on their way out as they tried to get to someplace safer?" Paige – the current most rational, clearheaded thinker of their young group – asks, trying to bring a new angle to the discussion before it escalated into complete unwarranted paranoia. "I mean let's not jump to any crazy conclusions or anything. We don't know anything about this area or the people that use to live here."

"No... no way Paige," Grant answers absolutely before Levi has a chance to speak. "This... *thing* has been slept in. And recently by the looks of it."

"Yeah I agree with Grant completely. You'd have to see it to understand exactly what we mean. We don't have to call it a bed if that what's throwing you off but the pile looked.... I don't know, organized somehow or something. Like it had been laid there for a reason. Whatever made it, made it on purpose." Levi is nodding to himself and rubbing the back of his head as he speaks out loud but it is evident that his words are meant more for himself than to the rest of them. After several seconds slowly tick by he looks up and says conclusively, "I think we need to get back to the dr.'s office and tell my dad and Ray about this. This might be something that could endanger the entire group and the job at hand."

"I agree and soon," Grant says moving to stand next to Levi.

"Ok guys, fine. We believe you. Do you think we should call off the search of the third house until we find out what the others have to say about it?" Laura asks, her voice growing thick with nervous worry.

"Everyone stop.... let's just calm down. We need to think about this for a minute. If it was a bed, there isn't anyone in it now so I say we continue to search the houses just like we planned," Paige says. She speaks with assertive confidence and her voice carries a tinge of authority and leadership within it.

"We haven't found that much in here at least not as much as we did in the first house anyway. And what time we have out here to find supplies and get back home is quickly running out. Also, and I'm sorry to have to say this Levi, but your dad isn't getting any better. He looked awful this morning when I went in to check on him. I gave him the only real medicine we had at the time which was just plain old aspirin. We **need** to keep searching for supplies and more medicine," Paige states flatly to the others.

"The group is depending on us to do our jobs and we can't let them down just because we got a little spooked. Our packs are only half full if you don't count the gas can we found and most of what we have are things like mouth wash, a few toothbrushes, and other odds and ends stuff like that." Paige pauses her lecture for emphasis, then turning to look directly at Levi she continues.

"Levi I think your dad is really, really sick. We have to keep searching for some antibiotics for him. I don't know how he can get better without them. And the sooner we find them, the better off he will be."

Levi looks down at the ground to avoid Paige's gaze. Afraid that even behind the mask and in the dark she would be able to see the shame held within his eyes that she was the one that had to stand up and be the voice for what their responsibilities were to the group; both here with them out on the sortie and to their family members and loved ones that were depending on them back at the compound. But most of all he was ashamed that she had actually needed to remind him of the grim situation that was his sick – and growing sicker – father.

"OK, well we all heard her so let's get to it. I do have one condition though," Levi says quietly. He looks up finally able to meet Paige's gaze hoping that she can read the "thank you" in his eyes.

"We stay and search, but in the next house no more splitting up. We stick together as a group for the rest of this outing." The group nods in agreement as an answer to Levi's half question, half order about how the search of the last house was to proceed.

"Good. Did you two get a chance to search the kitchen yet for any can goods?" Levi asks Paige and Laura.

"No, we had just finished searching the bathrooms when you guys came in from the garage," Paige answers. Her hand placed caressingly on his forearm was the only "you're welcome" that he needed.

"Alright then…" Levi begins, taking in a deep breath through his nose and exhaling it slowly through his mouth, "Grant and I will go bring the wagon over while you two go ahead to the kitchen and begin opening up the cabinets. We'll meet you guys in there in five minutes or so," Levi finishes. The air of uncertainty hangs thick about them as they begin carrying out their responsibilities with a new sense of purpose. Levi and Grant step out into the cold, damp air pulling up their coat hoods to protect themselves from the light icy rain that has begun to fall. Levi thinks he catches movement out of the corner of his eye causing him to draw his sidearm, turning quickly towards the dr.'s office. Intensely focused and full of nervous anxiety, his heart is racing as he mistakenly sees danger in every flickering shadow and in every twitch of a tree branch caused by the wind or rain.

"Dude are you OK?" Grant asks, darting his eyes nervously around the immediate area. Levi's quick, anxious movements startle him; causing him to feel uneasy.

"Yeah… I'm OK," Levi answers as the tension in his stance – but not his eyes – eases up ever so slightly. "Sorry man."

"Are you sure? You're being jumpy all of a sudden and it's kinda freakin' me out," Grant states flatly.

"I thought I saw something move across the street in front of the dr.'s office," Levi admits.

"Well…. do you see anything now?" Grant asks with nervous annoyance.

"No, I don't think so. It must've been a shadow or something, I'm not sure," Levi answers. "Maybe it was just a trick of light from the rain."

"Well the sun almost seems like a wannabe moon today so there actually is enough light to cast a shadow or two. Come on man, let's just grab the damn wagon and get back inside," Grant says looking up despairingly at the swirling sky overhead. The cold chill that rushes over him causes him to shudder, the day's events still weighing heavily upon him. The discovery of the sleeping area in the garage apparently still had them both shaken up a little more than their pride would allow either of them to admit. Levi continues to cast unsure glances towards the street as they collect the wagon and begin pulling it inside. They spend the rest of their time outside in uncomfortable silence, neither of them able to shake off the distinct uneasy feeling – *that they were being watched*.

Her eyes never leave them from her hiding spot on the opposite side of the street as she watches them re-enter the house pulling the wagon in behind them. For a second she thought the big one had spotted her even though she felt she was able to quickly get under cover and out of sight. Scolding herself she knows she will have to be more careful if she planned on making it back home with her supplies safely. Her group hadn't been able to search this area of town yet because of all the gashers that still roamed and lived over here. Her heart sinks as she notices the can goods that were stacked up in the wagon. Her stomach rumbles and gurgles in protest as she thinks about the food she had come over here to find in spite of the dangers. Food that now seems to have gotten even further out of her reach with the introduction of these newcomers. The food and supplies that were so desperately needed back at the house that her own small group called home.

"Sometimes what you are most afraid of doing is the very thing that will set you free."

-Unknown

CHAPTER TWENTY

Ally slipped out of the back door as quiet as possible so that she wouldn't disturb Mrs. Jackie or her dad, who were both still asleep. Mr. Broderick (or Brick as he constantly asks her to call him) was already awake and checking the houses defenses with his and Mrs. Jackie's two young sons, Benny and Larry. The look on Brick's face as he had let her out of the back door that morning had said everything; full of the guilt and shame he felt for letting a sixteen-year-old girl go out searching for food and medicine alone. But it also showed the grim desperation of the current situation that all in their little group were currently facing. Mrs. Jackie had been growing more and more ill with a case of the flu that had almost certainly turned into pneumonia as it seemed too settle deep within her chest and lungs. As the days slowly passed by her breathing had taken on a raspy tone that gurgled when she exhaled. Her inability to move around, mixed with the ashes that dusted everything despite their constant cleaning efforts, no real medicine available to them, and the constant cold were all proving to be accelerators in the transformation from the flu to pneumonia.

"You be careful out there, you hear me girl?" Brick whispers to Ally as she exits the house, his deep baritone voice always reminded her of the huge black guy from that movie about the man on death row with special healing powers. She allows herself to wish for a second that Mr. Brick was that man and that at any second he would walk back to the bedroom and suck out the sickness that was currently raging through the body of poor Mrs. Jackie and fix her dad's broken leg. "Any sign of trouble and you double time it back here." Brick continues.

"Yes sir, you know I will. Wish me luck," she whispers back. He nods at her sadly before simply stating,

"Good luck Ally."

Ally hears him quietly add "Thank you" as the door closes, locks, and the sliding sound of the barricade moves down the door behind her. Oddly she finds herself smiling at hoping she doesn't forget the secret knock that they had developed last night so they would know to let her back in. She was never much into secret agent stuff. Still smiling, she lets out a small sigh as she pulls her mask up over her mouth and nose. The silence unnervingly settles in around her as she mentally prepares for whatever it is that lies ahead of her.

It was the bright beams of white light being cast by their flashlights that first alerted Ally to their presence as the unknown group searched through the houses lining the opposite of the street. She quietly scolds the strangers under her breath for being so careless and foolish. This close to the gasher dens extra care was needed to conceal yourself as you moved through the otherwise vacant and polluted suburban streets on the outskirts of town. Brick had taught her to always use red lenses on her flashlights unless it was absolutely necessary. Both for concealment and to protect your own night vision in the event of an emergency. She marvels at why this group is being so bold moving about in and around the houses without any visible attempt to shield their presence or to protect their night vision. They had to know that the white light made their eyes have to re-adjust to the dark after it was turned off making it that much more difficult to defend yourself, delaying your reaction time against something that was already used to the dark. Didn't they? Ally grows increasingly more nervous as she broods over this unexpected quandary she has stumbled upon. Her assumptions do nothing to ease her worries as she finally concludes; either they were out here in the safety of great numbers or they were fools. Or worse yet…. they were both.

Ally is too lost in her thoughts and reflections trying to figure out just what the hell was going on inside the house, who these people were, and what they're doing out here to notice the two figures exit out of the back door. Luckily, she spots them just in time for her to get under cover and avoid being detected as the bigger of the two shines his light in her direction, alert and pulling his sidearm as he does. She chastises herself at her foolishness before saying a small prayer of thanks for her good luck at not being discovered. She is disappointed that she let herself become so dangerously distracted with her contemplations and she quietly scolds herself. Telling herself angrily that she needed to stay focused, to stay alert as she begins to stealthily maneuver into a more strategic surveillance position. She keeps the two figures in sight as she watches them re-enter the house, pulling a wagon in behind them as they do.

CHAPTER TWENTY-ONE

"Heck yeah guys we got lucky as crap in this house, the wagon is completely full!" Grant exclaims happily to his companions.

"I know right! This is twice as much food as we got from the first house," Paige cheerfully agrees.

"Whoever left here must have been in such a panic that they completely forgot to pack any food or provisions at all for their trip," Laura observes, questioning the reason for their good fortune.

"Or it could have been in the very beginning. When people were still crazy enough to believe that the government was actually going to take care of them if they reported to the FEMA camps that were set up in designated areas to house local families. Foolishly believing that they wouldn't need any of this," Levi states flatly, picking up a can of fruit cocktail and studying it as he turns it over in his hand. "My dad said that after the government pulled out and left the cities to their own fates. That the retreating FEMA agents and soldiers didn't even bother unlocking the gates. They just left all those poor people inside the fences to fend for themselves until they either killed each other or starved to death."

"Or worse," Paige adds solemnly. "I heard over the radio that after the government pulled out cannibalism and infanticide ran rampant inside what was left of the camps." The group stands in a hypnotized, reflective circle around their collected bounty for what seemed like an age. Silently thankful for the things they had been able to find. It is Grant that finally breaks the uncomfortable silence as he quietly says,

"Yeah, that sucks. Does everyone still think we need to hit the next house today since we were able to gather so much from this place? I can't help but to feel a little greedy now, after hearing that story."

"I know what you mean dude, but yes I definitely think we still need to continue our search. Paige is right, we are running out of time out here and we need to find as much as possible to take back with us to the compound. It's not greed Grant, in this world its survival," Levi says looking out over the group and the gathered supplies as he speaks. "It seems like a lot now, but we'll go through this pretty quick back home and I don't know about you guys but I'm not in any hurry to come back out here and do this again anytime soon."

"Amen brother," Grant says in response, exaggerating his words and drawing out the syllables. "But the wagon's full. Do you think we should go back and unload it, then come back out?"

"No that's too much back and forth. We should have searched the house farthest away first then it wouldn't be that bad," Paige says. "We should have thought about that before we started out."

"A valuable lesson learned for next time," Levi agrees. "What we can't fit in the wagon, we'll just have to put into our backpacks. Laura, Paige let me have your packs. We'll put everything in your packs that we consider medicinal or hygienic. Then Grant and I will load our packs down with whatever food or bottled water we hopefully find in the last house. Leaving the wagon loaded the way it is."

"Sounds like a plan" Grant says as he starts going through his backpack, taking everything out that could be put into either Laura or Paige's.

"And since we can't fit anything else in it anyway, we'll just leave the wagon outside the back door of the house we're all in now so it's one less thing we have to carry with us to the next house," Levi suggests. "We can pick it up as we make our way back the dr.'s office when we're done." They all nod in agreement and continue separating out the packs in preparation for what they hopefully might find when they search the next house. A rare sense of optimism surges through the group's mood as they kneel on the floor together re-arranging their backpacks. Lost in the moment all of them remain oblivious to the knowing set of eyes that now watches their every move from a short distance away.

They move in a straight line with Levi on point, followed by Paige and Laura with Grant covering the rear as they move stealthily toward the final house that was selected to be searched that day. Reaching the backdoor Levi is surprised to find it unlocked and standing slightly ajar, the door jamb is broken and shows signs that the door has been kicked in from the outside. Turning away from the door he gives the signal for them to regroup on the small, red brick patio the leads up to the door.

"The door has already been kicked in," Levi whispers to the others.

"Shit, are you serious?" Paige states more than asks, frustration evident in the tone of her voice.

"What does that mean? Is there someone else already inside?" Laura asks.

"I don't think so, but I guess it's a possibility," Levi answers.

"What it means," Paige begins, sighing her annoyance, "is that most likely we're not going to find much of anything we can use in there because the house has already been broken into and someone has already scavenged anything of value." Paige lets out another sigh as she places her face in her hands showing her frustration.

"Well we're already here, so we might as well go inside anyways. There's no sense sitting out here speculating on what we might or might not find by going inside." This time it is Levi that surprisingly represents the voice of reason, giving Paige a well-deserved and much needed break from being the backbone of the group.

"I agree. And you never know, there could still be something we can use in there. I mean, like Levi said, we're already here anyways. And things that didn't seem all that important when things first went to hell could be something we really need now. There's no way to tell how long ago someone kicked the door in," Grant says. Shrugging indifferently, he stands up and carefully begins pushing the door the rest of the way open, planning on leading the group into the house to get the search started. The quicker they got started, the quicker they could get back to base camp. He had his fill of the Ashland for one day and was ready to be done with it. He wanted to be sitting around a fire drying his clothes and warming his hands around a nice hot cup of coffee or tea.

The arms that reach out for him from the dark are accompanied by the crackled, gargled moan that could only escape from a throat that is either already dead or close to it; abused by time, volcanic ashes, and malnutrition. Whatever owned them sends Grant scrambling backwards tumbling over the others mumbling incoherent, frightened words as he teeters on the edge of shock and panic. The rest of the group – who were all still squatted down in a semi-circle – are caught off guard by Grant stumbling clumsily back into their midst. Wrapping up their talk over what their next course of action should be, all three of them aggravated at Grant's impatience and complete disregard of caution as he pushes open the door.

CHAPTER TWENTY-TWO

"I don't think he's doing very good Ray," Jim says worriedly, sharing his concerned opinion of Clay as he sits down and begins to pour himself a much-needed cup of coffee.

"Don't I know it? When I went in to check on him this morning his skin felt so damn hot it nearly burned my hand. And I think he was having a nightmare," Ray says, shaking his head in defeat before adding, "Damn if know what to do about any of it though. We need them kids to find some antibiotics' out there…. and soon."

"Have you noticed the red bumps that have popped up on the right side of his face?" Jim asks raising his eyebrows questioningly.

"Yeah Jim…. I noticed those too," Ray says in a breathy whisper. "I think we need to get him out of his clothes and gear, check him for a spider bite or something. The only thing I can think of that would cause all of his symptoms is that he got himself poisoned somehow. And seeing that we've all been drinking the same water and eating the same food, but he's the only one that's developed any symptoms…." Ray says with conviction, pointing in Clay's direction for emphasis.

"I believe that rules out both of those things as possible causes. So it's gotta be something else. We've come up snake eyes with everything that we've tried so far. I think it's time we started thinking outside of the box."

"But a spider bite? Really? Ray you can't be serious." Jim asks sarcastically, not looking at Ray laughing lightly to himself at the absurdity of the idea as he absently swirls what remains of his coffee inside of his cup creating a little caffeinated whirlpool.

"Why not?" Ray shoots back defensively, trying not to let himself be offended by Jim's blatant disregard of the idea. "Nothing else makes any sense either and none of the rest of us are sick."

"Ray I understand that, but when was the last time you even saw a spider? Or any other kind of insect for that matter?" Jim asks leaning back against the chair, his hands held out palms up in the universal sign of "show me".

"Well…it's been awhile I can admit that! But that doesn't mean that they're still not around," Ray answers sternly, unsuccessfully fighting back the rising anger that was welling up inside of him.

"And…. well…. shit Jim we need to try something – *anything* – to figure out what's wrong with Clay. The group needs him and…. Well damn it, I don't know about you but I don't feel like losing any more of my friggin' friends out here in this godforsaken shithole of a doctor's office!" Ray finishes his statement slamming his right fist into the open palm of his left hand.

"Alright, alright. I'm not sayin' I don't agree with you. That we need to try *something.* Just try to calm yourself down," Jim says holing his hands out in front of himself in mock surrender.

"I didn't mean to come across as such a smart ass or like I don't care as much as you do," Jim says placing his hands slowly back down to rest on the tabletop. Picking up his cup he downs the rest of his coffee. "I'm sorry Ray, you're right. We need to do something. So…. well come on then. There's no reason for us to keep sittin here thinkin about it. We might as well get to peeling all that stuff off of him. It'll probably be a lot easier without the kids around."

"Yeah ok, you're probably right. Look Jim…I didn't mean….." Ray tries to explain himself before Jim interrupts him,

"You can just go ahead and stop right there Kemosabe'. You don't need to apologize to me. Hell, after the fiasco over what to do with poor Colt over there," Jim pauses looking away from his friend to stare off in the direction of the room where Colt's body was still laying waiting to be moved to the Jeep.

"Well let's just say that I'm the one that should keep apologizing to you. Let's just get up and go see if we can figure out what's wrong with Clay. I'm tired of losing our friends out here too." Ray finishes his cup of coffee and sets it down on the table next to Jim's as they stand up and move towards the exit.

"Son of a bitch!" Ray exclaims shaking his head in disbelief. "I didn't think it was possible, but damn if he doesn't feel even hotter now. His fever has got to be approaching dangerous levels for him to feel this hot to the touch." Ray points out as they begin unwrapping the blankets they have Clay wrapped in, trying to stop him from shivering.

"In this cold.... to be this hot, it's not a very good sign Ray. The infection has got to be spreading throughout his entire body for him to have a fever like this," Jim says, visibly shuddering as he speaks. "Hey... not to be a downer or anything but do you think whatever he's caught is contagious?"

"No," Ray answers simply. "Infections shouldn't be contagious unless you got an open cut or something. He's not coughing or sneezing or anything so I don't think it's the flu or anything like that either. Help me sit him up so we can get these filthy shirts off of him."

"Ronnie... is... that......." Clay murmurs weakly in a dry, cracked voice as his friends' jostling him around momentarily rouses him from his fever induced slumber. "I'm sorry Ronnie, I'm so sorry. I... I told him not to drive... I told him to be careful... the mud was bubbling as it sucked them down into the depths... we couldn't... couldn't stop... couldn't stop them from drowning... Ronnie... don't cry..." Clay mumbles to no one in particular.

"What in the world is he talking about? Is that like a suppressed memory or something?" Jim asks, his eyes wide with wonder. Ray shakes his head sadly from side to side.

"No. He's just dreaming about an argument he and Veronica must've had after Roger died when we came out on our first trip. Although super high fevers can cause hallucinations and deliriousness, he's probably just reliving a past memory is all."

"Oh," Jim says sharing in his friend's concern. "I keep forgetting this is only my first time out away from the compound, not everyone else's."

"Hoooly shit," Ray breathes, his breath thick with surprise and worry as the last layer of clothing covering Clay's body armor is finally removed.

"What? What do you see Ray? Is it bad?" Jim asks apprehensively.

"You could say that...come over here on my side and take a look at this. The whole right side of his body is covered in dried blood and puss," Ray says taking a half step back so Jim can get a better look at Clay's side.

"Damn Ray, are you sure? Is it his blood or could it be Colt's blood that got on him from accident?" Jim asks concerned.

"It looks like his own but I guess it could be Colt's. He was bleeding out an awful lot when we were trying to help him in the waiting room," Ray says questioningly.

"Ah man that smells awful," Jim exclaims.

"Let's get this body armor off him and see if we can't find out." They begin to un-do the Velcro straps that stretch out across Clay's chest, carefully loosening the bullet proof vest one strap at time. Different members of the group had started alternately wearing the vests since they had lucked into a handful of them while rummaging through a cluster of police cars they found abandoned at an old, deserted road block. Clay lets out a long, ragged groan from the pain and discomfort caused by removing the vest. The puss that continues to slowly seep from the wound oozes out to mix with the dried blood inhumanely gluing the vest to Clay's body. The wound which is now raging with the infection brought on by the festering, untreated arrow wound fills the area with the foul, sickly smell of necrosis. Grimacing with disgust, Ray and Jim turn their heads as the smell and the repulsive sounds of separating Velcro fills the room for the second time as they peel off the vest that clings to Clay's body, stubbornly glued to him by the oozing infection. Lifting it up and over Clay's head he moans and squirms uncomfortably from the pain caused by removing the vest. A vest that had begun to masquerade as a sponge as it saturated itself with both filth and infection.

"Oh... my... god," is all Ray can say as he sees the festering wound caused by the arrow in Clay's side for the first time. Abscessed, swollen, and seething with infection it is undeniably the cause of Clay's sudden and severe illness.

"What the hell is that…. and how in the hell did he get it?" Jim asks as he bends over to inspect the wound more closely. Clay coughs and flinches as he takes in a sucking breath through his clenched teeth, trying to bite back the intense agony and painful throbbing that had been brought on by removing his body armor. Awakened by the discomfort caused by the jostling of his friends undressing him he exhales sharply as he clumsily tries to sit up. Clearing his throat, startling both of his caregivers as he answers Jim's question with one easy statement,

"I got shot with an arrow."

"You got shot with what? An arrow? How in the hell did that happen? **When** did it happen?" Jim blurts out once he realizes Clay is truly awake and not suffering from another delusion.

"Whoa, slow down Jim. Clay go ahead and lay back down before you do more damage to yourself," Ray says addressing them both while propping up a few of the pillows from the storage racks for Clay to lie back on.

"Jim, would you go grab a bottle of water from the corner over there please," Ray says pointing to the stack of bottled water just to the left of the entryway. They had thankfully built up quite a stockpile from searching the houses surrounding the small medical plaza and had almost five full cases stored inside the breakroom.

"Let's just have you lay back and take it easy for a minute Clay. We need to get some fluids in you."

"Here ya go," Jim says returning and handing over the bottle of spring water. Ray immediately untwists the cap and offers it to Clay. Clay sips the water slowly spilling a little out of the corner of his mouth to run down his chin and drip onto his chest. Ray knows it his imagination but he would have sworn he could hear the water sizzling from the heat of Clays fever.

"Feeling a little better yet chief?" Jim asks Clay when he finally pulls the bottle away from his lips and rests it in his lap.

"A little. Thank you guys," Clay says nodding weakly in appreciation at his friends. Meeting their gaze for the first time in over a day, he can't help but to notice the worry etched onto both Ray and Jim's furrowed brows as they glance down at him from the side of his bed.

"Ok, so then let's have it. How on earth did you get shot with an arrow?" Jim asks as soon as Clay seems to regain enough of his old self to help them diagnose his ailment.

"It happened when Colt fell through the table a few days ago. Apparently when he found what was left of the lovely woman sitting in the corner, it must've startled him so bad that he immediately staggered backwards stumbling over the glass topped table in the middle of the isle. I'm sure he had an arrow notched and drawn in case of any dangers in the room, I know I did. We hadn't cleared the whole place yet at that point so we were all still a little edgy. When he started to fall, he must've

114

instinctually threw his hands down to break his fall, releasing the arrow in my direction when he did. The arrow slammed into my right side, knocking the wind out of me as it passed through my vest and into my ribs like a hot knife going through butter." Clay's breath comes in short quick inhales and exhales as he recounts the series of events that led him to him developing the infection that now rages through his body. The pain inflicted by his broken and bruised ribs makes breathing uncomfortable and labored as he speaks.

"No shit. Talk about being in the wrong place at the wrong time," Jim whistles as Clay takes a break, trying to catch his breath. Then throwing up his hands as he adds mockingly, "I mean seriously, what are the odds?"

Ray sits as still as a stone, unmoving in the silence that follows Clay's recollections of the events in the waiting room. The "Shut the hell up" look he shoots at Jim is unmistakable even in the low light of the room as Clay coughs and winces, trying to continue.

"In all the chaos that followed…. well I kind of forgot about it honestly. Later when the pain reminded me it was there, I didn't think it was important enough to raise any concerns. I just figured I'd clean it out the best I could as soon as I got the chance and muscle through it," Clay states, chuckling weakly at how foolish it all sounds now.

"And with all the blood from Colt's slit wrists it would have been impossible to tell your blood from his," Ray says, finally able to speak as the severity of Clay's situation begins to fully dawn on him.

"Yeah that sounds about right. Anyway, as soon as I got a free minute I did the best I could to clean it up but hell that was……" Clay looks up at the ceiling as he tries to recall how many hours passed before he could get away and wash out the arrow wound. "Damn it must've been late that night, right before I went to bed before I had a chance to inspect the damage or clean it out. Even then, all I could find was some peroxide. I didn't want to waste any of our water stores. At the time we didn't have much left and we still didn't have any way of telling if we would find anymore out here or not." Finishing, Clay closes his eyes trying to catch his breath.

"Take it easy Clay. Try not to tire yourself out," Ray coaxes his friend. The diminished state of Clay's health weighs heavily on him – not for the first or last time that day. As Clay seems to slip back into a restless slumber tormented by the pain of the infection and his fever, Ray turns to Jim and says,

"I wonder if there are any diagnosing medical books in that dr.'s office we can look through. If we can at least figure out what type of infection Clay might have, well maybe then we can at least come up with some type of game plan to try and fight the damn thing."

"It's as good an idea as any I suppose," Jim says before sadly adding, "Anything's better than just standing here feeling helpless and watching Clay die. I'll go grab a couple of flashlights so we can get started with the search." Jim stands up and turns to walk out of Clay's room to retrieve the flashlights from the break room when an odd noise stops him mid-stride. With a worried look he quickly turns to look back at Ray. Both of their eyes go wide from surprise and fear as the muffled but unmistakable sound of distant gunfire flies through the room.

CHAPTER TWENTY-THREE

Levi reacts in an instant. Moving more out of instinct than strength of mind as Grant stumbles backwards over Laura landing on top of Paige, pinning her to the ground under him. His newly found hatchet is put to solid, quick work as Levi stands drawing the weapon up high over his head to bring it crashing back down – flat side first – to land heavily on the forehead of the would-be attacker. There is an audible *'crack!'* as the hatchet hits home, like the sound of a ripe cantaloupe falling to hit the floor, it simultaneously sounds both solid and wet. The woman – Levi can see now that it is or that it at least used to be a woman – collapses at his feet. She lands flat on her back sending up a little cloud of dust around her from the ash covering the houses worn and dirty kitchen floor. Blood begins to ooze out of the woman's ears and the wound on her forehead, the force of the hammer style blow Levi had delivered with the hatchet cracking her skull on impact.

"It's a zombie! Holy shit! *It's a fuckin' ZOMBIE!"* Grant is crying from his position on top of the pinned down Paige, looking like a turtle that has fallen upside down trying to right himself as he struggles to escape the undead he believes is massing to devour them all. Paige quickly grows more aggravated and frustrated with every passing second from her trapped position.

"Get off of me you dip shit!" Paige growls from beneath the hyper ventilating Grant as he continues to scramble backwards over the top of her.

"You idiot be quiet, it is *NOT* a zombie. And don't curse like that, if dad were here he'd pop you in the mouth for saying the "F" word," Laura shoots back over her shoulder at her brother from her position next to Levi; they both stand above the hideous form of the fallen woman looking down at her pitifully. Grant is finally able to scramble off of Paige letting her up from the trapped position he had her in under him. He stands up continuing his clumsy backwards retreat, stumbling over an old flower pot he falls again landing hard, hurting his tailbone on the houses bricked back steps in the process. Paige joins Levi and Laura as they continue to stand over the starved and shrunken form in a loose semi-circle. Looking down at the fallen form laying in front of them they stare in pity and disbelief at what little is left of her. Her open eyes glaze over gradually, her face upturned towards the ceiling locks in death's stare as a last solitary tear escapes to make its way sluggishly down her right cheek. The symbolic last piece of proof that the woman was ever alive as even the tear tries to escape from it's now dead hostess, tumbling from her cheek to land and die on the ash covered floor. It is the final sadistic twist in the desperate act of cruel irony that has become the reality of the world that they all have come to live-and die-in.

"Oh my God. This poor woman," Paige whispers barely loud enough to be heard through her mask. "Look at her lips. They look as if she has been *gnawing* on them."

"And her hands," Laura gasps. None of them are able to take their eyes off of the fallen woman. They stare unblinkingly at the horror laying prostrate on the ground at their feet.

The skin on the woman's face is drawn tight over her cheek bones and orbital sockets from severe starvation and dehydration, making it appear leathery and thin. The skin on her body is a direct contradiction to the skin on her face, hanging loose off of her from the atrophy of extreme muscle loss. Apparently in the world before the darkness she had actually been a plump woman, possibly even borderline fat. However, it is only the excessive amount of loose skin that is left to hang off of her in loose, wrinkled curtains that would give someone any indication of it. Whatever excess fat she had once carried had been used up by her starving body a long, long time ago. The rims of her eyes were red, bloodied, and swollen from the constant attempt to rub out the tiny shards of glass that make up volcanic ash. What teeth she has left appear unusually long and sharp from her receding gums, brought on by prolonged malnutrition, they are broken and jagged from the constant abuse of attempting to eat whatever uneatable things she could discover. Including her own lips. In starving, Donner party desperation she had gnawed at them to the point of leaving them in tattered shreds giving her a grotesque maniacal smile as irony once again shows off its malevolent sense of humor. Only her thumbs, pointer fingers, and ring fingers remained attached to her hands. Her other, non-essential fingers had apparently been cut off and eaten along with most of her toes. Naked except for a tattered skirt that was poorly tied about her at the waist, her ribs could be counted with ease. What were once her breasts are now nothing more than saggy flaps of skin only discernible as breasts from the dried up nipples that stood out from the ends of them like hardened, dried out raisins. Emaciated, dehydrated, and starving to death the hatchet blow is more of a release from a world that she was no longer strong enough to survive in than it is a punishment.

"See! I told you! I told you it was a zombie!" Grant cries as he comes running up behind them. Growing even more hysterical as he sees the abject form of the woman and the withered condition of her body in the full glow of the flashlight for the first time. Paige and Laura look at each other rolling their eyes in annoyance, both becoming increasingly more irritated at Grant's persistence of the ghoulishly supernatural of the undead.

"Grant.... calm down. It's not a zombie," Levi says sighing, "It's just what remains of some poor woman that didn't have a place like the compound to escape to after the eruption. She couldn't make it out here in the harshness of the Ashland on.... her.... own...." Levi's words trail off gradually into silence as he finishes his sentence. He spots a dull glow coming from beneath a door at the far end of the house's sole hallway causing the hairs on the back of his neck to stand up as the fear of the unknown washes over him in a wave.

"What is that?" Paige asks in a low controlled whisper as everyone turns to follow Levi's gaze down the hallway. A coldness seems to settle around the group as they all at once begin to realize that the woman in the kitchen may not have been alone in here after all.

"Levi?" Laura asks urgently in a soft pleading whine. "I don't know," Levi whispers. Suddenly realizing his flashlight is still turned on he quickly turns it off motioning for everyone else to do the same. Taking a more aggressive stance he gives the signal that everyone is to go silent and to form up behind him in the formation they use as they sweep houses. As

Grant, still visibly shaken by the incident, walks by to fall in line Levi grabs him by the elbow and holds it until Grant looks at him. Levi gives him a reassuring nod and lightly strikes him on the shoulder. Grant inhales deeply and exhales slowly as he tries to clear his head and refocus before returning Levi's gesture of goodwill. They fall in formation as Levi motions for them to cautiously begin making their way forward down the hall towards the door with the ominous ghostly glow emanating from something on the other side. Grant can't help but to cast one more nervous glance over his shoulder in the direction of the dead form sprawled out on the kitchen floor. An involuntary shudder ripples through his body, either from the chill that has begun to swirl in the air around them or from the sight of the dead woman's unsightly condition Grant can't be exactly sure which. Satisfied that the woman wasn't rising up to tear at their flesh from behind he turns and quickly catches up to the rest of the group falling back into formation behind his sister Laura.

Ally watches in disbelief at the absurd ignorance taking place in front of her. Cursing to herself as the small group apparently heads deeper into the house even after they have already confronted and killed one of the gashers in the kitchen! Didn't they know that gashers almost never roamed alone? That they were now voluntarily heading deeper into one of their dens? How could they be so foolish and utterly oblivious to the danger they were in? She had to try to warn them before they alerted every den left in the area that they were out here and got the gashers on the move again. Ally swallows her own fears of the gashers and of the strangers as she emerges from her hiding place and begins making her way swiftly across the street. She has just reached the driveway to the house when the first round of gunfire bursts out from inside to echo through the streets of the neighborhood, ringing out like a sonic boom in the deafening silence.

"Oh my god! ***Stop shooting!***" Ally exclaims aloud as she breaks into a full run forgetting about being cautious. "You're going to alert all of them!"

Contrary to the kitchen, the hallway shows signs of frequent use as they make their way towards the curious light. They could tell by the way the light flickered and danced that someone had actually started a fire inside the room behind the door. It was impossible to tell the size of the fire as they begin their approach to the mouth of the hallway, the amount of light coming from underneath the door stays constant, never wavering. A positive indication to Levi that the fire was at least contained to the inside of the room. Weapons at the ready (they only carry firearms now, ditching the bows after the discovery of the dead secretary in the waiting room and the cannibalized condition she was found in) as they cross the homes living room, entering the hallway cautiously making their way towards their destination. They scan the area continuously with the lights Levi and Grant both had mounted underneath the barrels of their weapons; the clear lenses having been replaced with the more dark friendly -and less ambient – red lenses after the incident in the kitchen. They pass by pile after pile of blankets bunched together like make shift bedding, eerily like the one Levi and Grant had found in the garage of the last house. More can be seen littered all over the entire area of both the living room and the adjacent dining room. After a brief pause, Levi begins to strategically work his way through the room towards the targeted door, the discovery of the beds brings on more and more anxiety with every new step they take leading them deeper into the house. The sheer number of bed piles alone makes Levi nervous as he momentarily rethinks the wisdom behind continuing to search this particular house. Curious light or not. As they reach the door with the fire glow Levi notices something just at the edge of the red light from his flashlight. He swings the red light slowly up and around until it comes to rest on an object propped up in the corner of the hallway which causes him to gasp involuntarily. The condition of the body that now rests in the glow of his flashlight making him take a staggering step backwards bumping into Paige. He is both shocked and nauseated at the sight of the body which still shows signs of life despite having both of its legs hacked off at the pelvis and both of its arms removed at the shoulder. The hideous, dismembered form that rests in the center of the red beam of light is repulsive and nauseating as Levi takes another step backwards, pushing even harder into Paige. This time it is Laura's gasp that fills the hallway as the torso looks up pathetically into the light uttering a low, mournful wail that is both frightening and pitiful in its hollowness. With bloodied eyes and its lips eaten away, its face looks shockingly similar to the woman Levi had slain in the kitchen. It sits alone in a small pool of its own blood as it slowly bleeds to death from the wounds that still seep fluid despite the crude attempt at cauterization. The abuse the torso's vocal chords had taken from the extended breathing of the non-filtered ashes had caused it to lose any ability to make any type of coherent sounds a long time ago. The group stands immobilized in shocked awe and disgust, staring down at the form in stunned silence as it continues its pitiful wailing. Grant barely rips his dust mask off in time before he turns and vomits. Trying to control his heaving and to be as quiet as possible Grant turns away embarrassed and takes a few steps away from the group. The gruesome sight of the butchered man propped up in the corner is just too much for him to handle in his current and fragile state of mind. Mercifully, Levi finally steps forward and in his second act of morose sympathy that day, he puts the flat side of the hatchet to work once again. Thankfully a single blow is all it takes to release the man from his agony. Finishing quickly Levi turns away from the expired form and steps back to face the group. They wait patiently together for Grant to regain his composure before turning their focus once more on the fire glow that still emanates from beneath the closed hallway door. A glow that now seems much more menacing than it had only a few moments before. Laura takes a plaque down off of the wall, then walks over and places it beside the body. As Grant rejoins them looking pale and exhausted, it seems as if he has aged 10 years in the span of ten minutes. Levi glances over at the memorial Laura had placed next to the body and in the shine of the red light reads the single word engraved across the top; "Footprints". Overwhelmed he looks at Laura knowingly and sees the tears filling her eyes. He offers her a respectful nod showing her his understanding of her heartache.

The door swings open slowly, revealing the smoke damaged room within. Lit only by the fire that burns within the ring of a crudely made fire pit at its center, it is enough to make out the details of the small room as their eyes adjust painfully from the dark to the light. A primitive metal tripod hangs over the open flames roasting the calf and foot of a severed leg like a grisly Flight 571 Andes Mountain rotisserie. Every head in the room turns to look at the group as the door comes to a slow, creaking stop. In the minute-long standoff of shocked silence that follows Levi notices that some of their mouths are ringed with the blood of whatever limb the "people" inside were busy eating. It seems that some of them had either been too impatient or too hungry to wait for the meat over the fire to cook and had decided to eat what they had been given raw. Before Levi can stop him Grant walks into the room and is horrifically greeted by the gruesome sadism being played out by its desperate and the starving occupants. Drawn together by the most basic primitive human instinct to gather in groups even in their desperate, emaciated state. Every last one of them are as withered and as sunken as the pathetic forms of the woman dead in the kitchen and the discarded torso lying in the hallway. How any of them were still alive was and always would be a mystery to everyone in the group as they stand their taking it all in. It is a scene that could be plucked directly out of any apocalyptic nightmare that fills the restless nights of every survivor in the world. They all stand there in consternation and silence at what they are witnessing. Appalled and lost in the shock of finding something as unexpected and ghastly as the sight of blatant, deliberate cannibalism taking place before them. The gunshot that abruptly fills the room dances grimly on the dead, stale air causing all of their ears to ring and their hearts to skip a beat as they jump up into their throats.

Grant is unable to bear the sight of the monstrosities seated on the floor of the room – most of which are busy dining on the flesh of another human being. They are seated in a rudimentary circle around the fire the burns in the rooms center. Grant shoots the form closest to them directly in the face as it looks at him with the twelve-gauge shotgun he is holding; subsequently decapitating it in a gruesome spray of gore, brains, and blood that sprays out covering the wall behind the victim in a grisly display of art that only Josef Mengele' could have appreciated. The rest of the group jumps backwards startled from the shock of the unexpected shotgun blast, instinctively drawing up their own weapons into a fire ready position. The withered forms that occupy the room begin standing up and moving towards them with their arms extended out in front of them, pitifully attempting to reach out and capture what they hoped was more food. With blood still smearing their mouths from eating the sacrifice in the hallway, they open them releasing the desperate cry of the starving and the ash-mute alike. Grant pumps a new round into the shotguns chamber and shoots the next one in the chest, sending the body flying backwards to slam against the opposite wall. Taking Grants cue the rest of the group begins to systematically eliminate the rising occupants of the room one by one. Nine starving, withered, but still monstrous forms lay dead or dying about the room as the last of the gunshots stop ringing out. Paige walks from one dying form to another, mercifully ending the lives of any that were still struggling to hang on. Hang on to what however, Paige couldn't say. Laura is right behind her ready to assist if necessary. As Paige reaches the closet she notices the door move ever so slightly. Paige motions to Laura and points at the flimsy but closed closet door. It is one of those cheap apartment French style three panel doors that open in an accordion fashion. Paige reaches out sliding back the first panel to reveal whatever it is that lies waiting for them inside. What she finds within the closet causes her hands to drop by her sides releasing her weapon which falls to land at her feet on the blood soaked carpet. Laura gasps and brings her hand up symbolically covering her mask at the spot where her mouth should be. From her place behind Paige she stands watching the wasted away form of a child eating fingers it had apparently stolen from the rest of the group. Evidentially to avoid detection of its thievery it had hidden itself inside of the closet to eat its prize in mock relative peace. Its hair had fallen out almost to the point of baldness and as it turns its red rimmed, bloody eyes up to look at them the look they hold within them is almost unnervingly apologetic. Appearing to try to smile – although it's hard to tell if someone is smiling when they don't have lips – as it notices them it reaches out its hand offering what is left of the finger it had ravenously been eating just moments before. Holding out the finger towards Laura and Paige with the hand and arm it still possesses, it begins to crawl out of the closet. Unable to walk, due to one of its legs having already been hacked off and eaten along with its other arm. The shot that rings out elicits a startled scream from the girls as the child's head snaps back and it collapses on the floor. The form of the child expires with a single dying twitch as its last breath escapes in an unearthly, snakelike hiss. Paige and Laura jump clumsily in their surprise causing Paige to trip over one of the many dead forms lying at her feet, seating her on her butt in a congealing pool of violence. Sitting there with blood seeping into her pants she begins to cry as she looks up to see Levi holding the .357 magnum Clay had found in the chiropractor's office the first day they had arrived here. He had it pointed directly at the fallen form of the child, a thin line of blue smoke slowly rising from out of the end of the guns' barrel.

Entering the house thru the same side door she had watched the group use Ally bursts into the kitchen, tripping over the dead woman to fall prostrate onto the floor. Scrambling up to rush down the hallway she pulls up short as the gunfire finally stops. She stands in the hallway listening closely for any warning of what was happening inside the room. She allows several tense seconds to pass before she decides its ok to alert the strangers to her presence. Swallowing her fear, she positions herself to the left of the doorway and prepares herself for whatever waits for her on the other side of the wall.

"You! Inside the room! Don't shoot me! I'm not like the others!" Ally screams from her position in the hallway just outside the door.

"My name is Ally and I'm a survivor like you. I'm coming in now please **DO NOT** shoot me." Ally calls out before stepping cautiously through the door and into the room. Still apprehensive she walks with her hands held over her head and slightly out in front of her.

"We all need to get out of here and back to someplace safe and we need to do it as quickly as possible. That video game style shootout just alerted every gasher for ten blocks that we are in here," Ally declares to the group, still standing just inside the doorway to the room with her hands held high over her head. Levi, Laura, Grant, and Paige – who has managed with great effort to finally pick herself up from where she had fallen – all turn to look at the newcomer standing in front of them in a new wave of absolute shock and utter surprise. Feelings that seemed to be in great supply that day.

"Well don't just stand there looking at me. **We need to go**, NOW!" Ally exclaims in an attempt to convey the dire situation they all now found themselves in. Sighing with frustration she turns and quickly walks back out of the room, swiftly making her way down the hallway toward the kitchen to exit the house.

"It is not the strongest of the species that survives, nor the most intelligent. It is the one that is most adaptable to change."

~Charles Darwin

CHAPTER TWENTY-FOUR

The group exits the house the same way they went in, Levi on point with Grant defending the rear still trying to process everything that has just happened. Ally stands waiting for them impatiently just outside the doorway next to a line of dead trees that line the yard leading back towards the house that they had searched before this one. Their wagon, with all of the previously collected supplies, laid hidden there beneath a crudely placed tarp and a few handfuls of leaves thrown over the top of it.

"Ok good, you decided to join me. Now that you guys are done ringing the dinner bell maybe you'd like to grab your supplies and get back to where ever it is that you're using as a base camp. It's not safe out here anymore. Every gasher within hearing distance of all that gunfire is going to be crawling out from under every rock and shack they're calling a bed at the moment," Ally hisses desperately as soon as they all gather around her by the tree. One by one they cast defiant and untrusting glares upon her and her words of warning. Paige is the first to gather her thoughts into words as she voices what they are all thinking out loud to float on the cold dark air.

"Whoa now, you just hold on for a freaking minute," Paige says irritably to Ally. "We're not taking you anywhere with us until we find out just exactly who the hell you are and where you came from."

"I've already told you who I am. My name is Ally, where I come from isn't important right now, and we don't have time for this," Ally shoots back at Paige, quickly becoming annoyed at being questioned – a feeling Paige shared with her in spades.

"Well then we'll make time," Levi answers. "Who the hell were those people in there and what the hell is a gasher?"

"And how long have you been watching us? How do you know about our supplies?" Paige asks with more than a little attitude.

"Look," Ally sighs holding her hands up in the rudimentary form of surrender. "I apologize if I seem hasty. Coming off as rude is not my intention. But like I've already stated inside the house, what you guys did in there was foolish and careless. Anything within ten blocks of here now knows exactly where we are and because of that…. we really need to get moving to a safer location. I promise that I'll explain everything in greater detail once we're out of sight and under cover." As Ally finishes her statement she stands up, cutting off any opportunity for anyone to continue the argument any further. Turning her back to them sharply she begins swiftly marching back towards the house with the wagon full of supplies that she already knew was poorly hidden beneath the camo colored tarp. The band stands up together outside the back door of the house and watches Ally walk away. Taking turns looking back and forth from Ally's back to each other until finally Laura simply shrugs and begins to follow Ally back towards the neighboring house. Everyone falls in line following Laura's lead as Levi breaks into a slow jog, attempting to catch up to the young girl simply named "Ally" that seemed to manifest out of nowhere. His curiosity and lack of trust getting the better of him as he goes searching for answers. Paige, Laura, and Grant begin to jog also; not only mimicking Levi's steps – but echoing his suspicious feelings on the mysterious newcomer as well.

The group quickly makes its way back to the second house and the stashed cans of food and water they had left hidden there. The rest of their bounty still safely stowed away in their backpacks. A storm had blown in during the pandemonium of the day, making the gathering gashers barely visible in the dark and rain. The occasional haunting moans and streaks of lightening are all that give them away as they stealthily make their way up towards the house with the backroom shooting gallery, approaching it from all sides. Hunching down and getting behind whatever type of cover they can find, they carefully army crawl the final twenty or so yards remaining between them and the line of dead trees. Pleading silently for the relative safety the trees had to offer, they are blessed that the property line had been marked with a variety of pine trees instead of something smaller. Even though the color of their needles would have faded from a bright green to a rust red they would still clung stubbornly to the branches, offering them more concealment than they could have ever hoped for otherwise.

"Well guys, it looks like you've drawn about every gasher living in the area right to us. I've never seen this many in one place before. Well done," Ally chastises in a quiet whisper. Throwing away the PC attitude she had adopted at the door, doing little to cover up the aggravated dread in her voice as the rest of the group crawls up to rest next to her.

"Look, we already told you that It wasn't intentional," Levi points out irritably casting worried glances over his shoulders as he whispers. Even through the dark and driving rain he is astonished at the sheer number of shuffling figures that can be made out as the lightening streaks overhead to light the area in brief strobe light flashes. Clothes hang from them like giant rags as they make their way silently through the neighborhood towards the little house and the possibility of a fresh meal.

"We've never seen things like this before. I'm sure you can appreciate the shock it was to all of us to see them now," Levi whispers with clenches jaws, growing more defensive as Ally continues to be annoyed at their lack of knowledge of dealing with the dangers that roamed within the city.

"Besides… it doesn't matter now anyway. Right or wrong it's over and done with. It's not like we can go back and change it," Paige adds. Amazed that there were this many people hidden in the region around them without their knowledge. She shivers as she spies the increasing numbers of them now slithering in and out of the houses around them like sickly, opportunistic vermin.

"And like it or not we all have to deal with it together now. So why don't we start acting like we're all the same team here guys," Laura puts in trying to defuse the situation before it got completely out of hand. "At least for the time being anyways, until we're out of danger."

Levi looks from Laura to Ally, then from Ally to Laura before letting his forehead drop to rest on the ground releasing a heavy sigh. Picking his back up he nods at them both and utters,

"Agreed." Levi turns his attention back over to the growing dangers that are steadily rising around them. Worried and tense he looks over at Grant trying to get a gauge on his condition. Grant – the instigator of small room massacres – who has been lying there in stunned silence. Even while killing Grant hadn't uttered a sound since the conclusion of the incident in the kitchen, when he thought the woman Levi had slain had been an actual zombie. Ally nods at the group wearing the apologetic look of the fearful and the defeated.

"I… I'm sorry everyone," she whispers. "I've been out here searching alone trying to find anything I can for my group and I let the fear and stress of it get the better of me."

"Apology accepted. But we can talk about all of that later. Right now, we have to figure out how we're going to get this food, and ourselves past these *"things"* and back to the doctor's office. Keeping all of us in one piece while we do it," Laura says, thankful that the tension seems to have abated between the newcomer and the rest of the group.

"Well there's no way we're all just going to get up and waltz in between them across the yard pulling a wagon full of food behind us," Paige observes pessimistically.

"Yeah…even in this weather I can make out way more of these things…"

"People. You keep calling them things. They're not **things**, they're just people," Ally interjects. "Starving, weak, and yes sometimes dangerous but still people."

"Fine, I can make out more of these **people** than I'm comfortable with," Levi says looking at Ally irritated, echoing Paige's sentiments.

"Well I've still got quite a bit of room left in my pack. We didn't really find anymore…." Laura pauses as she looks up at Levi and then looks back down at her pack before quietly finishing her statement, "We didn't come across anymore medicine or anything."

Levi appreciates the empathy contained within the gesture and places his hand on Laura's shoulder appreciatively before speaking.

"I think I know where you're going with this Laura and I think she's right guys. If we combine what we already have into one or two of the packs, we can fill the emptied packs with the scavenged food from the wagon. That way we can move slowly and stay low to the ground as we make our way back to the dr.'s office. We can come back out later to get the wagon and anything that doesn't fit in the packs later after things out here have calmed back down."

"Sounds like as good a plan as any. Once we get around the other side of that little brick house over there," Paige says, cautiously pointing at a little house about fifty yards in the distance off to their left. "We should be mostly in the clear and out of sight. From there it's a straight shot back to the office building."

"I like it. Hey Grant?" Levi whispers as loud as he dares trying to draw Grants attention away from the gathering gashers and back to the group.

"Grant!" Levi hisses again thankfully causing Grant to finally pull his eyes off of the wave of bodies entering the house. Looking in Levi's direction but still saying nothing.

"Look man, its ok. You did the right thing in there. No one here is upset with you. But we really need you here with us right now and focused so we can all get out of this alive. Alright?" Levi pleads with his friend, trying to pull him back from wherever it is his psyche was trying to take him to cope with all of the day's horrors. Grant's eyes seem to lose a little of the cloudiness that had settled in them lately as he nods at Levi, sighing loudly. Too loudly for Ally's comfort and she instantly begins casting nervous glances in every direction hoping that their luck was holding up and that they still hadn't drawn any unwelcomed attention to themselves. Grant nods at the rest of the group before dropping his eyes and removing his pack, handing it over to his sister Laura. Levi trades a look of concern with Paige over the Grant situation and the predicament they now found themselves in as he hands his pack to her for the transfer of goods from one pack to the other. They utter silent, thankful prayers along with their sighs of relief that they were in fact able to fit all the found food from the wagon inside the packs without making them weigh a thousand pounds. Finishing the task of re-loading their packs they all begin to cautiously, but purposefully, crawl beneath the protective boughs of the dead pine trees towards the little brick house off to their left in the distance. The chaos of the feeding frenzy and the sounds of the melee over the newly dead escaping the house behind them is all the motivation they need to keep moving forward as it provides the battle hymn for their dedicated march back to safety.

CHAPTER TWENTY-FIVE

"Thank the Lord above!" Ray exclaims embracing his children as they re-enter the dr.'s office.

"What in god's name happened out there?" Jim asks eagerly, looking hard at Levi. Everyone is still overly animated from the overdose of adrenaline as they excitedly begin to give a detailed recount of everything that had happened while they were out on the search. Ray and Jim both sit and listen in stunned silence, astonished as they listen about the gashers and about how they had accidentally stumbled into one of their dens. Levi describes the room full of repulsive atrocities, trembling uncomfortably at what they had witnessed hidden inside of it. Laura, Paige, and Levi explain in turn the fragility of Grants psyche, the meeting of Ally, and their desperate crawl back to safety as the newly motivated gashers began gathering in dangerous numbers searching for anything or anyone that was deemed edible. As the trio finishes the recounting of the day's events, the jolt of adrenaline plays out as exhaustion and the feeling of safety finally overtakes them. As they collapse into their sleeping bags they fall almost instantly into the deep sleep of the overly tired and weary. Too tired to even eat or drink, the stress of the day had worn them down to completely. Ray shows Ally to an area where she can lay down and get some much-needed rest, sighing sadly as he hands her Colts now unused sleeping bag. "I'm glad you ran into each other out there Ally. For their sake and for yours. We will be fine in here. This room doesn't have any windows and the rest of the building is locked up tight. Hopefully things will calm down outside while you all get some rest. Then we can get everything packed up, get you to the rest of your group, and get headed back home to the safety and comforts of the compound," Ray tells her as she crawls tired eyed into the sleeping bag, yawning widely.

"Thank you, Mr. Jones." is all she manages to whisper before she too is overtaken by her own fatigue and weariness, quickly falling into a deep and heavy slumber.

"I can't believe this Ray. This is some fucked up crazy shit! All I want to do is to get back home to the safety and comfort of the compound." A visibly shaken Jim blurts out as soon as he and Ray are alone once again in the breakroom of the dr.'s office. Both men hastily begin the task of preparing everything to leave. Ray nods at him in agreement adding,

"You can say that again brother. And we still have the unfortunate issue of Clay to deal with." Ray sighs as he glances in the direction of the room he knows Levi is now sleeping in peacefully.

"Yeah, I've been thinking about that too. Hell, other than the arrow wound we still don't really know what's wrong with Clay," Jim says standing up and placing his hands on his hips.

"You know what? You guys can have this *'going out on supply runs'* bullshit. This was my first and last time. I don't care who's having a baby," Jim states with conviction, shaking his head.

"I understand. Coming out here isn't for everyone. Hell, I wish we didn't have to come out here at all," Ray says softly. "But I do think I've figured out what's wrong with Clay," he says as he continues working on the preparations.

"I'm sorry Ray, what did you say?" Jim asks shaking his head.

Ray stops and looks up at Jim feeling his eyes expectedly on him, waiting for him to elaborate on his statement. Ray takes in a deep cleansing breath sighing as he releases it slowly before he begins;

"Before the gunshots, when we were going to look for a medical diagnosis book, I started trying to think of anyone that I had ever known or heard of that was as sick as Clay seems to be. And then it hit me! Keith Brown."

"Who's Keith Brown?" Jim asks curiously.

"I remembered this pal of mine named Keith Brown from back when I went to trade school for auto mechanics. Must be about thirty years ago now, but *he* was the sickest person that I had ever heard of until Clay." Ray takes in another deep breath, stopping what he's doing to go sit down at the table. Deep in concentration and momentarily overtaken by the emotional stress of the memory he pours himself another cup of coffee to help calm his nerves.

"We were learning how to hook up engines to the hoist and lift them up out of a car. We got it all hooked up and got it lifted out of the car fine but when we started pulling it back Keith tripped over the frame and fell. Unfortunately for him though he was still holding the large flat head screwdriver we were using to pry the engine loose from all the grime and muck that had stuck it in place to the mounting brackets when he did. The screwdriver was covered in all that old oil, grease, and road dust that was caked up around those mounting bolts. When Keith fell he drove the screwdriver into his left thigh. It entered just above the knee and drove in all the way to handle only about a half inch below the skin. Nastiest thing I've ever seen," Ray explains, wrinkling up his face in disgust of the memory.

"I mean Jim you could actually **SEE** the impression of the screwdriver underneath his skin!" Ray exclaims pausing for a moment to collect himself. Waving his hand dismissively in the air he continues with his memory,

"Anyway, so there's poor Keith rolling around on the shop floor screamin' and hollerin' with this fourteen-inch screwdriver sticking in his leg. He's bleeding like a stuck pig; blood is going everywhere. I mean all over the damn place! Hell, that damn thing was as big around as my damn pinky finger! Needless to say, with all the blood and grime covering the damn screwdriver, we couldn't get a good grip on it to pull the damn thing out. Especially with him rolling around screamin' and cussin'."

"Damn that sounds awful," Jim says wearing a look of sympathetic disgust for Ray's old friend.

"Yeah... Well... that's not the end of it. Just wait, it gets better. So there we are wrestling around on the floor, none of us even knowing exactly what the hell it is we're supposed to be doing at this point. Finally, after putting about a dozen shop rags around the screwdriver we got Keith to hold still just long enough to pull the damn thing out and get him to the hospital. We all thought that would be the end of it. Keith would have an odd scar and one hell of a story to tell. We'd all get a good laugh out of it around the shop making fun of him for always being so damn clumsy. That was the last time any of us ever saw Keith. He never left the hospital." Ray sighs sadly as he finishes recalling the memory of his lost friend.

"What d'ya mean he never came back? What happened to him?" Jim asks confused.

"Well the hospital cleaned him up the best they could but the screwdriver had driven so deep into his leg that evidentially they couldn't get all the dirt and grime out of his wound. Nowadays, or at least before the blackout, they would make an incision along the length of the wound. Open it up and clean it out that way before sewing him back up. But no one thought to do that back then. At least no one did on that day. He developed septicemia and died about a week and a half later," Ray finishes.

"Damn," Jim says softly. "I didn't see that coming."

"None of us did either. We were all shocked," Ray says.

"I feel a little dumb for asking this Ray, but what the hell is septicemia?" Jim asks after a few long minutes.

"I didn't know what it was before that happened either so don't feel bad. Sophia and I went to check on his wife Meredith a few days after the funeral and she described it to us like this; Septicemia is an infection you get in your blood caused by other infections – like kidney or bladder infections – or they can come from wounds that are either too deep to be cleaned thoroughly or by extremely filthy conditions," Ray explains.

"Or wounds that are both to deep and to dirty," Jim adds grimly, looking sadly in Clay's direction.

"Yeah or both. Anyway, your blood goes everywhere in your body so the infection spreads like wildfire. It can spread into all of your organs – even your brain – causing your body to start shutting down bit by bit." The direness of Clay's situation is beginning to dawn on Jim as Ray continues explaining the symptoms of a severe blood infection. As Ray finishes Jim asks hopefully,

"Ok, so now that we have an idea of what's wrong with Clay, isn't there something we can do for him?"

"Super duty antibiotics would work, but we would need a lot of them and we'd need them now. Aside from that…. No Jim, I don't believe there is."

"So basically, Colt not only killed himself but Clay as well all in one unlucky, fatal blow," Jim exclaims. Slamming his fist down onto the table Jim startles Ray as he hisses angrily, "Son of a bitch!"

"Yeah it certainly appears that way. The last thing Colt told Clay before he slipped into his coma makes a lot more sense to me now," Ray reflects. "I couldn't figure it out before."

"What's that? What did Colt say to Clay?" Jim asks curiously, leaning forward and placing his elbows to rest on the table. Ray raises his head looking directly into the eyes of his friend as he recites Colt's last legible words;

"He said: "I'm sorry… I'm so sorry Clay. Please tell Veronica I'm so very sorry.""

CHAPTER TWENTY-SIX

YEAR ONE, DAY THREE HUNDRES AND TWENTY-SIX

"I don't understand any of this Mr. Jones. How did Colt shoot my dad? **WHY** did Colt shoot my dad?" Levi exclaims. Visibly shaken by the seriousness of his dad's illness and with the unfortunate expected outcome of the infection. All of which was apparently brought on by Colt somehow accidentally shooting his dad with an arrow during their search of the waiting room.

"From what we can piece together with the information your dad was able to give us, we figure that Colt was searching the right side of the waiting room when he was startled by the corpse of the dead secretary," Ray begins trying to explain to the distraught young man.

"Which is what we think caused him to stumble backwards in the first place, tripping and falling into the table," Jim adds.

"Exactly. Evidently, Colt had an arrow knocked, drawn, and ready to release in preparation of whatever danger he felt may have been waiting for him as they searched the perimeter of the room.""

Your dad said that's how his was," Jim interjects matter-of-factly. Nodding Ray continues,

"When the corpse startled Colt and he fell through the glass table, he must've released the arrow in your dads' direction as he threw his arms back to break his fall. The arrow flew across the room striking him in his right side. Unfortunately, bullet proof vests – especially older ones like this – are exactly that. Bullet proof, not blade proof." Sighing Ray continues;

"The dirtiness of our conditions, the unexpected calamity with Colt possibly bleeding to death, and the inability to properly clean it or to keep it clean, led to him developing what we think is an illness called sepsis or septicemia. That is, we think he has a severe infection in his blood."

"You think or you know?" Levi asks mournfully, looking up at the two men with teary, bloodshot eyes.

"You know we can only speculate here son, but he shows all the signs," Ray answers softly.

"Plus Ray knew someone before the darkness that developed an infection like this. And just to make sure we weren't talking ourselves into an assumption, we double checked everything with this." Jim walks over to where Levi was kneeling, handing him one of the medical books he and Ray had collected from the office at the far end of the hall. The room sits in dazed silence, stunned by the unexpected diagnosis of Clay's fever and its unpromising outcome as Levi takes the book from Jim. Levi's tears fall to land on the sooty, worn cover simply titled; The Merck Manual of Medical Diagnosis and Therapy: Nineteenth Edition. Soft tears roll slowly down Laura's face to fall in her lap as she grieves openly for two key members of her adopted family. Paige sits next to her slowly shaking her head back and forth quietly uttering, "No, no, no" over and over again to herself. Grant says nothing from his spot in the corner where he sits segregated from the rest of the group, still wearing the same vacant expression he had worn since the encounter with the gashers yesterday. Ally had also positioned herself just outside of the circle, observing the interaction within the tight knit group she has become a pseudo member of. Urgently trying to gauge the severity of the situation and her fragile place within it. Levi rests on the floor where he had fallen to his knees. Dropping the book, he buries his face into his gloved hands, his body spasms, stricken by the sobs that escape him. Ray and Jim walk up to him in turn, each placing a comforting hand on one of his shoulders. Neither of them bother to speak, both knowing that any words of offered sympathy would only ring hollow given the bleak, grimness of the situation. Understanding in the fact that nothing could quench the burning pit of despair or the scorched feelings of loss that were now erupting inside the young man over his father. Feelings that were beginning to become far too common within the group as of late. They exit the room one by one in a metaphorical funeral precession to give Levi a few minutes of understanding, sympathetic privacy. They needed to check on Clay, finish preparations for their departure, and discuss the situation of Ally, along with the rest of her group that they have still yet to meet.

"Ok everybody, simply put here are the facts. We just don't have enough room in the vehicles to carry Ally and everyone in her group back to the compound with us this time out. So, what we're suggesting we do is this; first, we need to drive like hell back to the compound in hopes of saving Clay. There we can unload everything we've managed to salvage from the area. After that we can come back out here with only a few people carrying the bare essentials to pick up Ally and the rest of her group," Ray begins.

"With the supplies, Colts body, and the size of the group taking up all the available space within and on top of the vehicles......"

"And with Clay being so sick," Jim interjects, nodding at Ray to continue after his interruption.

"Yes and of course there's that. Unfortunately, that's the only real option I can see that we have here guys," Ray finishes. Jim's interruption seeming to break his concentration.

Levi, Paige, and the others sit and listen to what Ray and Jim are saying doing their best to take it all in.

"We can't just leave Ally at the dr.'s office to fend for herself or leave her to reconnect with her group alone," Laura pleads. "Not after we've discovered what's actually out there waiting for her. We have to at least help her get back to the safety of her own group."

"Yeah, we can't just leave Ally here," Levi adds. "No matter how sick my dad is he wouldn't want us to do that. He'd demand we took her to someplace relatively safe."

"We couldn't agree with you more," Jim says.

"Absolutely," Ray begins, turning to speak with Ally.

"How many people did you say are in your group again Ally?"

"And about how far away do you think is it from here?" Jim adds. Ally stands up to face the group addressing Ray and Jim's questions in turn, looking at them directly before respectfully meeting the gazes from everyone else in the group. Instantly earning more respect from everyone with her show of confidence in what they understood was a difficult situation, especially for someone so young. Facing this situation with people that are (for all intent and purposes) total strangers took courage. Courage was something they all could relate too. And the fact that she's doing it in spite of only being fifteen, raises the confidence level of everyone in the group even more that Ally at least, would be a welcomed addition to their group back at the compound.

"My group is relatively small. It consists of me, my father, whose name is Alexander but everyone just calls him Xander. The owners of the house that we all now live in are Mr. Broderick Thomas, his wife Jackie, and their two sons Benny and Larry."

"Ok so when we come back to get you we'll need to be able to seat six additional people plus any belongings or supplies that you would want to take with you as well. What aren't personal possessions we could just add to the stock pile already at the compound," Ray says more to himself than to anyone else in the room.

"Maybe…. maybe not," Ally says quietly dropping her gaze to the floor, playing with the discarded top of a water bottle with her foot.

"What do you mean by that?" Levi asks her. Ally looks up in time to see Levi, who has only just walked into the room, walk over to stand next to her in the center of the congregation.

"Mrs. Jackie is very ill with what we think started out as the flu and has since turned into pneumonia. That's why I was on this side of town. I was hoping to find some antibiotics in one of the offices over here. We thought since they were kind of out of the way on the edge of town, they might not have been looted by the townies as badly as the rest of the local area." Levi sub-consciously looks back in the direction of his sick and dying father as Ally tells of her own hopes in finding some antibiotics to help a sick member of her group. Just as they had hoped to find some for the sick member of their group as they searched through the houses yesterday.

"We haven't found anything like that yet. Just some over the counter cold and flu remedies," Paige tells her. "But you're welcome to look through it if you think some of it will help your friend."

"You have no idea how much that means to me, but honestly, I don't really think any of it will. Sadly, I think her pneumonia is too far advanced. But I appreciate you offering it to me just the same," Ally says wearily. The smile she wears contradicts the tears that have welled up in her eyes.

"Ok…well anyway, let's get a move on everyone. Times a'wastin. Jim and I already have all of the supplies loaded in the trucks, we took care of that while the rest of you were sleeping."

"And we need to toot the whistle on the boogie train while they're aren't so many of those freak-a-lopes out there roaming around," Jim adds.

"That we do my friend. All that's left to do is to get Clay situated and we can all be on our merry little way," Ray says absolutely. Standing up, Ray motions gloomily towards the room where they have Clay resting.

"Levi why don't you and I get your dad. Jim, you and Laura get the basic directions from Ally and start getting everyone buckled in and ready to move. Laura, with Clay like he is you'll have to drive the jeep and I'll take over as lead vehicle, do you think you'll be ok with that?"

"Yes sir. You don't think Jim should do it?" Laura answers.

"No, Jim will need to navigate. He knows his way around a map pretty well, the rest of you don't. Everyone got it? Good, let's move like we have a purpose. Paige, you and Grant give this place one last walk through to make sure we're not forgetting anything useful. I don't know about you guys but I'm ready to get the hell out of here and back home to the compound. Maybe Ol' Willy or Sophia will have an idea on how we might be able to help Clay. Sophia took some nursing classes when we were younger," Ray says optimistically. Saying the last part looking directly at Levi, giving him a reassuring nod that says it's ok to still hang on to a little bit of hope. Levi returns the nod, appreciating the symbolic gesture contained within the words from the closest friend his father had aside from his mother.

Ally sits patiently in the passenger seat of the Tacoma next to Ray, lost in her thoughts as she absently helps him navigate through the suburban streets as quickly and as quietly as possible. She is astounded at how different her home town looked in its current abandoned and ruined state. Ally had wisely taken the time to trace out several alternative paths on the map that Jim was carrying as he played navigator for Laura in the support vehicle that followed along behind them, just in case. With the decaying condition of the city, along with the roaming bands of the insane and starving, you could never be too sure that some unforeseen obstacles wouldn't pop up since it had unarguably been quite some time since anyone had driven a vehicle down these dilapidated city streets. Only the engines of the trucks speak as both groups ride in silent concentration. Tension hangs thick in the air as everyone stays on high alert, watching for any signs of the gashers or anything else that was alive and potentially dangerous that they had still yet to discover.

CHAPTER TWENTY-SEVEN

He stands alone at the edge of a small rise watching the bright red taillights of the trucks disappear over the next hill. He is full for the first time in what had to be months from the buffet of the fallen dead inside the house. Most of the blood that smears his face has yet to be washed away by the rain that now falls lightly around him. It begins to dry to a sticky paste as soon as he turns his face into the subtle breeze, enjoying the sensation as it washes over him causing the blood to cling stubbornly to his nose and chin. The nauseating sounds of people vomiting drifts to him on the wind from several directions as some hunch over heaving from eating too much of the raw meat and fresh blood. Their shrunken stomachs unable to handle the heaviness, ingesting so much of it so fast. Unable to chase after the mini convoy (in spite of the energy that surges through him from his protein dense meal) he stands and watches them futilely inch further and further away. No longer able to take in full breaths due to his lungs slowly filling with the unfiltered ashes he looks out over the houses panting in quick shallow breaths. Unknowing in the fact that the ashes he was breathing were causing silicosis – mixing the ashes with his natural body fluids gradually turning the ashes inside of his lungs into a crude form of cement, asphyxiating him slowly from the inside. So he stands there, alone in the rain watching the tail lights in hopeless desperation and panting. His belly extends out unnaturally, like a snake, from gorging himself on the opportunistic feast. His horribly dehydrated and oxygen deprived body won't listen to his mind as he begs it to follow the lights, to chase them. Muttering a gargled moan, he takes a convulsing step forward in the direction the taillights had disappeared in, accidentally kicking something previously unnoticed lying on the ground in the dark and the mud. Hypnotized and drawn to the red lights set in the canvas of blackness like a moth to a flame in the dead of night, he hadn't noticed anything lying at his feet as he had taken his stumbling step forward. Bending over awkwardly he picks up the mysterious object and does his best to hide his surprise and excitement as he quickly looks around scanning for anyone that would have noticed him find this treasure of treasures. Seeing that no one is looking in his direction, he hastily makes his way around the far side of the little house as quickly as his drowning lungs and emaciated legs will allow him to. No longer able to remember his name, who he is, or even who he was. He is no longer able to read, write, or to even possess the ability to speak so it is his natural, primitive instinct alone that understood the value of what luck had just allowed him to find. Struggling to twist the cap off of the bottle he begins to weep small, thick tears, causing his eyes to burn all the more hotly as the tears blaze their trail through the ash-raw wasteland of flesh that rims them. His moans of pleasure from the relief that the sweet, cool water provides to his scorched and ruined throat are thankfully swallowed up by the rain and the darkness that saturates everything around him. Weak, hopeless, and slowly dying with both his thirst and his hunger quenched for the moment, he begins to long for warmth and rest. Weeping at his own disparity, it is the first time in over a month that his throat doesn't burn as his slow controlled sips of the life-giving water temporarily extinguish the flames that the ashes and thick salty blood had ignited. He slowly emerges from his hiding place, no longer able to see the now forgotten taillights off in the distance, he is hidden and shadowed in the dark from the light the now burning house emits. Evidentially, during the chaos of the feeding frenzy someone must have kicked the fire burning in the back room out of the fire pit setting the entire house ablaze. He slowly turns away from the fire and the haunting moans of the unlucky that were trapped inside the burning house and heads towards a garage where he knows a warm, bunched up pile of blankets waits for him. There he knows he will find a short, peaceful reprieve. Until the pangs of hunger and thirst drive him back out to hunt through the darkness once more.

Ray leads Laura up and over the hill towards the outskirts of town and the rest of Ally's group. Consumed by the cruel contradiction between his longing to be home with his beautiful wife and the dread he feels at having to tell Holly about the loss of her husband and her young daughter

Belle about the loss of her father. He's still having difficulty wrapping his head around the whole Colt incident. And now on top of everything else there was the Clay situation. He was going to have to tell Veronica – the unspoken matriarch of the compound – that her husband and partner of almost twenty years was most likely going to follow in Colt's mortal footprints step for step. And then there was Cain. How in this whole dark world was he going to find the strength to break this tragic news to Cain? His sigh fills the truck as he begins to imagine how all of this was going to affect everyone at the compound. Life there will undoubtedly never be the same. He grits his teeth as he looks out at the damned godforsaken darkness! He shakes with anger at the unfairness of this new world. The unfairness of this current situation. But most of all he is angry at the feelings of helplessness he has at not being able to do a damn thing about either one of them. He looks up into his rear-view mirror to check on Laura and the position of the second truck, wishing he had been a little more forceful on his insistence of Levi riding up here with him. Squinting into the mirror he notices that a house a few streets over from the doctor's office had been set on fire. The irony of the flames standing out against the darkness in this paper mache version of the world, like a sadistic burning representation of the sun shining against the perpetual blackness of space, was not lost on Ray. Recognizing the endlessly rising worry he was developing for both his own family and Clay's, he recognizes that he needs to get his mind on something, *anything* else. Turning to Ally he asks curiously,

"Ok… tell me something Ally, why do you guys call the people left roaming around town gashers?"

"If you are depressed you are living in the past, if you are anxious you are living in the future, if you are at peace you are living in the present."

-Lao Tzu

CHAPTER TWENTY-EIGHT

Broderick sits in the kitchen watching through a slot cut out in the boarded-up window for any signs of movement that would signal Ally's return. His stomach eats itself with worry and nervousness at the thought that something might have happened to the girl. He glances over at Ally's father, Xander. Thankfully he had finally fallen asleep on the couch with his leg propped up to help ease the swelling. Broderick had finally convinced him to accept some pain medication for the severely broken leg he had sustained falling through the weakened, water damaged steps that led down into the basement of a house they were searching the last time the two of them had been out on a scavenging run. Tall and gangly Alexander may have the appearance of frailty, but his actions had shown Broderick on more than one occasion that he was anything but frail. It was the last supply run any of them had been able to take and they were now running uncomfortably short on several necessities prompting Ally to take the chance of going out alone. Broderick had persuaded him to take the meds and to try to relax, that sitting here watching out of the window and staring out into the darkness wasn't going to make his leg stop hurting or bring Ally back any sooner. Assuring him that the gashers that had harassed them during their frantic return home were only roamers and not part of a den. And now, despite all of his assurances to Alexander, he finds himself sitting in the exact same spot, at the exact same window, doing the exact same thing. His idle sigh is full of despair and worry as it reverberates through the kitchen of the house, sounding far louder than it should have in the stillness of the dark.

Sitting there alone, he lets his mind wander, reminiscing back to how life used to be in the dazzling light of the sunshine, how the warmth of it felt against your skin. He travels back to the days of when he had met his wife Jackie while they were both attending classes at the University of Tulsa over in Oklahoma. He was enrolled on a football scholarship but was enough of a realist to understand that his future most likely didn't lie within the NFL. So he had been diligent in his studies as an education major, even minoring in biology. Oddly enough that's how he had meet his future wife, Jackie. Through his studies, not through football. And it was because of this that he had known instinctively that she was the one he had been waiting for, for all of his life. She wasn't an athlete or involved in the athletic department in any way. In fact, she didn't even like sports – *especially* football. The violence of it appalled her. Broderick chuckles to himself as he dreamily thinks about his pacifist wife and how mysteriously funny love can be sometimes. Even after all these years he can still hear her lecturing him; ***"Todays athletes are nothing more than modern day gladiators and slaves killing each other in a new arena. Fighting to the rhythmic applause of the masses over greed. Chasing the coin they falsely believe will release them from their masters in their burning desire to be free. All the while they are to ignorant and blind to realize that all they're doing is escaping one master just to spend the rest of their lives bowing to another. Constantly stuck in the groveling position of a bended knee."*** He smiles warmly at how she had always described football and most sports in general. Jackie had been a history major with a minor in education so all her analogies seemed to have some type of historical event at its base. His smile is broad and genuine as he thinks about how the only thing they ever had in common back in those days was their passion to teach and a desire to be positive influences on developing young minds. But despite the overall lack of common interests he had fallen so desperately in love with her that just being in her presence would make his body tremble with yearning and desire. Her simplest touch on his bare skin was enough to cause it to cover itself in goose bumps. So, he had chased her. With the same energy and vigor as if she were a running back going in for the winning touchdown in double overtime, he had chased her. Until finally, one clear beautifully clear spring morning as he stood rambling and fumbling over his words, she let him catch her. And once he had her, he knew that he would never let her go. Confessing his love for her in every way imaginable, finally winning her heart and ultimately her hand. She was his most desired obsession and he had loved her from the deepest parts of his soul every day of his life since the first day they had met.

It was through Jackie that they had come to meet Ally and her father. Ally had been a sophomore at the local high school where he and Jackie had worked as teachers here in the serene Ozark Mountains of Arkansas. Broderick had grown up here and once he introduced Jackie to its lush and rugged beauty, she had grown to love the area as much as he did. Ally was an exceptionally bright, but melancholy girl that Jackie had recognized suppressed greatness in – through of all things, her poetry. Jackie was one of the few guidance counselors at the small school and she had been assigned Ally just after she lost her mother in a horrific car accident the summer before beginning high school. Ally's freshman year had been full of obstacles and strife as she had fought to find some type of identity. Fighting an internal battle over the unfairness of life and the lack of value that she now saw lying within it. Jackie had begun tutoring and mentoring Ally after school, which before long led to them developing a genuine friendship. Ally's grades and attitude began to improve by leaps and bounds over the next few months as Jackie willingly seemed to fill the mother role in Ally's life that she so desperately needed. Her father Alexander had started bringing Ally over to the house to babysit for them on the rare occasion they were able to get a night to themselves and over time the families also birthed a friendship. Beautiful and sincere despite being born out of the tragedy of Ally's mothers' death. He is smiling sweetly as his eyes begin to tear up, overcome by the emotions caused by the fond memories of days and years gone past. Sitting with his back to the room still watching out of the window, Broderick hears his oldest son Benny rush into the room.

"Dad! Come quick, moms not breathing!"

"He who finds a wife, finds what is good and receives favor from the Lord."

-Proverbs 18:22

CHAPTER TWENTY-NINE

"Is mom going to be ok dad?" Benny asks from the doorway as Broderick continues administering CPR to his unconscious wife.

"I don't know Benny," he pants, out of breath from his efforts. "But can you do me a favor buddy?" He asks his oldest son, who is serving as more of a distraction than anything else in his valiant attempt to be helpful.

"Yes sir," Benny answers. Momentarily inflated with pride at the fact that his dad has ask him for help. "Could you go check on your brother and Mr. Xander for me please? They should be waking up anytime now and they're going to want to know what's going on." Broderick turns and looks at his son as he finishes his request, "Do you think you can you do that for me big guy?"

"Yes sir," Benny answers again. But his voice had lost some of its gusto this time. The way his father just looked at him raises even more questions inside the young boy as he starts to turn and leave. He pauses to glance at his father once more, those questions are answered by his father's falling tears. Benny slowly turns away from his parents' room with his head down staring at his feet as he goes to carry out his father's requests. The pride he had felt when he was first asked to help was all but gone now. The last time his dad had called him "Big guy" was when his cat had been run over by a car in front of their house. Benny walks down the hallway leaving a trail of his own tears in his wake as the realization that his mother has just lost the fight with her illness hits home. Gloomily he can't help but to wonder if she too will be buried out back beneath the old oak tree, just like his pet cat.

Ray swings the vehicle into the mouth of the driveway and begins making his way towards the house that sits off in the distance at the end of the driveway, a football field's length away.

"Nice place," Ray murmurs raising his eyebrows with surprised respect.

"It's been in Mr. Brick's family for like…. I don't know, generations I think. His great, great, grandfather supposedly fought in the revolutionary war and won his freedom, or something like that. His family were the first freed slaves to form a homestead in the state of Arkansas. There's a monument and everything that tells all about it in front of the courthouse on Main Street," Ally says. Ray whistles his astonishment at such an incredible piece of family and American history.

"That's Impressive. But I do have one question…" Ray says as he pulls up to the end of the driveway and kills the engine.

"Sure, what would you like to know?" Ally asks, raising her eyebrows questioningly at Ray.

"Why do you call him **Brick**?"

"Ask me that question again after you meet him Mr. Jones," Ally says smiling teasingly as she pulls her dust mask up before opening her door, chuckling warmly she steps out into the cold air stretching noisily. Ray squints his eyes curiously at Ally's back as she climbs out of the truck.

Broderick Thomas bends down and kisses his lovely wife's lips for the last time. The only moisture to be found on them coming from his own tears as they fall in a steady stream from his cheeks. Alexander cradles both Benny and Larry in the crook of each arm as they stand respectfully at the foot of the bed watching as Broderick gently pulls the sheet up to cover Jackie's face. The gentle giant of a man stands on trembling, unsteady legs and with sad hollow eyes he looks down onto his lost love lying motionless in the bed that they had shared together for thirteen years.

"Everyone form a circle around the bed and join hands please," Broderick asks with a trembling voice that threatened to break at any moment. As everyone moves into position around Jackie completing Broderick's wish they join hands and instinctively bowing their heads without being asked. Broderick begins his eulogy in an unsteady voice, his eyes never leaving the picture of Jackie taken on their wedding day that they had laid on top of her now lifeless form.

"I have never known a stronger or more passionate person in all of my life than Jackie. Her ability to see what lies on the inside of a person, instead of what lies on the outside, was an inspiration to everyone that knew her. It gave her the foresight to see the man I had inside of me, the man I never knew I could be. The kind of man…. I could have never been without her." Broderick breaks down into open sobs forcing him to pause. It is only through the strength he finds within holding the hands of his sons that he is able to remain standing and find the voice to continue his dedication.

"My whole young life I always felt like I was waiting for something, but I was never really sure of exactly what it was I was waiting for. At first I thought it was football. Then I thought it was college. But it wasn't until I met you Jackie that I realized what it was that I had always been waiting for. You were the embodiment of everything that was good in my life and my life will be forever changed without you." Broderick sighs heavily before drawing in a deep breath to continue,

"Your love for me gave me courage. My love for you gave me strength. I love you as much today as I loved you yesterday, and I will continue to love you tomorrow and for all the days that follow after that. Thank you Jackie for filling my life with love and laughter." Broderick reaches out caressing the circle with his name inside of it that Jackie had written in the bottom right hand corner of every picture and note she had given him since their wedding day. With the eulogy finished Broderick suddenly bolts upright, looking in the direction of Xander. As Xander meets his gaze both men hold intense looks of confusion at the sounds they both hear and recognize coming from the driveway outside. The unmistakable sounds of someone turning off an engine followed by the opening and slamming of a car door.

"If you love someone, put their name in a circle; because hearts can be broken, but circles never end."

-Jackie Taylor-Thomas

CHAPTER THIRTY

"Ally! Thank god you're ok, you had us worried sick girl," Broderick exclaims. Relieved, he opens the door to allow Ally inside the fortified old farm house they called home. Using his long arms which are still muscular despite the prolonged lack of food, he gently sweeps Ally behind him through the doorway. All the while his eyes never leaving the masked and armed band of strangers standing behind her in the gravel driveway.

"It's ok Brick, everyone just needs to stay calm," Ally says as she steps back out through door to stand between Broderick and the others. "The only reason I am here and safe with you now is because of them. They gave me a safe place to hide and protection while the gashers were out roaming last night." Xander slowly hobbles through the living room to stand behind Broderick who is still blocking the door.

"Stand aside Brick. If that's true, I owe this group of strangers a sincere showing of gratitude. Thank you all for helping my Ally," Xander says as he is finally able to struggle through the door and past Brick. "Dad!" Ally exclaims throwing her arms around her father's neck, almost taking them both to the ground as she does.

"I'm so glad you're home Ally girl," Xander says returning his daughter's hug joyfully.

"Ok. If Ally here says you guys helped her and you're ok, then I guess you're ok," Broderick finally says, seeming to relax just a little as he watches the reunion between Ally and Alexander.

"Yes, yes, please everyone, let's go inside and get out of this ash and cold," Xander offers as Broderick slowly turns and walks back inside the house leaving his housemates to temporarily deal with the newcomers on their own while he goes to get his sons from where they were still waiting for him by their mother's side. Xander steps to the side half leaning on the door for stability and half holding it open with one arm while motioning with his other arm for the strangers to come inside.

"Dad your leg seems to be getting worse. Have you been staying off of it and keeping it clean?" Ally asks her father frowning, inspecting his leg with a disapproving glare. The story Ray and Jim had told about Clay's wound becoming toxic after lack of treatment weighing heavy on her mind. She thinks about the compound fracture that had caused the bone in her dads' leg to puncture through his skin and the existing possibility of it becoming infected if they're not diligent in his daily treatments. She knew that if the leg started showing signs of turning gangrenous, it would have to be removed.

"My leg is fine sweetheart," Xander answers, affectionately looking down into his daughters face for the first time since her arrival. "I promise."

Ally recognizes the pain her father is hiding from her in the redness of his eyes.

"Dad, why have you been crying?" Ally asks him, scanning the room. "Where is Mrs. Jackie? Why haven't Benny and Larry come to see me yet? Dad? Oh dad, no…" Ally whispers as her eyes too begin to fill with tears. Xander says nothing as he looks at her and softly shakes his head from side to side. Knowing his daughter would be just as devastated as Broderick and the boys at the loss of the treasured Mrs. Jackie Taylor-Thomas. Compassionately Xander wraps Ally in the loving embrace of sympathy. Truly saddened for his daughter that she has now had to endure the loss of two mothers in her lifetime. As the rest of the group from the chiropractor's office cautiously begin climbing the steps leading to the front door of the house Grant turns to his dad and whispers nervously,

"Well at least now we know why they all call him Brick."

"Be quiet Grant," Laura whispers harshly. Her face pressed up directly behind Grant's ear. "They're all upset about something. I have a bad feeling that something awful has just happened here. My only hope is that we're not considered to be part of it, whatever *IT* is."

"Or maybe they're upset over someone," Levi adds, his voice dreary from the worry he has for his sick father. The final steps to the porch are taken in respectful silence for whatever this little band of survivors has just had to endure. Reaching the summit of the steps Ray turns to Levi and Paige as Jim and the others enter the doorway of the house in front of them,

"You two stay out here on the porch, keep an eye on the vehicles and Clay until we can figure out exactly what's going on here and make sure we can trust these people. No harm in erring on the side of caution here I think."

"Yes sir," Paige and Levi answer in unison sharing sideways glances at each other. Ray hopes that under their masks they are smiling at spending some peaceful time together despite the uncertainty of their present circumstances. Their blossoming romance becoming more and more obvious to everyone around them. Ray enters the house and shakes the extended hand being offered by Xander, under his mask, he can't help but to smile – even if only slightly – in spite of his overly cautious nature and apprehension over of their current situation.

"We are very sorry for your loss Mr. Thomas," Laura says to Broderick and his sons as they come into the sitting area just off to the left of the doorway.

"Mr. Richland filled us in on Mrs. Thomas's battle with pneumonia." Ally walks into the room somberly behind Broderick and the boys after paying her last respects to the woman she had come to love and respect most in all the world.

"Don't call her that please. She hated being called Mrs. Thomas. She thought it sounded too formal and that it made her sound old," Ally says to the room addressing no one in particular, never picking up her head as she speaks. Xander can't help but to smile at the reflection of how Jackie hadn't liked formalities. She used to say it caused people to be withdrawn and not to be who they really were.

"And while we're on that subject," Broderick interjects. "Everybody please just call me Brick. Everyone always has. No need for the Mr. Thomas bit, although I appreciate the respect intended in the title." Brick walks over to where Ray has seated himself in the chair closest to the door and extends his hand out in his direction. Ray stands up respectfully to meet him more formally as Broderick states sincerely,

"I'd like to apologize for the episode on the porch. In these dark days one can't be too careful," as he and Ray meet and shake hands.

"No apology necessary. I would have reacted the same way if a bunch of armed strangers showed up on the doorstep of the compound with one of our own. And I too would like to extend my condolences to you and your sons for your most unfortunate loss," Ray offers to Brick who is still visibly shaken from the loss of his wife. The men nod appreciatively at one another, both thankful at the fact that whatever possibility there had been for there to be a hatchet, it had just been buried deep in the fallen ashes and Arkansas mud. As formalities commence and conclude inside the house Ray and Brick walk outside onto the porch to share introductions with Levi and Paige, then they all walk down to the vehicles together to check on the condition of Clay.

Brick whistles as he places his enormous hand across Clay's forehead and cheeks.

"Man, you guys weren't kidding. He feels like he's hot enough to melt the seat! Let's get him up to the house and in a proper bed. If leaning against the door of this car all hunched over like that is as uncomfortable as it looks, he'll appreciate it even if he isn't aware of it," Brick says. Walking around to the other side of the truck to help extract Clay and carry him up to the house. Levi grabs him by the arm as he walks by;

"My dad might not know it, but I do. And words fail to express how much I appreciate it Brick. Thank you for allowing us to give my dad a nice place to rest before we get headed back to the compound." As Levi finishes he extends out his hand. Brick wraps his oversized mitt around Levi's, happily accepting the respectful gesture from the distraught young man.

"You're very welcome son. I hope someone would do the same for me if I were ever caught in the same situation. On another note; we've got some ibuprofen stockpiled in the medicine cabinet. If we can get some in him... it might help to take that fever down a notch or two," Brick answers, offering Levi a reassuring smile and patting him on the shoulder before turning back toward the truck and the task of getting Clay inside where he can more comfortable.

"There isn't a single one of us at the compound that wouldn't do all we could for you and your group any time you needed us too for showing all of us such hospitality. All you'd have to do is ask," Paige says to Brick as he gets his huge arms under Clay's upper body and eases him out of the back seat, being as gentle as possible given the awkward position and Clay's dead weight. As Clay's upper torso emerges from the truck Levi and Ray each take hold of a leg as together they begin to carry him inside of the house and out of the cold and sleeting rain.

"Thank you. It's nice to know that we're not as alone in this world as we had feared we were," is all Brick says in response to Paige as they pull Clay from the backseat of the Toyota Tacoma. Once inside Brick and Levi carry Clay to one of the spare rooms of the house laying him down softly on the bed while everyone else gathers in the den to warm themselves in front of the fireplace.

"Ma'am? My dad asked me to give these to you," Larry says walking up behind Paige, holding out a bottle of ibuprofen in her direction, never actually crossing into the room.

"He did? Well thank you very much. You're Larry, right?" Paige says walking over to him and taking the offered bottle from him.

"Yes ma'am."

"How are your dad and your brother Benny doing? Do they need any help?" Paige asks him when she reaches the doorway.

"No ma'am, they're fine," Larry answers meekly.

"Ally is in the room with them. She knows what mom liked to wear the best. Dad told me to tell you that you should give Mr. Clay three of those every four hours to try to get his fever down and that it might be easier to give them to him if you crush them up and put them in warm water. That's how we had to give them to mom at the end." Paige stands in the doorway looking after him with growing sympathy as she watches the heart broken little boy walking back down the hallway towards his parents' room, doing everything he can to try to hold himself together through all of this.

"Ok I will. Tell your dad thank you for me. I'll be right here if you guys need me for anything, alright?" Paige calls out to the young boys back. A short pause with a slight turning of his head back in her direction and a raise of his hand in a silent wave of recognition is the only response he could manage.

CHAPTER THIRTY-ONE

YEAR ONE, DAY THREE HUNDRED AND TWENTY-SEVEN

The group stands in a circle, hand in hand, around the freshly covered gravesite of the recently departed Mrs. Jackie Taylor-Thomas. Their stand with heads bowed in the universal symbol of respect for a woman that some of them never even knew. The fond memories shared last night by those that did know and love her while they basked in the warmth of the fireplace had been evidence enough of the type of woman Jackie had been and it was more than enough for those that didn't know Jackie in life to feel both a connection to her in death, sharing in the immense pain of her loss. Lightening dances through the clouds above their heads covering the hillside in brief flashes of light, aiding Broderick in gathering the strength he needed to begin his eulogy.

"Thank you, old friends and new friends for standing here with me today as we lay my beautiful wife Jackie to rest. But as we reflect, I ask you to remember that I'm not only losing a wife, but we are also losing a mother, a teacher, a mentor. And I am losing the piece of me that I promised to her on our wedding day, a piece of my soul that only she will ever hold. The world lost someone very special yesterday. The lives of those who knew her will forever be missing a brightness that stood out in stark contrast to the dark that has been cast about us violently from this crucible of despair."

The lightning that flashes behind Broderick serves to add a powerful, theatrical feel to his words as he speaks. It was as if God himself was watching and bestowing blessings of faith and optimism down onto the collective circle of survivors. Reminding the group that where there is *love*, there is *hope*; and where love and hope survive together, there subsists the possibility for *life*.

And now these three remain: faith, hope, and love. But the greatest of these is Love.

–1 Corinthians 13:13

CHAPTER THIRTY-TWO

"We can't thank you enough for the hospitality Brick. Especially at such a difficult time for you and your family," Ray says as the group begins to descend down from the hilltop.

"It was our pleasure Ray. We appreciate you sharing your supplies with us. We were starting to get dangerously low," Brick answers gratefully, truly thankful at the rest of the groups' willingness to help him and his family in this time of need.

"No thanks necessary. It's the least we can do. Especially for all of your assistance with Clay."

Ray reaches out and grasps the big hand being offered to him from an even bigger man. A man that has shown them in a very short amount of time that he is as big in heart, as he is in stature.

"Are you sure you won't come with us back to the compound?" Ray asks Broderick for the umpteenth time. "We could really use you and your family there. And we easily have the room to accommodate what would be such a tremendous addition to our community."

"We appreciate that Ray, we really do, but the way I see it we already are an addition to each other's community," Broderick says, smiling at his new friend pleased over this newly formed alliance. "In my opinion; with us being here next to the city and you guys being out there in the countryside, it makes us an even better community. Creating known, if only small places of safety and solitude in the middle of all this uncertainty and chaos." Broderick stops and looks back up the hill towards the far corner of the designated family graveyard. Ray stops to stand next to him as Brick asks him to follow his gaze.

"Take a walk with me Ray. Can you make out that grave marker resting beneath that old willow tree over there?" Broderick asks. Ray has to squint, straining his eyes against the dark as they begin to move around the border of the family cemetery towards the tree. He could just make out the stone Brick was pointing out to him in the flashes of lightning that still streaked overhead.

"Yes, I can see it," Ray says as they approach the marker. Noting that even from a distance you could tell that it was old and faded, worn away by both time and weather.

"That is the resting place of my grandfathers' ***grandfather.*** He was born on the central plains of Africa. He lost both his mother and father when he was very young in one of the many tribal skirmishes that have always seemed to ravage Africa. Orphans were disregarded by his people so he made his way by scavenging along the outskirts of the village and by the love of one of his older sisters. Living that way, he was captured and brought before the Portuguese slave traders along the Western Coast by the tribal elders. In the end he was betrayed by his own people for a surplus of tobacco and whiskey when he was only fourteen years old." Broderick speaks as he slowly walks around to a small bench that sits next to the gravesite of his great, great grandfather.

"You understand Ray that there has always been division between the have and have nots, even in the tiny villages within the central plains of old Africa. Segregation is nothing new to the world. It always crawls its way back out of the muck; you're to white, you're to black. You're to Chinese, to Irish, to Italian. To Christian or to Jewish… you get my point. Ultimately it has never really mattered what color you are or where you're from, it has always boiled down to one thing and one thing only: ***We*** are the rich and ***You*** are the poor." Broderick smiles and pats Ray on the shoulder as he sits down to rest on the small metal bench. Ray nods his head in agreement. A hundred thoughts swirl around in his head as he stands next to the generations old gravesite. Smiling, he even catches himself marveling that the small rusty bench could support such a massive individual such as the man that now rested upon it.

"Anyway, the traders put him on a ship and brought him across the Atlantic instead of the Mediterranean. Upon his arrival, he was sold at auction to an English settler named Henry Patrick Thomas in the seaport of Hampton, Virginia sometime during the year of 1773. Aside from being a slave of course, he was actually pretty lucky and treated extremely well for the time. He could have just as easily been shipped off to South America to work in the coffee fields or the sugar plantations ran by the French in the Louisiana Territories or the Caribbean. Most importantly as luck would have it, he had been taught to read and write in English by his sister and the missionaries that had come to teach the 'savages' all about Jesus and Christianity. I'm sure you can appreciate what a rarity that was for a black man in that period of history. Add in that he knew the teachings of the Bible and his puzzle of good fortune was complete as he grew to be well regarded by both Mr. Thomas and his family. When the war for American Independence broke out in 1776 he voluntarily fought alongside his plantation owner and was awarded his freedom, literally by the blood on his hands for his bravery and valor. You see, you need to understand that by this point in the war the English had started what was known as "Lord Dunmore's Proclamation". This promised the freedom to all slaves that fought against the colonies for the crown. A vocal participant of the Revolutionary War and a signer of the Declaration of Independence named William Whipple recognized the hypocrisy of fighting for one's freedom while still holding on to the ownership of an individual. He proposed that the newly founded American country offer this same right to its current crop of slaves, but the bill was denied. The English learned about this and seized an opportunity to create infighting within the new upstarts." Looking up at Ray, Broderick laughs slapping himself on the knee. "Sorry for getting so long winded Ray, but you learn a lot about the gray area that's taught regarding American History when you're married to a history buff like Jackie was. You still with me or did I lose you?"

"No... no. I'm with you. I've never heard much about any of this. It's truly fascinating actually. A little over my head, but fascinating." Ray laughs at himself over his ignorance of Revolutionary history.

"Most people never have so don't beat yourself up over it. Anyway, Whipple opened the eyes of a few of the other plantation owners by standing by his word after America won the war by releasing his own slaves. This prompted some of the other plantation owners to do the same."

"And Henry Thomas was one of them?" Ray states as much as asks.

"Yes, he was one of them. So, my great, great, grandfather was granted his freedom. He stayed for a time working for the Thomas's, even taking their name as his surname out of respect. That is, until the westward expansion started taking place. He saw an opportunity in moving west to new land, a new start. So, he packed up his family and they headed west. He knew it would be much more difficult for a freed and educated black man to make an honest living if he stayed on the already established and European dominated east coast."

"It sounds like he was a tough, smart man blessed with the gift of foresight," Ray offers as Brick pauses to take a breath. Brick nods appreciatively in response to Ray's comment as he continues the story of his family.

"Thank you. I believe he was. Anyway, this is where he settled. Along with his wife, who had also been freed as further reward for his extraordinary contributions to the war effort. They worked long and hard and made this land their own. Through the westward expansion and all of the Indian skirmishes that scarred this area throughout the 1800's and through the War Between the States. Through segregation and the civil rights marches of the 1960's my family has never left this land." Broderick turns to look at his new friend, "The point I'm trying to make with all of this Ray is that my ancestors fought for this land, worked this land, and they have lived and died on this land for a very long time. My family and I won't be the ones to leave it now in the face of this new adversity. My great grandfather's nickname was "Bug". That's how the farm came to be called 'Firefly Farms'. The townspeople and other settlers called him that because they felt that a freed black family in the world back then was nothing more than a bug that needed to be squashed at every opportunity. Things got rather tough at times as I'm sure you can imagine. The funniest part is that almost all of my families hired farm hands were white. They were the ones who suggested the name Firefly. They told my great grandfather that to them, if he had to be a bug, then he should be like the Firefly. That for them he generated this beacon of goodwill from within himself, shining his light on everyone around him from the inside, despite whatever darkness was going on in the world on the outside."

"Just like a Firefly," Ray says as Broderick finishes. "Sounds like we could use a place like that now. Standing out as a beacon of light and hope against the darkness that threatens to smother us all."

"I couldn't agree with you more. Anyway, with all that being said; my family and I will stay **here**. In **this** house. On **this** land. To be that light in the darkness away from the compound as we all fight alongside one another to survive. We'll serve as an outpost and safe haven of sorts for whenever anyone from the compound needs to come into the city to search for supplies." Broderick finishes his statement looking at Ray. Placing his hand to rest on Ray's shoulder he adds,

"We will be a place of security and stability as we *all* search the local areas for what we need to survive. Working together as a team so that what happened to Clay and Colt will hopefully never happen to anyone else in **OUR** group ever again." Ray recognizes the emphasis on the word 'our' and instantly appreciates the words of the groups' new found allies. Fully recognizing the good fortune bestowed upon them at the chance meeting between Ally, Levi, and the others in town, serving to bring the two groups together.

"Our beacon of light in an otherwise dark and cruel world. You know Brick, where I come from we called them lightening bugs. 'Lightening Bug Farms' doesn't have quite the same ring to it as 'Firefly Farms' though," Ray says smiling. Enjoying the fact that when you were outside after a good rain you could go without wearing your mask for a while since the moisture kept the ashes down. Broderick returns the smile as Ray continues,

"Well as much as I'd like to keep trying to talk you out of it, I can't argue with the logic or the sentiment behind your decision. And, if I'm being completely honest, I have to admit it will bring me a huge sigh of relief knowing we always have a safe place to go to whenever we need to come out into the city," Ray says, knowing that Broderick is right. He and his family did serve a much greater purpose staying out here in this Ashland border town than they would if they came back to live with everyone at the compound.

"And I feel the same way about having a place to go to if the time ever came that we couldn't hold out here at the farm."

"Hey guys, sorry to interrupt. We got Clay resting as comfortable as possible in the truck and the supplies that we needed to leave here have been unloaded," Jim says walking up to the duo. Then turning to speak more to Ray he states, "There should be enough food and water to last a good while as long as it's rationed properly." Then turning to Brick and offering his hand Jim adds, "I really appreciate the soft bed and the safe room so I could get in a good night's sleep before we head back to the compound Mr. Thomas."

"It was our pleasure Jim. We want you guys to know that you are welcome here any time," Brick answers shaking the man's hand heartily.

"I think this is a partnership that is going to benefit everyone of us and we are all that much better off now that it has been formed," Ray adds reaching up to pat Broderick's shoulder.

"Mr. Brick, we put enough gas in your truck to get you at least to safety and maybe even as far as half way to the compound if you should ever run into trouble and need to get away in a hurry," Levi says walking up from the driveway to stand with the group on the hillside.

"Also, I'd like to give you this for a little more protection and… well… you know… for trying to help my dad and everything. I think if he were able to, he'd give it to you himself." Levi holds out the Ruger .357 Clay had found in the chiropractor's office the first day the team had arrived in town along with the opened box of bullets that went with it.

"Thank you, son. Having a little more firepower lying around never hurt anyone," Brick says as he takes the offered sign of gratitude from Levi understanding the symbolic weight that the gift of the weapon actually carried with it. Levi quickly turns his attention to Ray and Jim in an effort to hide his emotions from the trio of gathered and respected friends.

"The trucks are fueled, loaded, and we're ready to get going as soon as you guys are finished here," Levi says, then turning around he quickly begins making his way back down the hill to where the rest of the group waited by the vehicles, slipping a little in the thick ashy mud in his haste. Brick, Ray, and Jim stand for a moment in silence before they finish their conversation, all three men sharing an extraordinary amount empathy and pride for the young man that has had to grow up all too quickly in an unforgiving, cruel world that ostensibly seems to always take, but rarely gives.

"Take care of yourself friend. We'll be back out this way in about three months or so to check in on you and for another excursion," Ray says to Brick as he and Jim finish gearing up and walking to the vehicles. "We'll be looking' forward to it. Now you drive slow and safe so you make it back to your families in one-piece Ray and we'll all see each other again real soon," Brick says with genuine concern. Ray turns the Tacoma around in the yard

163

with Laura following close behind in the Cherokee, waving as they make their way down the driveway. Traveling along the rutted and ruined road, they twist and limp their way slowly back towards town until they reach Main Street. Low spirits lift a little higher as they turn right and begin to head back towards the highway, ***and home.***

Broderick and Ally stand at the head of the driveway waving their good-byes, watching after their new friends until the tail lights from the trucks disappear in the distance.

"I hope we see them again soon," Ally says as the tail lights slip out of sight leaving her and Brick alone to turn and head back into the house.

"Ray said they would be back out this way in about three months or so," Brick says to Ally as they climb the steps to the front porch.

"Three months can seem like a lifetime with the way things are now," Ally responds cheerlessly, shivering slightly. "It feels like it's already starting to get colder too." Looking around and taking in their surroundings, Broderick scowls nodding his head absently.

"I was just thinking the same thing. Come on, let's get inside and relax next to a nice roaring fire," Brick says placing his tree trunk of an arm around her shoulders, pulling her in for a warm, affectionate embrace.

"How does that sound Ally girl? I can't be sure, but I think Laura said she left some of the hot chocolate they found. What d'ya say we go in and make some for everyone?"

"I think that sounds amazing," Ally answers, as she returns the much-needed hug.

"Soooo…. what did you think of Grant?" Ally asks as they reach the top of the stairs and cross the porch to the front door.

"What? Oh Lord help us all!" Brick says laughing as he opens the door so he and Ally can walk inside.

"What?! I was just asking. I thought he seemed nice," Ally responds shyly, her cheeks blushing a brilliant shade of red.

"And so it begins!" Brick shouts as he closes and locks the door behind them still laughing. Then turning around from the door, he throws his hands up in the air in an exasperated showing of surrender.

"What? What begins?" Alexander asks from his spot next to Benny and Larry in front of the fireplace. "Well it would seem that at least one bug has survived through all this mess the world has thrown at us" Brick says in a serious tone. A stern look on his face as he addresses Alexander and his boys.

"Oh no! Please tell me that no one has been bitten by a spider!" Alexander exclaims, visibly shaken up by the possibilities held within Bricks statement.

"No Xander, I'm afraid it's a much more serious bug than that," Brick says sitting down and stoking the fire.

"More serious than a spider bite?" Alexander asks alarmed.

"What bug is that dad?" Benny asks, overtaken by his curiosity.

"The…. *LOVE BUG*!" Brick shouts as he jumps up grabbing Ally and tossing her down on the couch to sit in her normal spot next to her dad as he bursts out with renewed laughter.

"What? Oh, OH! HAHA," is all Alexander can get out before falling into his own bout of laughter as he realizes what Broderick is talking about. Both ten-year-old Benny and eight-year-old Larry sit confused and disappointed. Anxiously waiting to hear what the joke was all about and exactly what kind of bug had bitten Ally, wondering if she was going to be ok. Still holding his side from laughing with Ally sitting next to him twenty shades of red Alexander is finally able to catch his breath enough to ask,

"I wonder what Mrs. Jackie would have thought about this blossoming love interest we have budding between the beautiful young Mrs. Ally and, I'm assuming, the handsome young Mr. Grant." He reaches over and pulls his daughter over to him in a fatherly embrace as he answers his own question,

"I'll tell you what she'd think. She would be absolutely thrilled for you." He leans over and kisses the top of her head. Broderick nods his head, his eyes growing misty as he adds,

"Yes she would Xander, she would indeed."

Morning turns into afternoon as one by one the group begins sharing their most cherished memory of the recently lost, dear Mrs. Jackie. The stories continue into the evening as no one is able to recount just one memory of how their lives were changed because of knowing Jackie Thomas. As the fire dies the cold settles in with the darkness that it is broken only by the glowing embers of the once roaring fireplace, while far away in the distance the red fading tail lights of a mini convoy longing for comfort, warmth, and family steadily makes their way home.

"Fireflies are truly natures' purest symbol of beauty, hope, and inspiration; for what other creature in all of nature better symbolizes that true beauty comes from within more than the firefly? Because without that inner beauty shining through showing everyone just how beautiful you really are; you're just another bug flying around aimlessly in the dark."

~Robert Bartlett

CHAPTER THIRTY-THREE

Year One, Day Three Hundred and Twenty-Eight

Veronica lets herself into Sophia and Ray's bunker to check on her friend who is still understandably grief stricken over the horrific loss of her daughter Rose and the gruesome way that she had met her end. Putting on a brave face for the majority of the compound Veronica knew how devastated her friend truly was.

"Oh Ronnie! I didn't hear you come in sweetie, let me get myself together," Sophia says as she notices Veronica standing in the entranceway. Trying her best to clean her face of the tears she had been softly crying just moments before, Sophia stands up pulling her jacket on as she does.

"You're quite alright honey, take your time. I just thought I'd ask you if you'd like to sit by the fire with me this morning and help me make the coffee for everyone," Veronica asks not letting on that she had heard Sophia quietly weeping as she had made her way up the tunnel that lead to the main living chamber of the shelter.

"Cain gave me this bracelet he found with his dog Buddy's name on it that he made when he was in middle school." She holds the gift out to Sophia who is still rummaging in the dark for the rest of her clothes.

"I thought we could take it by and lay it on Rose's marker as we made our way to the pavilion." Veronica assumed that Sophia and Lily went by Rose's grave marker first thing every morning as they made their way to the wash house and the pavilion.

"That sounds wonderful sweetie. Please tell Cain thank you for me," Sophia says as she emerges from the dark of her room, her clothes wrinkled and disheveled. "He doesn't still think that was his dog that did that to Rose and attacked poor little Belle, does he?" Sophia asks stopping next to Veronica and grabbing her by the arms, clearly distraught at Cain feeling any type of guilt or blame over the gruesome death of Rose.

"He does. He swears it actually. He claims that the dog stopped and looked at him, actually wagging its tail for a moment after he called its name out loud." Veronica pauses not sure of how to finish her thought before Sophia finishes it for her, her voice shallow and empty, void of emotion.

"That's when it stopped attacking Belle, bounding off into the woods and running away. After snarling and snapping at Dylan of course. But it was already too late for my poor Rose by then."

"Honey, Cain and Dylan killed the two dogs responsible for what happened to Rose. Remember?" Veronica speaks gently, placing an arm around Sophia's neck pulling her close in a motherly embrace as they begin to walk down the exit tunnel together.

"Oh, that's right! I do remember!" Sophia exclaims dreamily. "The little one was awfully tasty the way Willy served it over rice with a little brown gravy and green beans." She finishes her memory with the kind of sadistic grin usually reserved for only the demented and criminally insane. The look makes Veronica feel a little uneasy but she offers a reassuring smile to her friend as she agrees with her, grabbing onto any excuse she can that could possibly help to pull her out of this spiraling depression.

"Yes sweetie, it sure did." As they exit the bunker Veronica utters a small prayer that Ray and the group get back soon. Their return is all she can see that stands between Sophia possibly making a recovery or being lost forever.

"Good morning Jackson," Veronica says as she and Sophia walk up behind him. Jackson's head is down but they can hear him softly crying as he pays his morning respects to the only other occupant in the compounds newly designated cemetery, Gracie.

"Morning Ronnie, Sophia," Jackson responds never leaving his knees or even bothering to turn around. His eyes stay fixated on the grave marker that stands in front of him.

"How is Marie doing this morning?" Veronica asks placing a comforting hand lightly onto Jacksons' back. Reaching out to one of the two markers in the plot Sophia places the bracelet Cain had sent over on top of the one for Rose.

"She's fine. She's still sleeping. Aubrey is attending to her," Jackson says quickly rising from his kneeling position and shrugging off Veronica's hand. Detesting any touch of empathy or pity. He bends over and runs his left hand down the side of Gracie's grave marker and whispers to the dark "Everyday" then abruptly, he turns and begins making his way back to his bunker.

"I should really get back and check on Marie now." And just like that, with his words trailing after him, he was gone. Veronica sighs as she watches him walk away for as long as the dark will allow her to. As Jackson's silhouette is swallowed up by the darkness she turns around to pay her own respects to the two members of their community that had been laid to rest here. Finishing her respects to Gracie, Veronica places her attention back on Sophia who sits on the ground next to Rose's gravesite. She watches as Sophia obsessively brushes away any leaves or debris that had fallen to settle on Rose's marker during the night. She leans over and hugs the marker as her anguished tears leave little round drops of wetness on top of the stones surface. Veronica can't help but shed a few tears of her own, saddened by this new morning ritual that the compound has been forced to accept for Sophia and Jackson. As Sophia finishes saying her good morning to Rose, she stands and grabs Veronica by the hand.

"Thank you so much Ronnie for coming here with me this morning," Sophia says thankfully.

"You are very welcome Sophia. Thank you for allowing me to come," Veronica responds sweetly. Then looking around curiously she asks, "Where is Lily? I thought she came here with you too." Sophia's eyes fill with a new round of tears as she looks off into the distance towards the water station.

"No, Lily doesn't like to come here with me. She hasn't been here since the funeral."

"Oh, I'm sorry Sophia I didn't know," Veronica stammers not realizing that she had inadvertently stumbled upon a sensitive subject. "It was so recent...maybe she just needs a little time to pass. Let her own wounds heal before she can come by."

"I hope you're right Ronnie," Sophia says, then quickly changes the subject. "Hey I thought you said we needed to get the coffee started for everyone? I know some people who will be awfully grumpy if we don't." Sophia pulls on Veronica's arm with both hands as the pair begin to leave the cemetery and make their way to the pavilion.

"Yes we do. Willy is grumpy enough already, we don't need him going through caffeine withdrawals," Veronica responds with a soft giggle, hugging the arm Sophia has wrapped around her while patting her hand affectionately.

Willy walks into the circle of firelight just as the two women set the coffee pot on the tripod over the fire to begin brewing.

"Mornin' ladies," Willy says as he approaches the duo, his voice still heavy with sleep.

"Good morning Willy," Veronica and Sophia respond in chorus.

"We have a little of the beans left over from last night Willy, would like me to heat some up for you?" Sophia asks as Willy sits warming himself happily by the fire.

"I would indeed Mrs. Sophia! Thank you very much!" Willy answers excitedly. Then while wearing a sly grin, he turns to Veronica and asks her,

"How come you never offer to warm me up some beans with my coffee first thing in the morning Ronnie?" Then adding, "A man could definitely get used to this" as Sophia places the steaming bowl of beans if front of him. Wearing a broad smile, he begins to eat as the fog of sleep pleasantly begins to lift away. Veronica walks over smiling and places the coffee down next to the beans commenting,

"And that's exactly why I don't do it Willy. We don't want you going all soft and lazy on us around here. The only thing I want you getting used to is work."

"The hell you say woman, I thought I left my wife and boss back in town," Willy responds good naturedly. The laughter that spreads out through the pavilion reminds them of how grateful they are to have each other to lean on as they try to survive during these difficult dark days. Sitting together under the pavilion enjoying the light conversation of friendship and the warmth of the fire, the trio finishes up their morning meal of beans and stale bread as the talk turns to a more serious topic.

Speaking quietly as if it were something that needed to be kept a secret, they begin to discuss the nuances of the compounds most recent addition – The oddly peculiar, Aubrey Bryant.

"Ok, so what do you ladies really think about the newest member of our little club?" Willy opens the discussion up with the easiest and most obvious question.

"I don't get a good feeling about her at all. Something about her persona just rubs me the wrong way," Sophia chimes.

"I know what you mean. I don't get all warm and fuzzy around her either. I can't put my finger on it but something about her just seems… Off" Veronica adds.

"Well for starters," Willy bursts in, "how about the way she gained access to the compound in the first place!" He places a sympathetic hand to lay over Sophia's as he speaks. Sophia returns the gesture with her free hand patting Willy's.

"Willy has a point. She was supposedly out there just wandering around for days or weeks, all alone? Just to show up on our doorstep right at the exact moment the dogs attacked the girls? Now I don't mean to sound ungrateful for what she did for Lily and Belle," Sophia says, pausing to catch her breath, "But something about it just doesn't add up."

"Exactly my point. If she really was out there alone all that time, how is it that she is miraculously lactating? Which to me raises a more important question… if she's lactating, what the hell happened to her baby?" Willy points out excitedly, like a detective who has just discovered a bizarre new clue in a decade long cold case. "And what's up with that book she's always carrying around and writing in?"

"It's supposedly a journal she keeps, like a diary. She claims she keeps it to document her ordeals during what she calls the 'afterlife'. And I agree with both of you. I know a woman can keep lactating for weeks, sometimes months, after a baby stops nursing but the flow usually slows down to a trickle. It doesn't stay as full as hers seems to be," Veronica says puzzled.

"I'm with Willy. I would still like to know where her baby is and why she never talks about it," Sophia says comparing the feelings she has for her own children (both living and dead) to how Aubrey seems to have no emotions about her dead or lost child at all.

"Or its father. Or anyone else for that matter. And no one survives this long out there by themselves," Willy adds, growing more agitated with every word. "And another thing, where did all those scars around her lips come from? And why does she sound like someone who just drank an entire bottle of whiskey and smoked a carton of cigarettes?"

"I don't know where the scars came from Willy, or why she sounds the way she does. But what I do know is that the three of us sitting out here in the cover of darkness, underneath the pavilion whispering about it like an old sewing circle isn't going to change anything or cure any ones' curiosity," Veronica states flatly. "But if she wants to be part of the compound we need to find out more about her, it's as simple as that. But we shouldn't be out here doing it like some sort of secret inquisition. I think we should talk to her about it."

"I agree Ronnie. I think we should to have a community meeting about it," Willy says nodding his head.

"Yes, I think getting us all together in an open forum to talk about it would help to curb these uneasy feelings that we all seem to be having about the mysterious and peculiar Mrs. Aubrey Bryant," Sophia states with conviction.

"As do I, but we need to make sure that it doesn't turn into an interrogation or a persecution. And we especially need to be gentle with the whole Jackson situation," Veronica says. "His psyche is hanging on by the thinnest of threads as it is."

"Ok. When should we get everyone together? You don't think we should we wait for Clay and the others to return?" Sophia asks.

"That's a great question Sophia, but can we wait that long to take care of this? We don't need this situation to escalate any more than it already has."

"I think it should be sooner rather than later," Willy interjects with conviction. "There's going to be enough to fill Ray and the rest of the group in on when they return. We don't need to add anything else to it if we can help it." As the three senior members left at the compound absently nod their agreement to one another, they sit together and finish the rest of their coffee in silent contemplation. Apprehensive at how Ray will take the news of his daughter Rose's gruesome and untimely death.

The scream that jolts them awake from their thoughts is so loud it seems to shake the very foundation of the mountain the compound is nestled in. Startled, Veronica and Willy jump to their feet spilling what was left of their coffee to run off of the table and pool on the ground to be swallowed up greedily by the pavilions wooden floor. Sophia stays seated unable to move. She begins weeping softly into her hands as she slowly brings them up to cover her face. Thinking to herself that there has been far too much screaming and crying inside the compound lately. Unable to face yet another despairing event Sophia gradually rises and makes her way away from the direction of the screams. She averts her attention on getting back to check on how Lily was doing. Lily had stayed with Holly last night to help take care of Belle's mangled ankle and foot. Every step towards Holly and Colt's bunker reminds her of just how much she wished Ray was already home and by her side. She didn't know how or if she was going to be able to make it through all of this without him.

Veronica and Willy make their way through the dark in a frenzy towards the sounds of the frantic screaming that is still emanating from inside the communities' kitchen and pantry. Bursting through the door they are immediately met by the overpowering, sickly-sweet smell of burning flesh. From somewhere in the back of the room they can make out the glow of flickering firelight as it cast haunting shadows that mimic a desperate struggle dancing over the walls. A dance of desperation, broken only by the indiscernible, frenzied screaming that was booming out in chaotic intervals from someone inside the room.

"The Darkness that surrounds us cannot Hurt Us. It is the Darkness in Your OWN Heart that you should Fear."

–Bernard Silvetris

CHAPTER THIRTY-FOUR

Veronica and Willy charge through the back of the kitchen and burst open the door to the pantry. They are startled and confused at the initial sight of Jackson violently slamming Aubrey up against the wall over and over again. Finally throwing her into the far corner of the room on the opposite side of the fire; a fire that had foolishly been lit for some unknown reason in the center of the room. Jacksons screaming sobs continue to fill the room for another moment until they finally end abruptly with one final dreadful yell, full of pain and rage. The eerie silence that follows is tenuous as their ears continue to ring from the ear-piercing volume of Jacksons screams. With another kick into Aubrey's ribs he falls back, collapsing against the wall and running his hands over his face. He smears the blood oozing from the scratches across his forehead through his hair appearing like the gory highlighted streaks of the macabre'. Veronica covers her mouth audibly sucking in her breath as she takes in the revulsion being played out inside the little back room used to store food and other perishables.

"Oh dear God, oh sweet Jesus no" Willy repeats over and over from where he is standing just inside the door to Veronica's left. Aubrey, who has managed to struggle back to her feet, squats over the fire slowly turning the little spit she had crudely mounted over it. Incoherent mumblings in her raspy, repulsive smokers' voice escape from her as she works the spit creating a haunting image of the insane.

"Hungry, hungry, hungry, no more crying, no more hungry." These are the only words Veronica can decipher as Aubrey mumbles them over and over working the spit and blowing on the fire to stoke the embers.

"Hungry, hungry, hungry." Willy and Veronica are turned into statues, petrified by the ghastly atrocities being performed in front of them by Aubrey who continues to mumble over the fire never bothering to wipe away the blood that was streaming out of her nose. The most visible result of an apparently good right hand from Jackson that she endured during their struggle in the corner.

"Aubrey... can you hear me Aubrey? Listen to me Aubrey... listen to my voice. This is Veronica, you know... Ronnie. Remember? Aubrey, where is the baby? Where is Marie Aubrey? Can you tell me that please? Can you please tell me where Marie is Aubrey?" Aubrey stops turning the spit, looking up at Veronica with insane, maniacal eyes as if she is surprised to see her standing inside the room in front of her. Either from her split with reality or during her struggle with Jackson she hadn't even noticed that anyone else had come into the room.

"Baby?" Aubrey rasps out in response to Veronica's question. "No baby. Hungry, hungry, hungry." Aubrey begins her chanting once again. Breaking out of his daze Willy moves stealthily over to stand next to Veronica.

"Ronnie, do you see those piled up blankets over there against the wall?" Willy says from just behind her, thankfully coming out of his trance in time to help with this most dire of situations.

"Yes, I see them Willy," Veronica stammers out. Her voice barely above a whisper as she begins to cry at the thought of baby Marie being crumpled up somewhere inside of them cold, hurt, or worse.

"Willy, the blankets... the blankets are covered in blood Willy."

"Hungry, hungry, hungry," Aubrey rasps out tauntingly from her hunched over position hovering above the fire methodically turning the spit. Up and down... up and down. A slight squeak coming from the spit now, caused by the heated metal rubbing together as she turns it, up and down... up and down... squeak... squeak. Veronica takes a cautious step towards the blood covered blankets as Willy takes over the hopeless efforts of trying to get through to the all too clearly and now completely insane Aubrey Bryant.

Veronica reaches the blanket pile and carefully begins to peel the blankets back layer after layer. The feelings of déjà-vu flood her emotions as she remembers Jackson doing the very same thing when she and Holly had brought Marie out to where he sat waiting beneath the pavilion to meet him for the first time.

"WHAT ARE YOU *DOING*?!" Aubrey suddenly begins shrieking at Veronica as she notices her rummaging through the pile of blankets, no longer paying attention to Willy's gentle prodding.

"Hurry up Ronnie!" Willy calls out from the opposite side of the room as he springs into action, trying to grab Aubrey. Veronica begins throwing the layers of blankets back now, no longer worried about being discreet as she hears the shuffling from the struggle going on behind her as Willy does his best to keep Aubrey from getting to her and the pile of blankets. Aubrey's screams turn into an ear-piercing, high-pitched shrieking as she desperately fights against Willy's grasp,

"No attachment! We can't form an attachment!"

Finally, after it seemed like Veronica had searched through every blanket they had at the compound she reaches the bottom. There, laying on the concrete covered in bloody rags, unconscious from trauma and loss of blood she finds the mutilated, bruised, and bloody Marie stubbornly clinging to life.

"Oh, thank you God!" Veronica sobs out loud, finally able to breathe again. Sighing with relief that the child was still alive and that her worst fears hadn't come to fruition as she quickly scoops her up from off the cold, damp floor. Swaddling Marie in the cleanest blanket she can find in the pile she clutches the baby to her chest as she stands up, turning back towards the door. The gunshot that suddenly thunders through the room is deafening in both its volume and magnitude as it reverberates of the walls.

Willy reaches out and grabs the suddenly hysterical Aubrey as she jumps to her feet and begins racing towards the side of the room where Veronica was desperately searching through the blankets. Hearing Veronica call out that she had found Marie and that she was still alive was the last thing Willy heard as Aubrey's head explodes in a shower of gore in front of his eyes, his ears instantly ringing painfully from the deafening crack of the gunshot that came from the doorway behind him. Behind Aubrey on the wall is a splattered self-portrait painted with bits of her brains, blood, and tiny white pieces of her skull. Willy – realizing that he is still holding onto Aubrey's body – suddenly releases her as if he has just touched something that was red hot, allowing Aubrey's now lifeless form to slump to the floor and lay grotesquely at his feet. Veronica walks up yawning purposely trying to get her ears to work again to stand next to Willy, both of them stunned that the furious figure standing in the doorway that greets them is not Jackson… it is **Dylan.** Standing in the doorway crying, still holding and pointing the smoking gun in the direction of the crumpled up, fallen figure of Aubrey as if he had become flash frozen into place and time.

As time sluggishly begins to run again, Veronica rushes over to catch Dylan as he falls into her outstretched arm, utterly exhausted from the expenditure of such extreme emotion and adrenaline.

"It's ok Dylan, it's all going to be ok. Marie is still alive and she's going to be ok. You're going to be ok," Veronica begins telling Dylan. Trying to sooth his anxiety as he openly sobs into her shoulder.

"She was going to hurt Marie! I couldn't let her hurt Marie!"

"I know Dylan, I know. But you saved Marie and she's going to be just fine because of what you did. See…. look here. I have her with me, **with us**, in my other arm. Shush now, it's all over. It's all over now," Veronica says, continuing her efforts to comfort the distraught young man. Willy is finally able to stand upright again after he had collapsed to lean against the wall following the shock of watching Aubrey's head explode and then turning around to find Dylan standing in the doorway. Looking around he realizes that they were the only ones left in the room.

"Ronnie… where's Jackson?" Willy nervously calls out loudly, still trying to get his ears to clear.

Veronica turns to look about the room before finally bringing her eyes back around to rest on Willy. They both are wearing looks of concern and worry on their faces as she questioningly answers,

"I don't know Willy, but I definitely think we need to find out."

Willy's legs feel as if they're stuck in mud as he walks over to help Dylan up off of the floor. He shakes his head from side to side trying to chase away the fog, opening and closing his mouth like a fish gulping for air to ease the incessant ringing in his ears. Picking Dylan up from under the arms he buries his head into Willy's shoulder without a word, continuing his persistent sobbing. Leaning on one another for support they walk out of the back room and exiting the kitchen, come out into the courtyard of the compound. A few steps behind them Veronica holds Marie close to her body doing her best to keep the baby warm. Already thinking about getting to the infirmary so Marie's wound could be properly cleaned, wrapped, and covered. Behind them, forgotten in the mayhem of the moment and left hanging over the now dying fire, hung what was left of Marie's amputated and partially cooked left arm still skewered to the squeaking cooking spit. Aubrey had removed the arm at the shoulder, cauterizing the wound after the procedure was complete so that the baby wouldn't bleed to death. She shudders at the horror that had just played out in the little back room of the community pantry. Veronica walks dazedly behind Willy and Dylan as they enter the courtyard. Lightly she kicks something lying on the floor on her way out. Looking down curiously, Veronica furrows her brow in an attempt to focus her dulled senses on the heavily worn book that was oddly lying on the ground at her feet. Bending over and picking it up she reads the faded words written across the front cover:

"THE JOURNAL OF AUBREY BRYANT. A DETAILED MEMOIR OF THE AFTERLIFE."

Quickly tucking the journal under her arm, Veronica walks hurriedly out of the building trying to catch up to Willy and Dylan who were already sitting beneath the pavilion as the rest of the community begins to gather around them, almost certainly drawn out by the screaming and the gunshot that has just resonated through their little community.

"Be careful who you trust; remember that the devil too was once an angel."

~Unknown

CHAPTER THIRTY-FIVE

Reaching the pavilion Veronica quickly does a head count as Cain and Willy do their best to tend to Dylan, who seems to have unfortunately slipped into a sort of mild shock. No longer crying, he sits silent and monotone as he stares unblinkingly off into the distance. Holly and Sophia rush into the pavilion followed shortly by Lily and Belle who are the last ones to arrive. As Willy quickly fills everyone in on that morning's atrocious and revolting events, both Holly and Sophia rush over to help Veronica tend to Marie.

"Here Ronnie let us help. We need to get her cleaned up and that wound properly dressed to avoid a possible infection," Holly says reaching out for the baby. Veronica, still clutching Marie protectively to her chest looks up vacantly at Holly.

"My god, this poor child. Still so young and innocent yet she has had to endure so much pain and loss already," Sophia says, shrinking back at the sight of the trauma Aubrey had caused to Marie's left arm and shoulder.

"Is this all that we have left to offer a child in this drab version of the world? Is every child that is to be born in this dark and dismal hell only being born to endure pain and suffering?" Holly asks weakly as she openly begins to weep. Pulling her arms back from Veronica who has yet to release Marie to anyone, she steps out from beneath the pavilion to look up into the swirling black sky and whisper,

"Isn't there any hope anymore?"

Falling to kneel in the cold mud Holly places her face into her hands and allows herself to wallow in her own self-pity. Her last words are barely audible as her voice transforms into the squeaky whisper of fractured emotions and heavy sobbing. Coming out of her fog Veronica goes over to kneel beside her awkwardly embracing Holly with her free arm. They kneel there together as Veronica hugs both Holly and Marie in comforting, motherly sympathy doing her best to console Holly and chase her fears away in this epically miserable time of need.

"There is ***always*** hope Holly. As long as we hold on to each another and love each other, there will ***always*** be hope," Veronica whispers into Holly's ear as she strokes her upper arm soothingly.

"Do you really believe that Ronnie?" Holly asks, desperately looking up at Veronica with red, tear stained eyes. "Do you ***Really?***"

"Yes Holly, I really do. I have to. Otherwise what's the point?" Veronica answers as she places a kiss softly on Holly's forehead.

"I have to go and find Jackson now sweetie, will you be ok while I go and do that?" Veronica asks. Then grinning she adds, "You can cuddle with Marie while I'm gone."

"Yes, I'll be ok. Sorry about losing it like that. I just don't understand how someone could do this to something as precious as helpless baby," Holly answers as a fresh stream of tears break from her eyes to roll down her cheeks.

"No apology is necessary. Believe me, I understand exactly what you mean," Veronica says to Holly as she gently lays the sleeping baby into her arms. Then standing up, she readies herself mentally to begin the search for the now missing and undoubtedly distraught Jackson. Walking over to where Willy and Cain were busy with Dylan she hears Holly call out to her back,

"Oh! Hey Ronnie! The girls and I saw Jackson as we were on our way to the pavilion!"

Veronica turns swiftly back towards Holly who was just standing up cradling Marie lovingly to her chest. Trying to hide her annoyance that Holly was just now remembering this little factoid, Veronica questions her trying to pry any more pertinent details from her about their run in with Jackson.

"You did? Did he say anything to you? Could you tell where he might have been headed?"

"No, he didn't say anything. In fact, now that I think about it he never even picked his head up. He just kept staring at the ground and walking fast," Holly says seeming to remember more details about the encounter as she speaks.

"It looked like he was heading to the cemetery, so we didn't really think too much about it at the time," Holly says, shrugging indifferently. "He spends a lot of his time up there sitting next to Gracie."

"OK. Thank you Holly," Veronica says as she turns back around and begins making her way over to Willy. She had an uneasy feeling that she was going to need his help for the second time that morning.

Jackson reaches the cemetery as everyone is gathering at the pavilion and begins to find out about the true monster that had been secretly hiding amongst them, disguised inconspicuously as Aubrey Bryant. Leaning the bundle he was carrying against the trunk of the dead tree next to Gracie's marker, Jackson falls heavily to his knees to kneel in front of the stone.

"I'm so sorry my love. I am so damn sorry that I failed you and our beautiful baby daughter," Jackson cries to Gracie's marker; sobbing and begging her for her forgiveness.

"I thought Aubrey was a sign from you up in the heavens. A sign that you and god were watching over us and that everything was going to be ok," Jackson sobs. "But I was wrong Gracie, I was so terribly wrong. Now Marie is with you in heaven where she belongs. Where she can be safe. And I'm left down here to suffer in the darkness… withered and broken… all alone. I know I don't deserve any better than this, but I can't do it Gracie! I can't survive down here on my own without you, you know that! So now I finally understand what you want me to do. What you always wanted me to do. I now know what you meant when you said we would always be together. I can do it. I want to do it! I will be strong enough. You and Marie will be my strength." Jackson stands up in front of the grave marker and running his left hand down the side of the marker he bends over and kisses the crown of the stone softly whispering, "Everyday" in a play of the ritual that they had shared everyday of their marriage. Then standing up straight he adds, "For all of eternity." Turning, he picks up the bundle he had carried with him up the hill from leaning against the tree. With unwavering determination Jackson steps back and places the barrel of the shotgun into his mouth and pulls the trigger all in one practiced motion.

Veronica and Willy had just begun to make their way up the small hill that leads to the cemetery as the gunshot blasts out loudly to echo through the compound, reverberating through the countryside beyond its protective walls. Jackson's body falls awkwardly backwards to land on its back in the spray of blood and brains that now trailed out behind him to lie lifeless in front of the marker of his one true love. Running now, Veronica and Willy come upon the scene of Jackson's suicide just as the splash of gore settles back to earth. Veronica falls to her knees screaming, kneeling in the mud with her face buried in her hands unable to look at the horror laying on the ground in front of her. Willy stands halfway between Veronica and his fallen friend with slumped shoulders and tear filled eyes, slowly shaking his head from side to side in defeat. Jackson's lower jaw had been entirely removed by the shotgun blast that had almost completely severed his head from his shoulders. Mud and bloody water mix to fill his now hollow skull, rushing to fill the space once occupied by his diluted brain. Jackson's open, dilated eyes stare up into the menacing watchful sky almost as if he is calling out to the lightening that now dances through the clouds to come down and carry him home to be with his lovely wife.

"A cheerful heart is good medicine, but a crushed spirit dries up the bones."

—Proverbs 17:22

CHAPTER THIRTY-SIX

Veronica's nights are no longer peaceful and sleep for her has become a distant, faded memory. As she lays on the cot she has set up in the back room – she won't sleep in the actual bed of their bunker without Clay, it feels to empty without him – she listens to Cain toss and turn through his own demon filled nightmares from inside his room down the hall. She closes her eyes and is welcomed by the insanely sadistic look in Sophia's eyes from this morning when they spoke of eating the wild dogs. She opens her eyes and is greeted by the cold, black, and lonely room of her bunker. She closes her eyes and this time is greeted with the vision of baby Marie's left arm being slowly turned on a spit over open flames while the words "Hungry, hungry, hungry" echo maniacally through her mind over and over again, being muttered in that horribly raspy voice that seems to resonate from everything that is dark and menacing. Her eyes snap open and for a brief moment she almost believes she can hear the words echoing in the shadowy recesses of her own room. On and on the pattern repeats dragging into the night – she closes her eyes and she is met by her dark memories, opens her eyes and she is met by her dark surroundings – until finally, sighing in exasperation and rubbing her sleep deprived eyes, Veronica rolls over and turns on the battery powered lantern that she keeps on the table next to her cot. As the light fills her little section of the room she notices the notebook she had found on the ground coming out of the pantry that fateful morning. Picking it up and looking it over, she picks up the crank handle flashlight she kept next to the lantern and begins turning the handle to give it a charge. Once it is charged she turns on the flashlight, then leaning over and she turns off the lantern to conserve the batteries. Sighing heavily, but acting before she loses her nerve, she pulls back the cover of the journal and apprehensively begins to read:

"The Journal of Aubrey Bryant. A Detailed Memoir of the Aftermath."

Thursday, September 22ND:

It has already been eight days since the volcano erupted so I've decided to write a journal about how life has changed in what we've playfully started calling "the aftermath". The cities have been over run and are in a state of complete chaotic disorder. People are running around everywhere looting and fighting. The military has already began to pull out in most places, leaving everyone still in the city and the surrounding areas to fend for themselves. It seems to me that everyone has gone crazy or something. Just yesterday we watched a group of teenagers beat and gang rape an elderly woman over a gallon jug of water for Christ's sake! Not beer or liquor, but water!! Owen yelled at me because it made me cry. He said I'm going to have to toughen up if I want to survive in the midst of all this calamity. The only place left that still has any semblance of law and order is the FEMA camp the government set up to the west, on the outskirts of town. Owen says we have to stay out of sight and be as inconspicuous as possible; he made me hide while the woman was raped. I felt ashamed for not trying to help.

Saturday, September 24TH:

I begged Owen for us to report to the FEMA camp again this morning. I call tell he's getting aggravated with me over the situation. I just don't get why he insists on believing that we can't go to the FEMA camp, even though the police said over the loud speakers as they drove through town last night that it was the safest place to go! With plenty of food and water for everyone! Owen say's that they're lying and that it's just a place to round everyone up for orderly disposal; "Execution by starvation and dehydration" he keeps saying, "so that the rich elite can have what's left of the

PLANET FOR THEMSELVES." I UNDERSTAND THAT HE'S JUST TRYING TO PROTECT US, BUT ALL OF THAT CONSPIRACY MUMBO JUMBO JUST SEEMS LUDACRIS TO ME. I DON'T THINK HE KNOWS WHAT HE'S TALKING ABOUT. AND NO MATTER HOW HE JUSTIFIES IT, I DON'T LIKE STEALING OUR FOOD FROM OTHER PEOPLE THAT NEED IT JUST AS MUCH AS WE DO.

Veronica flips through the pages, absently skimming over the words. Her thoughts becoming pre-occupied with the vivid memories of the many obstacles her own family had faced during their furious exodus from the city. Stopping at a random, she once again begins to read;

THE FIRST WEEK OF DECEMBER, DAY OF THE WEEK UNKNOWN, IT IS THE 6TH I THINK:

I AWOKE THIS MORNING TO THE SOUND OF PURRING AND THE FEELING OF SOMETHING BUMPING ITSELF AGAINST MY SHOULDER AND NECK. I WAS SURPRISED TO FIND THAT A KITTEN HAD WANDERED INTO THE CAMP DURING THE NIGHT. PROBABLY DRAWN IN BY THE WARMTH OF THE CAMPFIRE AND THE SMELL OF WHAT LITTLE FOOD WE HAD COOKED THE NIGHT BEFORE. IT WAS HARD TO TELL EXACTLY WHAT COLOR IT WAS; IT WAS SO DINGY FROM RUMMAGING THROUGH WHATEVER HELL IT HAD CRAWLED UP OUT OF. NOT TO MENTION MY EYES ALWAYS HURT NOW, THEY NEVER STOPPED BURNING ANYMORE. THE BURNING MADE THINGS BLURRY AND HARD TO MAKE OUT ANY FINE DETAILS IN ANYTHING. IT IS A REAL STRUGGLE JUST TO FOCUS ON MY WRITING, CONCENTRATING MAKES THEM BURN MORE. AND I'VE DEVELOPED A WONDERFULLY NASTY COUGH WHICH MAKES THE BACK OF MY THROAT BURN AS WELL. I HATE IT, IT MAKES ME SOUND LIKE I'M SOME SORT OF OLD BARMAID THAT JUST SMOKED THREE PACKS OF CIGARETTES AT AN EIGHTIES HAIRBAND CONCERT. BUT I'M DIGRESSING, IT WAS NICE TO SEE THAT SOMETHING ELSE WAS SCRATCHING OUT A LIVING (PUN INTENDED) OUT HERE ON THE EDGE OF TOWN BESIDES US.

DECEMBER 10 (?), STILL NOT SURE OF THE DAY:

I HAD TO CHASE THE KITTEN AWAY TODAY, THEN LIE TO OWEN THAT I HADN'T SEEN IT AROUND LATELY. I GOT TIRED OF HEARING HIM TALK ABOUT HOW EVERYONE ELSE THOUGHT THAT WE SHOULD EAT IT. I MEAN I'M HUNGRY

TOO, BUT FOR SOME REASON I JUST COULDN'T BRING MYSELF TO EAT THE KITTEN. I HOPE IT FARES BETTER ON ITS OWN THAN IT WOULD HAVE FARED IF IT HAD STAYED WITH US. OWEN AND CHARLES HAVE BEGUN TO THINK AND SAY CRAZY THOUGHTS AS OUR LITTLE GROUP GROWS MORE AND MORE DESPERATE FOR FOOD AND WATER. CHARLES'S WIFE GRETCHEN LOOKS LIKE SHE IS ABOUT TO GIVE BIRTH AT ANY MOMENT.

UNHAPPY NEW YEAR!

I'VE BEEN THROWING UP EVERY MORNING WHEN I WAKE UP FOR THE PAST WEEK NOW. AT FIRST I THOUGHT IT WAS FROM MY DISGUST AT THE ATROCITIES I HAVE ALLOWED MYSELF TO TAKE PART IN. BUT NOW I KNOW IT IS WHAT I HAVE COME TO FEAR MOST; I AM IN FACT PREGNANT. THE LOOK FROM THE REST OF THE GROUP WAS NOTHING SHORT OF DISTURBING AS THEY ALL REJOICED HUNGRILY AT THE NEWS. THE THOUGHT OF BRINGING MY OWN BABY INTO THIS WORLD WHILE THE TASTE OF GRETCHEN'S STILL LINGERED ON MY PALATE IS ALMOST ENOUGH TO MAKE ME GET SICK AGAIN. BUT SICK OUT OF GUILT OR ANTICIPATION, I CAN'T BE TRUTHFULLY CERTAIN.

Veronica's hand covers her mouth in a weak attempt to cover up her shocked cry of astonishment. Appalled and disgusted at the words contained between the covers of the journal. She backtracks to read a little of what she had previously skipped over, trying to comprehend what exactly went wrong and why. Going back several weeks she reads about how Aubrey and Owen had to hide and fight for food, keeping out of sight whenever possible. She reads about how they stumbled upon Charles and his wife Gretchen hiding in a dilapidated old storage unit behind a convenience store. Then about how Owen had convinced her that they were like-minded people and about how he felt that they would stand a better chance of survival if they joined forces. Then she read about how they had killed and eaten their first victim. Then about how cannibalism had become a mainstay in the little band of survivors' diet. Even birthing and eating their own young in horrific infanticide, growing jubilant at any news of pregnancy. Then she reads about how they purposefully sought out and hunted victims that were pregnant to add to their food storages as they slipped further and further down into the depths of insanity. She reads about how Charles teaches them to be patient, only cutting-off and eating certain parts of the victims at a time. Then about cauterizing the wounds as you cut, significantly lengthening the time that the food source would survive as they literally ate their victims' alive, piece by agonizing piece. She finds a passage about how they had been forced to cut off and eat their own non-essential fingers and toes when times became extremely lean. Veronica wonders how they chose which fingers or toes were "non-essential" as she reads what Aubrey says about how the sealing of the wound had in fact hurt more than actually cutting off the digit in the first place. Crying uncontrollably, Veronica lays the open book down to rest against her chest unable to continue as she desperately fights to get her sobbing under control. All the while the smell of Marie's arm cooking over the fire pit invades her senses as the words Hungry, hungry, hungry, echo over and over again, accompanying the repulsive smell of burning flesh that will forever remain within her nightmares.

Sickened to the point of nausea by the horrors written about inside the journal, Veronica pinches the bridge of her nose in a futile attempt to further dam up the flow of tears that run down her cheeks in steady streams to hide inside of her ears or land to dry up on the surface of her pillow. With steeled reserve, she sighs heavily and forces herself to pick the journal back up and continue reading; thumbing quickly through to the last few pages of entries. Not wanting to know, but ***needing*** to know exactly what the hell happened out in the wilds that could create something like Aubrey Bryant and her demented companions. A change in the heading grabs her attention so she stops flipping and once again bravely enters the world of the desperately insane;

<u>**DAY THREE OF THE AFTERLIFE**</u>

OWEN AND CHARLES MANAGED TO KILL A DOG YESTERDAY! THEN IN A MORBIDLY, IRONIC TWIST THE DAMN THING WAS ACTUALLY PREGNANT! MY CHEEKS AND SIDE WERE BURNING FROM LAUGHTER AS WE ALL COOKED UP OUR VERY OWN PUPPY! CHARLES KEPT CALLING THEM PUPPY SKEWERS, LIKE THEY WERE SOME SORT OF APPETIZER, MAKING US ALL LAUGH THAT MUCH

HARDER. IT WAS THE BEST NIGHT'S SLEEP THAT I COULD REMEMBER HAVING IN A VERY LONG TIME. FEELING DRUNK WITH A BELLY FULL OF PUPPY, I FELL ASLEEP SITTING UP WITH MY BACK PROPPED UP AGAINST THE WALL OF THE TOP FLOOR APARTMENT WE HAVE CURRENTLY SET-UP TO USE AS OUR HOME. WITH THE HEAT OF THE FIRE CHASING AWAY THE CHILL IT WAS REALLY QUITE COMFORTABLE. IT'S BEEN THREE DAYS NOW SINCE THEY TOOK THE BABY FROM ME. I DON'T KNOW IF I WILL EVER BE ALLOWED TO HOLD HIM IN MY ARMS AGAIN.

DAY SIX OF THE AFTERLIFE

IT IS GETTING COLDER AS THE NIGHTS TICK BY, ONE RUNNING INTO ANOTHER. THE DOG HAS PROVEN TO BE A LASTING AND PLENTIFUL FOOD SOURCE OVER THE PAST FEW DAYS. CHARLES SAYS THAT WE COULD BE ENTERING INTO ANOTHER ICE AGE. BUT CHARLES SAYS A LOT, MOST OF IT I'VE COME TO REALIZE IS BULLSHIT. LIKE WHEN HE AND OWEN TOOK THE BABY AWAY FROM ME AND GAVE IT TO GRETCHEN TO NURSE. HE SAID IT WAS BETTER THAT WAY, TO AVOID THE CHANCE OF ME FORMING AN ATTACHMENT TO IT. 'IT' IS HOW WE ALL REFER TO THE BABY. CHARLES SAID THERE WAS NO NEED TO GIVE IT A NAME, ALTHOUGH OWEN ALMOST FELL THROUGH THE FLOOR FROM LAUGHING WHEN HE SAID THAT WE ALL SHOULD JUST CALL IT CUPCAKE BECAUSE HE WAS SURE IT WAS GOING TO TASTE SO DAMN SWEET. I DIDN'T THINK IT WAS ALL THAT FUNNY. EVERYONE LAUGHED EXCEPT ME. THE FLOOR OF THE APARTMENT IS BADLY DAMAGED FROM A PREVIOUS FIRE AND CHARLES MENTIONED THAT WE MAY HAVE TO MOVE TO ANOTHER APARTMENT SOON BECAUSE THIS ONE IS BECOMING TOO UNSTABLE. MAYBE OWEN WILL HAVE AN ACCIDENT AND FALL THROUGH FIRST. MAYBE BREAKING HIS LEG OR EVEN BETTER HIS BACK TO DIE IN SLOW, AGONIZING PAIN. A GIRL CAN HAVE A FINAL WISH, CAN'T SHE? OH, AND I WOULD HAVE CALLED THE BABY WILLIAM I THINK. AFTER MY GRANDFATHER. IN ANOTHER TIME, IN ANOTHER WORLD. YES, I WOULD HAVE CALLED HIM WILLIAM.

DAY SEVEN OF THE AFTERLIFE

THE BABY DOESN'T CRY ANY MORE, I THINK CHARLES CUT TOO MUCH OFF OF IT LAST NIGHT IN DESPERATION. I WONDER CURIOUSLY IF IT'S STILL ALIVE.

GRETCHEN WON'T LET ME SEE IT. AND THE SMOKED JERKY THEY MADE FROM THE DOG WITH THE PUPPIES IS ALMOST GONE NOW TOO. OWEN SAID HE KEPT HEARING SOMETHING FOLLOWING HIM WHEN HE WAS LOOKING THREW SOME OF THE OTHER APARTMENTS IN THE BUILDING EARLIER. HE AND CHARLES HAVE SET UP TRAPS AROUND THE PERIMETER JUST IN CASE SOMEONE WAS GOING TO ATTACK US. THE BOOBY-TRAPS LOOK MORE UNSAFE TO ME THAN ANY BANDITS MIGHT BE THOUGH.

DAY NINE OF THE AFTERLIFE

THE DOGS CONTINUE TO FOLLOW ME NON-STOP, PERSISTENT AND VENGEFUL. I HID INSIDE OF AN ABANDONED VAN YESTERDAY SO I COULD GET SOME REST. I'M COMPLETELY OUT OF THE CITY NOW AND MOVING DEEPER INTO THE WOODS. WHEN THE DOGS ATTACKED US THEY SET OFF THE BOOBY-TRAPS, COLLAPSING THE FLOOR OF THE APARTMENT CRUSHING CHARLES AND GRETCHEN. I WANTED TO HEAR THE CRY OF A BABY SO THAT I COULD RESCUE WILLIAM, BUT THE CRY NEVER CAME SO I JUST STARTED RUNNING, TRYING TO GET AWAY. I WAS SITTING BY MYSELF WHEN EVERYTHING HAPPENED SO I WAS LUCKY ENOUGH TO ESCAPE LANDING UNDER ANY FALLING DEBRIS. THE FLOOR FELL THROUGH ALL FIVE STORIES IN A TANGLED MASS OF BURNT TIMBERS, OLD FURNITURE AND CONCRETE. I COULD HEAR SOME OF THE DOGS WHO MUST HAVE ALSO GOTTEN HURT, YELPING AND WHINING AS IT ALL FELL.... AND OWEN. I COULD HEAR OWEN. CALLING FOR HELP, CALLING FOR ME. THEN I HEARD HIM SCREAMING AS HE WAS ATTACKED BY THE SURVIVING DOGS, BECOMING THEIR NEXT MEAL. I THINK THAT FROM NOW ON IN MY MEMORIES AND IN MY JOURNAL, I WILL HEREAFTER REFER TO HIM AS CUPCAKE. BECAUSE TO THE DOGS, I'M SURE HE TASTED SOOOO DAMN SWEET.

DAY TEN OF THE AFTERLIFE

I FOUND A TRAIL TODAY THAT RUNS ALONG THE SIDE OF THE MOUNTAIN BEFORE I CAME BACK TO HIDE INSIDE THE VAN AGAIN. WHAT REMAINS OF THAT DAMNED DOG PACK SHADOWS MY EVERY STEP AS SOON AS I LEAVE MY HIDING PLACE, WAITING FOR AN OPPORTUNITY TO POUNCE WITH EERIE PATIENCE. ON A HOPEFUL NOTE, THE TRAIL SHOWED A LOT OF SIGNS OF BEING USED RECENTLY. I AM SO THIRSTY AND HUNGRY! MAYBE I'LL FOLLOW THE TRAIL TOMORROW,

NO HARM IN SEEING WHERE IT LEADS. IT CAN'T BE ANY WORSE THAN HOW I'M LIVING NOW. NOTHING IS WORSE THAN BEING HUNTED. BESIDES, HELL IS HELL. WHOSE HELL – THEIRS OR MINE…. IS **IRRELEVANT.** I WONDER IF THERE WILL BE A BABY AMONGST THEM….

"Are you Ok mom?" Cain's words filter into the room from the dark recesses of the hallway that leads into the sitting room. Veronica is so taken aback by Cain's manifestation out of thin air that she emits a small, startled yelp out of her shock and surprise. She had been so focused on the journal that she hadn't even heard him get up or make his way down the short hallway to stand in the doorway to the room.

"Damn it Cain! You startled me," Veronica stammers, visibly shaken up from the fright.

"Sorry." Cain says rubbing his face roughly. "Where's Dylan?"

"It's ok bud, and yes I'm ok. Dylan stayed at Jackson and Gracie's old bunker with Sophia and Lily to make it easier to care for Marie. Thank you for checking on me." She hadn't realized she'd been crying, much less sobbing hard enough to disturb her fifteen-year-old son that for the most part, still slept with the sound luxury of teenage innocence.

"Oh, ok. Are you sure you're alright? I could hear you crying from down the hall in my room," Cain asks, his voice still groggy from sleep. Veronica shivers coldly as it momentarily reminds her of Aubrey's own deep and raspy voice.

"Yes honey I'm sure. I couldn't sleep so I was just reading a little. I hoped that it would help me to relax. Turns out I should have made my choice of literature a little better. I read some things that caused me to get upset is all. I'll be fine," she answers.

"What are you reading?" Cain asks, yawning widely.

"A book I stumbled on this morning that needs to be thrown away."

"Oh… Well maybe you shouldn't read any more of it if it's going to keep upsetting you," Cain says as he turns around and heads back down the hall to his room and fall back into bed. Falling back to sleep again almost as soon as his head hits the pillow. Veronica feels a slight touch of envy at her son's ability to fight through his nightmares and find the sweet bliss of sleep so effortlessly. She lets out an exasperated sigh and closes the journal of Aubrey Bryant for the last time, laying it face down on the table next to her cot. She lays there thinking about the words she has just read and revisiting the tragic events that have occurred at the compound over the last few weeks. Sighing sadly, she wipes what remains of the tears from her face, completely giving up on any chance of sleep. She knows that any attempts to sleep now would be nothing more than a pointless waste of time and effort. Frustrated and exhausted Veronica gets out of bed to get an early start to her day, struggling to forget the disturbing images still playing out inside of her thoughts. She hopes that a nice, hot cup of coffee and a warm, roaring fire will go a long way in helping her do exactly that.

Cain's dream picks back up with the same vivid intensity that it had before he had woken up to hear his mother crying down the hall. He re-enters the dream right where it had left off like he had never even gotten out of bed at all. It's the morning of his thirteenth birthday and he jumps out of bed excitedly. Overwhelmed with the pride that he wasn't a little kid anymore, not after today. Today he was a teenager! As he comes out of his bedroom the smell of his mom's famous buttermilk pancakes fills the house, making him instantly hungry and his stomach rumble in happy anticipation. He flies into the kitchen and jumps up into one of the barstools that line the island.

"Well, good morning sleepy head! Happy Birthday son!" Clay says smiling, looking at him from over the top of the Sunday morning newspaper.

"Leave him alone Clay, besides it's only noon," Veronica says sarcastically as she sets a plate of the steaming fresh pancakes down next to the butter and maple syrup in front of Cain. She gives him a wink and roughs up his hair before she turns back around to face the stove once again.

"Mom, don't do that. I'm not a kid anymore," Cain says embarrassed, quickly trying to smooth his hair back down.

"Oh really? I wasn't made aware of any such changes. And mothers are usually the first to know of such important evolutions in the stages of their children's lives. Let's see, I think I need to investigate this further; Clay? Clay honey were you aware of these rather interesting changes in our little Cain and that henceforth he is to no longer to be considered 'a kid'?" Veronica asks jokingly.

"Nope, that is news to me. How about you Levi?"

"What?" Levi asks, not even bothering to look up from his smart phone.

"Excuse us son. I'm sorry, but is being an active member of this family interrupting your texting time? Your father asked you if you were aware of your brother no longer being a kid," Veronica states sternly to Levi with more than a little edge to her voice.

"Uh, I'm sorry. No ma'am I didn't know anything about it either," Levi stutters, laying his phone face down on the table and placing his hands in his lap. A teenager's subtle showing of surrender, almost like he is saying 'See I promise I won't touch it again' with the gesture. Cain rolls his eyes irritated at the silly banter being played out between his family members.

"Ha-Ha-Ha, you guys are *soooo* funny. *NOT!*"

"Well, Mister I'm not a kid anymore, why don't you take that bag of trash out to the can for your ol' mom," Clay says playfully. "Awe man really? I'm not finished with my pancakes yet!" Cain whines. "True, but only kids get to finish their pancakes before doing their mother a favor, teenagers have to do the favor first." Clay grins as Cain places the fork down next to his plate and goes to take out the trash, shuffling his feet and pouting the entire way to the garage door. As Cain opens the door to go outside, he notices a box sitting on the ground. Huffing with annoyance he bends down to pick the box up so that he can carry it to the recycling bin. Picking it up lazily he feels something inside the box shift and then.... was that whining? Confused and curious, he quickly sets the box back down onto the garage floor opening it quickly. Inside he finds a black and white Alaskan malamute puppy with silver tips on its fur and bright blue eyes, a blue bow tied around his collar. The puppy sits back on his haunches and looks up at Cain, letting out a single yip followed by another soft whine. Cain places his hands inside the box and lifts the puppy out, holding him in front of his face to read the writing on the bow – Happy Birthday Cain! Take good care of him, we love you! Mom and Dad. – As he finishes reading the note the puppy sticks out its tongue and licks him on the nose. The bond is secured with that one simple gesture of love and faith. Jumping up, hugging the puppy Cain turns to run back into house. "Mom, Dad!" He yells as he comes through the doorway to find his parents and his brother standing there waiting for him, smiling. "Happy birthday buddy," Clay says happily as soon as Cain steps into the room. "He better not chew up any of my X-Box cables birthday dork," Levi says smiling. Bending over to rub the puppy between the ears. "Levi, stop being a bully. What are you going to name him Cain?" Veronica asks. "I can name him anything I want?" Cain asks with surprised excitement. "Yep, he's all yours buddy. You can name him anything you want to," Clay says walking over to pet the puppy. "Within reason!" Veronica quickly adds holding up her hand in the air palm towards her three 'boys'. "Nothing dirty or gross." Levi and Clay laugh loudly as Cain places to puppy down for the first time to run around and play. "Thank you Dad! Thank you Mom! He's awesome!" Cain exclaims. "You are very welcome. I think your mom picked some toys out for him if you want to go grab them from out of the car. I think she left them sitting on the backseat," Clay says, smiling warmly at his son. "Ok Dad!" Cain answers, beaming as he turns and runs out of the house and into the garage to grab the bag out of his mother's car. Levi has rolled the puppy over onto his back and is rubbing his belly when Cain comes back into the room. Seeing how happy the puppy was and how happy everyone else was around the puppy he finds himself uttering almost accidentally, "Buddy. I think I'll name him Buddy."

Cain awakes with a start, jumping almost completely out of his bed from the dreams powerful realism. He can't believe he has started having this stupid dream again. He angrily wipes away the tear that had escaped his eye to roll down his cheek. Sitting up in bed he notices that the light beside his mom's cot was turned off. He nodded to himself about how he was glad that she was finally been able to get some sleep. He however, was giving up on sleep for this night. Every time he closed his eyes all he could see was Buddy, then and now. He wasn't tired anymore anyhow. His mind was too jumbled and confused, going back and forth between the sickening memories of the dog attack and the happy memories of his birthday. He struggles with the painful memory of accidentally leaving Buddy behind, tied to a stump in the backyard with a blue nylon rope. His eyes snap open with the sudden memory of the blue rope! He had to know. Standing up he gets dressed as quickly and as quietly as he possible. One way or another he had to know if that dog was really Buddy, no matter what troubles the consequences might hold. Walking to the front of the bunker with newfound determination, Cain shrugs on his coat and steps out into the cold, disappearing into the dark with long purposeful strides.

"To think that the specter you see is an illusion does not rob him of his terrors...."

-*C. S. Lewis*

CHAPTER THIRTY-SEVEN

YEAR ONE, DAY THREE HUNDRED AND TWENTY-NINE

Veronica makes her way up the hill with the rest of the current members present at the compound with her left arm locked around Sophia's, her right arm locked around Holly's, it gave the funeral march a melancholy 18th century nostalgic look. Sophia has become too sullen and morose to cry any longer. With everything that has happened at the compound in the past week climaxing for her with the loss of Rose, an event that has sent her views of their existence after the eruption on a steady downgrade towards absolute pessimism. Holly, who has slipped into a sort of mild shock over the last week's string of horrific events, walks up the hill stiff legged and perfectly upright. Her face pale and blank, she wears the glum mask of disbelief and doubt. Lily carries the sleeping Marie in a sling across her chest as she walks hand in hand with Belle just behind the trio of women in morose silence with their heads tilted towards the ground out of both respect and sadness. Cain, Dylan, and Willy -the recently designated gravediggers of the compound – are already at the cemetery waiting on the procession to arrive so that they can, yet again, commit another beloved member of their community to the ground. The fact that there is only one open gravesite is not lost on Veronica as she curiously looks around for another open site.

Dylan quickly walks over to stand with Lily and Marie as soon as the procession arrives and assumes its ritualistic position around the open gravesite that was soon to be filled with the body of the late Jackson

Scott. Lily looks up and smiling at Dylan she knowingly hands Marie over to the protector that destiny had mercifully provided for the recently made orphan. Dylan took the responsibility willingly with great pride and affection for the child. In his mind he was finally given the opportunity to be the big brother he knew in his heart he was always supposed to be. Dylan cradles the tiny infant close to his chest and smiling down at Lily silently mouthing the words "thank you" to her. Lily's slight blush is the only indication that it's not just for the sake of Marie and Belle that she has so enthusiastically stepped into her role of compound Nanny. Their attention is soon drawn away from each other however as Willy begins the eulogy for their fallen friend. Dylan stands up straighter with his chin held high as he is filled with the pride of knowing that he will do everything in his power to provide the life for Marie that Jackson had been too weak to provide for her. As Willy asks everyone to bow their heads for the opening prayer Lily offers her hand to Dylan. With closed eyes and bowed heads Dylan readily accepts the offered hand, inside he can't help but to smile, blushing in the recognition of their fast-growing feelings for one another.

"Thank you for coming everyone. Today we gather together yet again under the prescience of the creator to sadly lay to rest another one of our own." Willy says, addressing everyone after the opening prayer has been completed. Every eye concentrates on Willy as they all do their best to avoid looking at the body of Jackson that has been lovingly wrapped in a decorative cloth but is still lying next to the open grave waiting to be lowered into its final resting place.

"It seems to me, that we have been filling far too many holes in the ground with the bodies of our loved ones here lately. Although I think Jackson's death presents us with a new form of sadness. Because in spite of everything this world had already thrown at him, in the face of everything that he had already had to endure; the world finally succeeded in driving Jackson over the edge." Willy pauses to catch his breath and to wipe at his eyes and nose with a handkerchief before continuing.

"How many times in our lives has it driven us all to that very same edge? A hundred? *A thousand?* But for most of us, we are fortunate enough to find the strength within ourselves or within our bond with one other, to keep us from letting it topple us over. For Jackson… that strength was found within Gracie and Marie. After Gracie was taken from him that strength was placed solely on Marie. When he thought that he had failed Marie by allowing her into the hands of a deranged psychopath as far as Jackson was concerned all of his sources for strength left in this world were gone." Willy looks up into the eyes of all his friends that were gathered around him one by one.

"So today we yet again, before almighty god and the damned devil that brought us here, once more commit a soul to the seemingly insatiable darkness that blankets us in its despair." Willy falls silent for a moment, allowing the silence to settle in heavily around them, doing its part to feed the groups growing feelings of sadness, doubt, and desolation. The darkness pairs with the silence seamlessly, recognizing and seizing an opening to tighten its icy grip even further on the hearts of the community that it has long held within its cold and lifeless left hand. Its right hand is kept squarely placed on their backs, waiting for the right opportunity to push as they all stand fretfully looking over the edge into the abyss.

Willy begins to speak again just in time to hold the darkness at bay, bringing shuddering sighs of relief from everyone except Sophia and Cain. Sighing himself and drawing in a large breath Willy begins to read from the open bible he was holding,

"For as much as it has pleased Almighty God, of his great mercy to take unto himself the soul of our dear brother Jackson here departed, we therefore commit his body to the ground; Earth to Earth, ashes to ashes, dust to dust; in sure and certain hope of the resurrection of eternal life through our lord Jesus Christ." Finishing the eulogy prayer Willy takes another breath before asking the gathered group "Whose father?" The group answers the question in chorus as they all begin the final prayer of the funeral service, saying it together as one voice, rising above the cold, dark wind the whistled through the willow's dead branches, and the choking dreariness,

"Our Father, who art in heaven. Hallowed be thy name. Thy kingdom come, thy will be done, on earth as it is in heaven. Give us this day our daily bread and forgive us our trespasses as we forgive those that trespass against us. Lead us not into temptation, but deliver us from evil. For thine is the kingdom, the power, and the glory, forever and ever. Amen."

The group breaks up slowly and begins to filter back either to their homes or to the tasks of their daily chores. Veronica hurries over to Willy and Cain who have already begun the unwanted responsibility of lowering Jackson's body down into the grave.

"Thank you Willy. That was a beautiful eulogy. I think Jackson would have appreciated it."

"Yeah, well I'd rather someone else be giving it. Or better yet, to not be giving it at all." Is Willy's only response as he bends over to retrieve the shovel that was discretely placed out of sight behind the skeleton of a dead, but still standing, tree.

"I know. Me too." Veronica pats him on his forearm as she turns to make her way down the hill toward the pavilion to begin preparing breakfast and more coffee for everyone. Stopping halfway down, her curiosity finally getting the best of her, she turns and shouts back up the hill,

"Hey Willy, how come there's only one open grave?" Willy stops with a spade full of dirt hanging over Jackson's body, turns and looks down the hill to stare at Veronica, meeting her gaze as he answers emotionally.

"Because that devil's whore doesn't deserve to be buried up here alongside our family and friends that's why."

"Fair enough," Veronica says nodding her head in agreement. "But then what are we going to do with her body?" Willy's demeanor turns calloused and dark as he turns away from Veronica. Wearing a slight maniacal smirk, he drops the hovering spade of dirt to land sickly on top of his deceased friend calling back over his shoulder,

"We're going to treat her just like she was going to treat baby Marie."

"We are **NOT** going to eat her Willy?!" Veronica asks shocked.

"No Ronnie, we're not going to eat her. I suffer from enough indigestion already," Willy says sarcastically. Then turning back to face Veronica, brooding once more, he states flatly; "**We're going to burn that bitch.**"

The funeral pyre for Aubrey Bryant had been unceremoniously lit and is in full blaze as Cain secretly slips out of the compound. He hurries to sit and wait with his back resting against a large rock nestled inside the woods about seventy-five yards off of the main path to the water station. Waiting, he catches a low slinking form out of the corner of his eye as it seems to slither up towards him from the deepest recesses of the black menacing darkness that covers the dead wilderness surrounding them. A low raspy cough followed by a mixture of hurtful whining and menacing growling comes from the form as it inches closer and closer to the outstretched hand holding the offered meal.

"Come here boy, its ok. I won't hurt you again. I'm sorry about before but I didn't know it was you," Cain says, prodding the form to come ever closer. Again, a low soft mixture of raspy breathing and growling escapes the form as it slithers up on its belly to rest just out of the reach of the boy's outstretched arm. Getting down on one knee Cain goes the final half yard to meet the slinking malnourished form of a dog. Ravenously snatching the small, burnt babies arm from Cain's hand the demonic form rushes back into the darkness to eat at its leisure. Resting within the comfortable embrace of the black that it has grown all to accustomed to.

CHAPTER THIRTY-EIGHT

Veronica stands hypnotized by the dying embers of the final contribution Aubrey would ever offer to the compound; A four-hour circle of light and warmth as the cleansing flames rid the world of the vessel that a blackened soul had once used in its animated form to commit haunting and horrific acts. Acts of atrocities that now keep Veronica awake at night as they run through her head stealing away any real chance she had of ever getting a peaceful night's sleep again while Clay was away. Acts committed to children. To the sick members of their party. To the scared and desperate they had met along the road. To their babies. Acts that this vile soul can no longer commit against anyone in this world. A .45 caliber bullet placed through her brain by Dylan had seen to that. The fire set by Willy had taken care of the rest. Veronica shivers as she looks down at the journal she is holding and the nightmares that she knows are contained within its pages. She lightly tosses the despicable manuscript into the center of the smoldering embers and watches as it slowly catches fire. Burning away all the evidence and written memories of how truly lost and evil some human beings are capable of becoming. As the flames devouring the journal reach their zenith, Veronica shudders coldly once more and turns away from the final resting place of the desperately insane and cannibalistic Aubrey Bryant for the last time. With ghostly timing the wind begins to swirl, fittingly spreading out her ashes to mix with those that had already fallen from the volcano.

Veronica somberly makes her way back towards the pantry, dreading the awful job of cleaning up the mess left behind from yesterday mornings twisted and deplorable events. As she rounds the corner of the pavilion she notices that it looked as if someone had been out here not too long ago sitting around the fire pit. The evidence left behind in the form of a dirty cup and a bundle of blood covered rags. Scowling to herself she examines the items perplexed. She can't shake the haunted feeling that overwhelms her as she walks a little faster toward the gore coated kitchen. She can't help but to feel that something akin to a poisonous cloud of misfortune had begun to settle over them all like a dense fog creeping up from the sea to lie heavily upon the beach. Thick and menacing, fear and distrust ebbing out from the swirling mist in twisted tendrils of evil threatening to penetrate every crack and crevice of the compound. She begins to shiver as she breaches the doorway to the kitchen, either from the cold or the uncomfortable atmosphere that presently shrouds them in its punishing uncertainty Veronica can't be sure which. Finally reaching her destination she huffs out a heavy cleansing sigh and timidly approaches the door to the pantry. Gathering up all of the remaining courage she can muster, she hesitantly pushes it open revealing the interior.

Holly stands in the center of the room with her back to the door, hands placed firmly on her hips. Hearing the door swing open she turns to see Veronica standing in the doorway.

"Oh Holly! Thank god…You scared me to death," Veronica chuckles nervously placing her hand on her chest above where her heart should be. Letting out an exasperated sigh of relief as she sees that it's only Holly standing there and not the demon she had envisioned waiting for her inside the blood-stained room waiting to devour her soul. Holly wears the mask of disappointment and regret as she addresses the state of the room.

"I thought I'd come here early. I saw you standing out by the pyre and you… I don't know, you just looked so *sad*. I thought since I didn't do anything to help yesterday I could at least come in here and get started cleaning up for everybody today," Holly says looking at Veronica. With a slight, dismissive shrug she adds,

"I was hoping that I could help anyway, but it looks like you already beat me to it."

"What? I didn't clean this up. When I walked in and saw you in here I thought you did," Veronica answers with more than a hint of confusion in her voice, "I was about to thank you for doing it."

"It wasn't me. I wish it had been. I don't feel like I've been much help around here lately. With the whole Gracie thing, then the attack on the girls, and now…" Holly pauses, fighting back tears as she spins in a circle raising her hands to the room, "this."

"No Holly, everything is fine. I promise. You have Belle to worry about. We all understand that."

Freeing herself from the initial shock of finding someone already in the room, she walks over to Holly, hugging her sympathetically.

"How is Belle healing up by the way?" Veronica asks Holly as she pulls away from the hug.

"I wish I knew," Holly huffs, sadly dropping her head to gaze at the ground shuffling her feet anxiously. Veronica doesn't say anything; she just gives Holly that "what are you talking about" look that all mothers characteristically seem to possess.

"Belle doesn't want much to do with me these days. She spends most of her time trailing after Lily. That was another reason I thought I could get in here and get everything cleaned up before anyone else woke up. Belle is asleep at Sophia's with Lily," Holly shares, the stress apparent in her voice at no longer being the shining light in her daughter's eyes was heavy and sad.

"Try to understand Holly, Belle and Lily have just shared a deeply traumatic event. Lily is like her security blanket right now that's all. It's just a phase, she'll bounce back before you know it. Children are nothing if not resilient, she'll come back around to you. I'm sure of it," Veronica says hoping to raise Holly's spirits. Memories of how the people in the journal had treated their children played through her head once more like the pin stuck in the temple of a voodoo doll, bringing forth the troubled memories with every new twist. Veronica closes her eyes trying to fight back the demons she had unexpectedly discovered hiding within the pages of Aubrey's journal. Realizing at that moment that even after the cleansing of the burning, that the demons would haunt her in her thoughts and dreams forever.

"Come on sweetie, let's go get a cup of coffee. I put some on to brew before I came over here. I know I can definitely use a cup or three," Veronica says smiling, then taking Holly by the hand she gently begins to lead her out of the room.

"Now that you mention it… so could I," Holly sighs allowing herself to be led away from the horrible little back room and its sinister memories. As the two friends cross over the thresh hold they both turn and give the room one last look.

"I wonder if we should just board this room up. We don't really use it that much anyway," Holly says noticeably trembling as she speaks.

"Funny…. I was just thinking the exact same thing," Veronica agrees pulling Holly in close once more. "Let's talk to Willy about it later this morning, see what he thinks about it." They turn and close the door to the room for the last time. Moments later as the two are walking arm in arm towards the pavilion, a light rain begins to fall playing nature's incantation that everything is going to be ok.

CHAPTER THIRTY-NINE

The rain has begun to fall more heavily now, slapping against the windshield in big fat drops as Ray leads the convoy up and over the last hill that leads them to the compound. He struggles to make out the turnoff for the trail from the main road now that it is set against the colorless backdrop of the grey, rain soaked mountain. Visible land marks are a convenient thing of the past amongst an erased landscape. Straining against the dark and rain Ray desperately tries to find the marker he and Clay had set up to mark the trail-head. Motoring cautiously along he is haunted by the labored breathing of his dying friend from the seat behind him. He remembers the difficulties they had finding the turnoff to the trail the last time they returned from a scavenging sortie and about their hike back out to the main road with Levi and Cain to build the landmark. Ray sighs at the memories of his friend, who's ever worsening breathing stands out even among the sounds of the rain and the engines. If breathing is what you could call it. His labored breaths going in and out more as ragged gasps than breathing and have grown countable seconds apart. Ray knows that it's only a matter of time before his friend stops taking breaths all together now – ragged or otherwise. The race he is in against time and death to get Clay back home to his family before he passes adds more pressure to the already volatile situation of getting home safely. Wiping away the sweat that has beaded up on his brow Ray glances in the rearview mirror at Levi cradling his father against him in an attempt to make what were probably his final moments as comfortable as he can. Ray is thankful that Levi chose to ride with them instead of with Paige when they packed up camp and got started towards home this morning. As the muddy turnoff to the trailhead finally manifests itself like a beacon of hope standing out against the darkness, Ray's sigh is audible even over the cacophony of the heavy rain that beats down heavily on the roof of the truck. The welcomed sound of tires over mud instead of asphalt soon adds its voice to the incantation that sings them home.

"We found it," Jim points out from the passenger seat, letting out his own huge sigh of relief. Ray is so deep in the midst of the contradicting thoughts of being happy at finally being home and being distraught at the news he is bringing home with him, that he doesn't even respond to Jim's declaration. Making their way little by little, but steadily up the trail the headlights of the vehicles cut a path for them through the darkness of the mountainside. The butterflies inside Ray's belly gradually begin turning into vultures as the words come from behind him that he has been dreading for the past two days now.

"I don't think we're going to make it in time Ray. My dad isn't breathing anymore."

Ray had been so lost in his own thoughts that he hadn't realized that Levi was right. Clay's labored breathing no longer filled the car.

"Are you sure Levi? I mean ***absolutely*** sure?" Jim asks turning around to check Clay's wrist for a pulse. A task that proves impossible inside of the truck as it bucks and twists down the rugged trail towards home.

"Damn it we're almost......" The look of grief on Levi's face as he sadly stares at Jim causes him to let his last statement trail off unfinished in the stale air of the truck.

"Yes, I'm sure," Levi says as he turns his gaze from Jim back to his father. From the driver's seat Ray is unable to speak, his own sorrow and regret for his friend crippling his voice.

CHAPTER FORTY

Veronica jumps up from her position of hovering above the fire as she was setting up the coffee percolator to begin a fresh pot for her and Holly. Looking quizzically in Holly's direction she asks excitedly,

"Did you hear that?"

Holly, who had slipped back into a state of being somewhere between being awake and going back to sleep, looks up groggily,

"What? I'm sorry Ronnie did you say something?"

"SHHH, listen Holly. Do you hear that?" Veronica asks as she takes an eager step towards the edge of the pavilion. Concentrating Holly strains to make out what Veronica is hearing above the noise of the now heavily falling rain and the popping logs within the fire pit. Then Holly too begins to hear what has gotten Veronica so excited. She looks up at her and for the first time in a week she has hope in her eyes excitedly exclaiming,

"The trucks! Oh my god Ronnie, I can hear the trucks!"

Holly jumps up and rushes towards the front gate of the compound almost knocking Veronica down in the process. Veronica can't stop herself from smiling as she follows Holly's lead and takes off running for the gate only a few steps behind her. Willy emerges from his hobbit hole just in time to see Holly and Veronica streak by its opening,

"Whoa! Hey girls where's the fire?" Willy asks, startled by the unexpected sight of the sprinting females that greeted him first thing this morning before he even had a chance to wake up.

"The trucks Willy! We hear the trucks!" Veronica and Holly both shout back over their shoulders in chorus to Willy.

"What?! Really! Hey, slow down and wait for me!" Willy shouts happily at their backs. Unable to contain the smile that breaks out across his face as he falls in line behind Veronica happily taking his place in line as the newest happy member of the compounds make shift welcome home committee. In spite of -or maybe because of- all that has happened over the last week since the scavenging group left the compound on a supply run, the trio can't help but to be ecstatic over the return of their family and friends. As much as they needed the supplies that the group was undoubtedly bringing home with them and the aid they would provide for the compound, it was the stress their return erased that brought the most joy and relief to the group that now ran to greet them.

Veronica runs right into the back of Holly as she comes barreling around the corner of the washrooms, running along the path that leads to the front gate. Holly had stopped so suddenly that the momentum of Veronica was almost enough to take them both to the ground. Willy's momentum however was another story as he slams into the back of Veronica who was holding up Holly taking all three of them down to land clumsily in the mud, a loud "HMMPF" escapes as they hit the ground hard and slide in an almost comical shower of muddy water.

"Damn it! Why did y'all stop like that? We're still twenty-five yards from the gate entrance!" Willy exclaims as he begins shaking mud off the palms of his hands and coat.

"Willy..." Veronica whispers, "Please be quiet."

"What? Why?" Willy asks grumpily before looking up from rubbing the mud off of his pants to see Holly and Veronica staring at the two trucks that were now parked inside the compound. The group was busy exiting the trucks and inspecting the supplies as Willy finally looks over at the gate. Standing there trying to take it all in Willy can't be sure, but it looked like... Yes, it looked like Laura was helping Jim and Grant unload what appeared to be a body wrapped inside a sleeping bag from off of the roof of the Tacoma.

CHAPTER FORTY-ONE

Ray had never seen a more welcomed sight than the front gate of the compound as it comes into the view of the trucks headlights. The gates, once well camouflaged with vegetation, were now only slightly concealed with the dead foliage of days gone past as the vines and trees around them withered and died from the onslaught of devastation executed by Mother Nature. Still Ray's heart fills with the warmth of content, simply being pleased with nothing more than the mere sight of it. His stomach however was a sinking pit of nervous anxiety that felt like it was being twisted and braided into tight knots. His thoughts of sympathy for the people he knew would be at first relieved by their return, then hurt by the tragedies that they brought home with them weigh heavily upon him as they approach the compound's entrance. Jim hops out of the truck to open the gate as Ray brings the truck to a stop about ten yards away allowing sufficient room between the truck and the gate to allow them to pass through easily. Jim opens the gates to their widest point and steps out of the way, waving the trucks trough. Following Laura's truck in through the gate as she slowly pulls into the compound to park next to Ray; Jim closes and secures the gates behind him as he walks over and begins to help unloading the vehicles. Believing the compound to still be asleep due to the early hour, the group carries what they had gathered over to the dispersing shed. Here the supplies would be held before they decided where they should be stored on a permanent basis. Finished unloading the packed vehicles they all gather together around the Tacoma somberly for the heartbreaking job of unloading the bodies of Colt and Clay. Two more unfortunate casualties of the harsh world they all now lived in that needed to be laid to rest in the communities growing cemetery. They had strapped Colt's body to the roof of the Tacoma dutifully in a painful decision that offered more room inside the vehicle for supplies. It was a calloused choice, but one that had rendered itself necessary due to the bountiful abundance of supplies they had been able to collect on their excursion. Not to mention that leaving Colts dead body behind was never an option. Not even at Firefly Farms with Brick and the others. They would have brought him home to be buried here with his friends and loved ones even if it had meant sacrificing some of the supplies to do so. The recent passing of Clay has also served to form a thick melancholy cloud over the group that is only thickened as they lower Colt's body to the ground. Just as they are about to finish Jim and Grant are startled by the sudden gasp emitted by Paige who was standing just behind them. The graveness of the situation is summed up in an instant with the two simple names uttered by Laura perched in the bed of the truck,

"Mrs. Holly, Mrs. Veronica."

Ray jumps up from examining how well the sleeping bag had held up in their travels like a child that has just been caught doing something that he knew was going to get him into trouble. Grant stands up slower than his father wiping his hands up and down on the front of his jeans like he had just touched something filthy or dirty. Holly's tears are rolling down her face as she asks the obvious burning question that was on everyone's mind.

"Ray where is Colt? Please tell me you do not have my Colt wrapped up in that sleeping bag? Oh god Ray, please tell me that's not my Belle's daddy?"

Ray walks quickly over to Holly to help her up from the ground where she was she still kneeling in the mud and the rain.

"Yes Holly, I'm afraid that it is. I am so sorry that you had to find out like this," Ray begins.

"How else was I going to find out Ray?" Holly whimpers, then asks in a weary whisper, "What happened to him?"

Laura hops down out of the bed of the truck and walks over to help her father with Holly. Together they begin trying to explain to her what exactly had happened out on the excursion and inside the waiting room of the chiropractor's office. Holly sits kneeling in the mud and falling rain that continues to fall heavily, listening to the story of her husband's demise. Her face is blank, staring expressionless at her husband's body lying on the ground between the Jeep Cherokee and the Toyota Tacoma. Next to her, Veronica turns to Willy who is sadly shaking his head at hearing the news of yet another tragedy that has befallen a member of the compound. Looking around she realizes that she has yet to see Clay or Levi.

"Willy, where's Clay? I don't see Clay or Levi. Do you? I'm sorry for interrupting Ray, but where is Clay?!" Her voice cracks threateningly as she struggles not to lose control of her own emotions. Frantically calling out Clay's name she rushes toward the trucks looking for her husband and her son. Levi cuts her off, blocking her path to the Tacoma as his own tears fall to mix with the rain on the muddy ground. His expression telling her all she needs to know about the fate of his father. He sullenly tells her everything she doesn't want to believe about her best friend... her lover... her soul mate.

"God no, not Clay too? Please god not Clay too," she whispers. Breaking out of Levi's grasp she sprints the last few yards to the truck where she can see Clay's motionless form leaning peacefully against the opposite window. Climbing inside the truck to sit next to him, Veronica impulsively throws her body across his in a lover's embrace of loss and regret. She sits there holding her husband sobbing in the regret of knowing that she'll never get to make up for the time she lost punishing him for the death of her brother. Something that she always knew was never really his fault. That the one person she was waiting for to help her take all the pain of the last week away was now the newest and greatest part of that pain. She cradles his head against her chest as she sobs her apologies to what is left of the man she knows she will never be able to replace. In this world or in any other version of it.

"Oh Clay, I am so sorry baby. You will never know just how truly sorry I am. I love you so very, very much," Veronica sobs over and over. She bends over and kisses his lips for the last time. Feeling their warmth, she realizes how close she had been from being able to confess her love and sorrow to him while he was still alive. Her sobs grow stronger as she begins kissing him over and over again, unable to stop herself in her grief. Whispering "I love you" in between each kiss placed on Clay's lips savoring the touch of warmth they still held from the fever that only an hour before had been raging through what was then, his still living body. The mystery of who had cleaned the gore from the walls in the little back room of the kitchen had all been washed away in the fresh tears and rain of the community's heartbreaking reunion.

"Those we love never go away, they walk beside us every day. Unseen, unheard, but always near, still loved, still missed, and forever dear."

–Author Unknown

CHAPTER FORTY-TWO

YEAR ONE, DAY THREE HUNDRED AND THIRTY-ONE

The despairing tragedies as everyone comes back together for the first time in over a week, brings with it more than enough sadness and heartbreak to go around. After almost a full year of living inside the compound the community has been forever shaken down to its very core by the tragic string of current events. They stand there together in a loose circle around the two newest members of the community's little cemetery that is growing larger far too quickly. Hand in hand with their heads bowed, they utter the Lord's Prayer together once again. All their voices coming together in chorus (even Cain and Sophia participate) as they lay their friends and loved ones to rest under what was left of the huge Black Walnut tree that would have once dominated the hilltop. Tears fall from their eyes and roll down their cheeks, to mix with the snow and the mud at their feet as the blackened skies swirl ominously above their heads. The lanterns provide a soft circle of light throwing haunting shadows to dance around them in the wind and the rain as lightning flashes through the clouds.

Later that night as the compound once again settles in for a long restless night, Veronica lays alone inside her bunker comforted only by the tears that fall onto what was once Clay's pillow. Ray sits propped up against a tree softly crying next to his daughter Rose's grave site, alone save for the empty bottle of whiskey that lies discarded on its side next to him. Holly cries herself to sleep alone in her bed facing the cinder block wall of her bunker. She cries over the emotional loss of Belle due to her attachment to Lily after the dog attack. She cries over the loss of Colt, the person that had been the center of her strength and optimism in this world. She cries over feeling angry at both of them for leaving her alone in this dark and desolate living nightmare. Belle walks with a visible limp from the attack that has left her foot maimed as she and Lily walk to the far side of the compound to sit with Dylan – who is busy feeding Marie cuddled up beside a warm fire with the formula the group had been able to bring back from town. Sophia withdrawals deep within her created inner walls as a shield from a world she no longer understands or has the will to survive in. Willy and Jim sit sipping whiskey, reminiscing over a game of chess and times long past inside of Willy's bunker. They do their best to avoid speaking about the manifest misfortunes that had befallen the compound as of late. Levi and Paige lay together in the sweaty entanglement of young lover's bliss. The tragic events that have unfolded before them in town and at the compound making them realize that waiting "for the right time" to fall in love was no longer a sensible or realistic option. Laura and Grant do their best to reach their mother. They tell her about Broderick, Ally, and the rest of the group they had met while they were out on the supply run. Trying urgently to convince her that all was not lost in the world, that there was still a tiny thread of hope that they all could still cling onto selfishly. They explain about how the compound had found a friend and an outpost with Broderick and the others at Firefly Farms. All the while Cain sits under an umbrella alone in the middle of a skeleton forest beside a rock, waiting patiently for a friend that was lost long ago to the evolution of madness that has become survival beneath the ashen veil of darkness.

"Do not submit yourself to wallow long within the throes of depression; For it is out of the ashes of despair, that the sprouts of opportunity often begin to rise."

–Clay Stratford

CHAPTER FORTY-THREE

YEAR FIVE, DAY ONE HUNDRED AND SEVENTEEN

Paige stands on top of the mountain that overlooks the compound and the valley below. Bleak and desolate in its vastness, the barren forest that had once been the Ouachita National Forest surrounds them in all directions; locked within the mini ice age brought on by the volcanic winter. She is still annoyed with the fact that Levi have drug them all up here without a real explanation, but his persistence finally won her over. Whatever secret he was keeping had him more excited than she had seen him in quite a while. The savagery of existence in the world of the aftermath following the volcanic eruption didn't allow for a lot of excitement and pointless frolicking. Paige is quietly preparing her scolding speech for Levi if this all ended up being a big waste of time and used up valuable energy and the limited resources of the compound for his little "field trip."

"What is it we're supposed to be looking for over here Levi?" Jim asks as he crests the top of the trail to stand in the small glade at the top of the mountain.

"What brought you all the way over here in the first place?" Willy adds.

"You'll see," Levi answers, slightly out of breath but smiling as he helps Veronica up the hill. Veronica's back kept her in obvious pain from the fall she had taken on the one, and only, excursion she had accompanied a scavenging party on. Even so, Levi's smile was brighter than the light from the flashlight he held out in front of them so that they could find their way up the path. Paige realized that it was the first time she had seen Levi smile like that since Cain had ran off into the barren Ashland, "chasing ghosts from days long past" Ray had said. None the less, it had devastated Veronica and, from association, Levi as well. Ronnie hadn't been the same since. Not that she ever fully recovered from the loss of Clay. Sophia had thankfully bounced back to life not long after Ray had come home. Dylan and Lily's relationship seemed to help out quite a bit with all of that as well. A relationship that, in spite of their age difference of just over three years, just seemed to make sense with the way that they had fostered Marie and Belle after Jackson and Holly's suicides. Paige shivers at the memory of the indifference in Belle's voice as she entered the pavilion that morning describing her mother's apparent ending.

Belle had been awakened by the steady sound of an eerie creaking, like the sound that comes from someone sitting in a rocking chair on an old porch. Not knowing what the sound was, Belle's curiosity got the best of her as she follows the sound into the sitting room of the bunker she now shared with only her mother. Standing in the entranceway to the room, gazing into the dark held within, Belle can just make out the silhouette of her mother as Holly slowly swings back and forth, back and forth. She had hung herself from the single support beam that ran down the center of the shelter during the small hours of the night. Standing there for several seconds Belle listens to the hypnotizing creak of the rope as it rubs against the beam. Her mother's body slowly continuing to swing back and forth, back and forth. Belle looks down at the floor and quietly turns around to leave her mother. Limping on her permanently damaged leg she exits the bunker to go and find Lily, sadly the only real mother she had known in quite some time. She would remain at Lily's side until Jim and Willy went into the bunker to remove Holly's body and lay her to rest forever on the little hill that overlooks the compound in the cemetery next to her husband. The only thing that Holly left for her only child to remember her by was a note that simply read,

"THE DARK HAS FINALLY SUCCEEDED IN PRESSING ME OVER THE EDGE. IT RISES UP OUT OF THE BLACK TO CONSUME MY SOUL. I HAVE NOTHING LEFT TO GIVE THIS WORLD OR TO ANYONE THAT LIVES WITHIN IT. PLEASE TELL BELLE THAT I AM SORRY."

"Again, why do you come all the way over here Levi?" Ray asks. His eyebrows raised in the questioning look of puzzlement.

"Dylan and I started coming up here to gather most of the firewood for the community about a year ago so that we wouldn't keep thinning out what little bit of cover the trees around the compound offered us by chopping them all down and burning them," Levi points out. Willy and Jim instantly nod in understanding, appreciating the foresight that process of thinking offered for the shared optimistic outlook on the future of the compound.

"That makes a lot of sense Levi, Dylan. That was good thinking by you guys," Ray says nodding to the duo as he does.

"Wish we would've thought about it a little sooner," Jim adds.

"Hey y'all look at the way this natural downgrade runs off over here. This would be an excellent spot for a third water filtration station," Willy points out, turning to Levi and Dylan adding, "Since you guys come over this way most days anyhow."

"That's a great idea Willy," Ray comments. You could see him working out the schematics as he adds "You know what just might work? If we widened out this natural run off ditch a little bit more…" Ray, Willy, and Jim automatically start mapping out the path and position for the barrel as everyone else chuckles at the expected response from the trio who are always looking out for ways to improve things around the compound.

"Hey guys! We're not up here to scout out new water stations," Paige jumps in putting an abrupt end to the planning. "Levi brought us all up here to see something, remember?"

"Ha-ha oh yeah. Sorry Levi," Ray says impishly, taking off his hat and running his hand through his hair.

"Just always looking for things to make life a little easier around here, ya know what I mean?" Willy adds.

"It goes without saying how much we all appreciate what you guys do for us to keep the community up and running," Paige says.

"Here and at the outposts," Laura puts in from where she was sitting on a fallen tree behind them. "The set-up you guys came up with for giving us hot water was like the second coming of the messiah." The group laughs with echoing agreement at Laura's mention of the boiler tank Willy and Ray had come up with for hot showers at the community washroom.

"Ok son, you have us all up here and thanks to Paige, you have our undivided attention. So, what is it you would like us to see?" Veronica asks from the folding chair Levi had carried up here for her to sit in.

"You'll see. Just be patient everyone." Levi says as he turns away from the group and stands gazing out over the horizon. Then suddenly, his voice barely above a whisper, he gasps,

"There. That's what I wanted you all to see."

"Oh Levi," Paige gasps.

"Daddy what is that?" Marie, who is now five, asks the only real father she has ever known, "Why does the sky look like that?" Dylan scoops her up into his arms and places her on his shoulders as he answers,

"Those are the colors that nature paints across the heavens during a miraculous and beautiful sunrise baby-girl."

Standing on the porch overlooking Firefly Farms, Grant and Ally stand holding each other next to Xander, Broderick, Benny, and Larry. The spectacle they are witnessing coming up over the horizon taking all of their breaths away in one shared, awed gasp. Levi had gotten word to them through the CB radios they had taken from the eighteen wheelers they had found abandoned on the side of highway 270. Every three days at what was previously designated to be sunrise, they checked in with one another to let everyone know that everything was ok. The gashers had long ago stopped being a problem but you could never be too cautious or take anything for granted. Infection, broken bones, even something as simple as the common cold could mean death while you were trying to scrape out a living within the darkness and the cold. So, they stayed in regular contact. Communicating every three days and getting the two groups together every three months. It had become a tradition that they all looked forward to. Especially since the group had begun to spread out to living at the outpost as well as the compound. Laura, for one, split her time between the compound and the Farm. Grant, with his relationship and subsequent marriage to Ally, had moved permanently to Firefly Farms some time ago. Now as they stood looking out at the horizon that laid over the family property of Broderick Thomas, they all wished that this was one of the times they were all together to witness the first unmistakable sign of the true healing power of nature.

The group that is gathered together from the compound stand in awe and cautious optimism at the view they are witnessing take place before them. Off on the horizon was an orangey, red globe standing out against the blackened ash cover that has blanketed the earth for more than five years. Thin red and orange tendrils filtered out from it going in all directions fading to light and then dark purple before finally fading back into the black they have all become so accustomed too.

"Isn't it beautiful," Levi whispers. "Dylan and I noticed it two days ago, but we wanted to make sure it happened every day before we got everyone out to see it."

"I think we needed a couple of days to convince ourselves it was real too," Dylan adds.

"It's the most beautiful thing I think I have ever seen," Paige whispers in his ear.

"Well, it's almost the most beautiful thing anyways," Paige adds shyly, kissing Levi on his cheek as she places something in his hand. Looking down he can barely make out the results of the positive pregnancy test that she handed him. Levi's tears of joy fall from his cheeks to wet his collar as he places his hand on Paige's belly and kisses her softly on the lips. Pulling back from the kiss he softly whispers

"I love you" into Paige's ear.

"And I love you Levi," Paige answers as her own tears of joy and hope begin to form and fall. Hope for herself. Hope for Levi. Hope for the community. Hope for their child. Hope…. for the future.

"If you can't fly, then run. If you can't run, then walk. If you can't walk, then crawl. But no matter what, you have to keep moving forward."

–Dr. Martin Luther King

EPILOGUE

When the satellite equipment started receiving signals from space again it had been the indicator that the underground facility beneath Fort Smith, also known as the FEMA residential housing center for western Arkansas, district six, sub-section nine, was to begin recon operations for the obtainment of any evidence that anyone or anything had survived the aftermath and calamity that followed during the years since the eruption. Master Sergeant Kenneth Brown stands looking over his team as they pack up camp and begin moving out again on their constant search for any type of life; flora or fauna. His heart strings are tugged on heavily by the dead and barren landscape that greets him and his team around every new corner. He hadn't known what to expect when they ventured out of the underground base for the first time, ***but this*** .... this was almost more than he could bear. The volcano was quick and efficient in its complete and utter annihilation of the life and civilization that had once scurried across the surface of the planet. As he looks around at the devastation the speaker in his ear fills with static as he can just barely make out his scout team reporting in from the outlying mountains that surrounded the lake and small town.

"Say again Fox Two, your last transmission was inaudible," he says into his microphone.

Looking down the barrel of his M4A1 Flat-top carbine, Pvt. Lynch is both shocked and amazed at what he sees resting directly in the center of the cross hairs of his ACOG scope. Over his ear piece he hears Sgt. Brown say,

"Come again Fox Two, your last transmission was inaudible."

"Fox One, I repeat, existence of survivors is confirmed. We are awaiting your orders sir."

As Pvt. Lynch sits waiting on his orders he watches as the man stares at something he is cradling in his hands, whatever it is it causes the man to become emotional. He continues to watch as the man then places his hand on the woman's belly and rubs it in slow, caressing circles before bending down and softly kissing the woman tenderly on the lips.